Mark

Stan Meihaus

Dedicated to my father, Stanley A. Meihaus, Jr., 1939-2012.

Rest in Peace, Dad.

ACKNOWLEDGMENTS

Thanks to my reading group, which handles all my beta testing:
Christine Brown, Christine Frost, Allison Holmes, Brian Krum,
Ellen Meihaus, Barbara Nosek and Karen Meihaus.

Thanks also to Patrick Schneider at Patrick Schneider Photography
for the great cover photograph of the Charlotte skyline during a
night of fireworks.

ALSO BY STAN MEIHAUS

$KIP

2011 Indie Gold Medal for Best New Suspense/Thriller Novel

1

I slipped my security card through the card reader and opened the door to the trading floor. The noise from the pit exploded on me. It was 7:30 on Monday morning and something big was happening. The domestic stock and bond markets weren't even open yet, so it had to be on the international desk.

An asset-backed trader I knew was scurrying by. I stopped him.

"What's up?" I asked, nodding toward the international desk, which was at the front of the trading floor closest to the windows. It was stacked three-deep with people.

"I don't know, some kind of meltdown in Russia, I think. The rumor is that the Russians are going to default on 'certain international obligations.' Everybody's trying to figure out exactly what obligations they mean, and whether we have any or not."

"Do we?" I asked.

He shrugged.

"I don't," he said, and hustled away.

Hint #1 that I was on the trading floor: a trader cares about two things, his book and his bonus. Most of the time he is barely aware that he works for a bank. My asset-backed co-worker could not care less about international exposure, and would only begin to care if it affected his book or his bonus.

I eased my way toward the international bond desk, trying to look inconspicuous. In times of market losses, nobody who works on the trading floor wants to see anyone who doesn't. They are angry and embarrassed and they don't care to share it with anyone except other members of the tribe. I knew a few of the traders but we were not friends in any sense of the word, and I would not be welcome right now.

The crowd at the international desk was mostly focused on a bank of television screens. The noise ebbed and flowed, now sounding like a rock concert, then turning to silence as the traders listened to a talking head on TV. To the right of me I saw a conversation that looked interesting, so I snuck up behind the two guys having it, and got Hint #2 that I was on the trading floor.

George Lamb. Head salesman of domestic corporate and asset-backed bonds. Pinstripe custom-designed blue suit from Savile Row, light blue shirt with a white collar and a dark blue tie, gold cufflinks and brightly polished black Italian shoes. Black leather suspenders, a big school ring on his left hand and a gold Rolex on his right. His outfit cost more than all the suits I owned. Forty-ish, tall, thick and meaty, with a big loopy black mustache that was waxed to fine points and turned upwards on the ends to make it curl. He was fighting a losing battle with a receding hairline and wearing his hair long in the back to compensate.

He was talking—or shouting, really, to be heard above the noise—to one of his salesmen whose name I didn't know. They were both facing away from me and staring at the pandemonium on the international desk.

"What do you mean, pull it?" George yelled. The veins in his neck bulged.

The salesman grimaced and yelled back.

"Look, George, I had this thing 90% sold yesterday afternoon: hedge funds, mutual funds, all our usual clients. I figured I would come in this morning, wrap up the last little bit, and put this thing to bed by lunch. Ham on rye, you know? But my voicemail was flooded with messages this morning. All of our investors are pulling out because of this Russia thing. I've talked to them all, and they are all on hold until this clears up. 'We need more visibility,' they say. 'Until we see how this affects the rest of the market we are on the sidelines.' So we're back to square one. We have no commitments to buy on this deal. No way we close today."

"You should have been here earlier, to take those calls," George accused.

"Come on, George, how was I supposed to know that this would blow up overnight?"

"What does this shit in China have to do with us?" said George.

"Russia," corrected the salesman.

George glared at him.

"I don't give a fuck if it's Easter Island. Why is it affecting a U.S. dollar-denominated corporate bond sale? This Seletrex deal is half a billion dollars. Do you have any idea how much money we are going to make on this? Why do you want to pull it?"

"I talked to a half-dozen other investors this morning, guys who weren't in the original group," said the salesman. "They're all saying the same thing: we are not buying anything until we see if this thing in Russia spreads. "Contagion" is today's buzzword. These guys are not writing any checks until they are sure that the problems in Russia are not spreading to other markets."

"Fuck," said George, and chewed on a fingernail. A shout and several groans came from the international desk; they were reacting to something that had been said on TV. George and the salesman looked at the desk, then back at each other.

"Any chance we could get the bank to take it on balance sheet?" said the salesman.

George shook his head.

"The whole thing? No way. If there was a stub that was unsold, $50 million or something, then we could probably put it on the trading book and tell them we would have it sold by the end of the quarter. But half a billion? No way those pricks in Credit would sign up for it. Hell, $50 million makes them nervous. They would probably all stroke out if you mentioned $500 million."

"What's the point of having this huge bank balance sheet if we're never allowed to use it?" the salesman asked.

George shrugged angrily. They both watched the action in the international area a little while longer. Then George said:

"Well, I guess we're pulling it. Call Seletrex and tell them what the deal is. Make sure you emphasize this is temporary, okay? Just one of those aggravating market disruptions. We'll have this thing booked and sold by the end of the week, no later."

The salesman looked glum but nodded.

"Go take care of it," George said. "I'm going to talk to Rajat and figure out what the hell is going on."

I slid in behind George as he walked toward the international desk. I stopped a few feet away and leaned on an empty desk, looking to eavesdrop some more.

"George," said Rajat, the head of the international desk, nodding as George walked up. The noise had abated somewhat and they were speaking in normal tones.

"Rajat," George nodded back. "What's going on?"

Rajat gestured at the TV. "Russia has been making noise like they are going to devalue the ruble and default on their international debt."

"Making noise? What does that mean?" asked George.

"It means that the people who are really going to make the call, like the prime minister and the president, are actually on vacation at their summer *dachas,* and the people left back at the Kremlin have no idea what's going on," Rajat said.

"Did something happen or didn't it?" George asked.

"Some official in the finance ministry said that currency controls were being placed on the ruble. He was then asked if that meant Russia was defaulting on its international debt, and he gave some vague answer. So nobody's really sure."

"Well let me ask you something, Rajat," said George. "Why is this fucking up my deal for Seletrex?"

Rajat looked at him with surprise.

"I didn't realize it had," said Rajat. "Are you saying that deal is not going to close today?"

"No it is not," said George. "My whole investor group just slammed their wallets shut this morning, and the deal was 90% sold when we went home yesterday."

Rajat rubbed his chin.

"Well, contagion, I guess," said Rajat. "They're scared about this default spreading to other countries. You have to understand, this thing wasn't supposed to happen, according to the politicians in Washington. 'Nuclear powers don't default' was the party line up there. It has caught a lot of people by surprise."

"So some foreign currency issue is spooking my guys?" asked George. "Seletrex is a domestic deal, U.S. dollars to a U.S. corporation."

Rajat looked bemused, then shrugged. "What can I tell you? That's the definition of contagion. People are worried that this 'foreign currency issue,' as you put it, is going to spread and create problems elsewhere."

George turned to go. "How long do you think it will be before this crap blows over?" he asked.

Just then somebody shouted at the TV:

"Could you please get this idiot off the screen and get us someone who actually knows what's going on?!"

The noise level jumped again, traders again shouting into their phones and at each other, and Rajat turned back to the TV bank without answering George's question. He obviously had his own problems to worry about.

George stomped off. I headed toward the trading desk door and the elevator bank that would take me up to my boss's office on the 12th floor. As I did I glanced into the trader's break room and got Hint #3 that I was on the trading floor.

The trading floor break room has a coffee/cappuccino machine, a soda fountain with a crushed ice dispenser, three snack machines, a mini-fridge full of imported bottled water (regular and sparkling), and six different types of hot tea. All of it accompanied by an attendant clad in black to help with your selections. And all of it free to the salesmen and traders who worked there.

It was a damn sight finer than the microwaved burrito smell that permeated the break rooms at the rest of the bank.

Most of them were lucky to have a coffee maker and a refrigerator.

But this was not traditional banking, the boring old business of taking deposits and making loans.

This was Investment Banking. Capital I, Capital B.

2

My boss, Lawson McCoy, was a fat-faced Virginian who fancied bow ties and suspenders over belts and ties. He had a deep, sonorous voice and was given to uninterruptible soliloquies. Whenever he spoke to the trainees in the management development program, you could later hear them trying to imitate his accent. "Now Ah woan y'all to remembah this heah…"

He had once been head of both Internal Audit and the Special Assets Group, but the two jobs had become bigger than one person could do, so last year he chose SAG and someone else got IA. He was highly respected in the bank, a man of unquestioned integrity, and if that meant putting up with his pipe and a whiff of Virginia tobacco coming from his office in a no-smoking zone, then most everyone was happy to look the other way. I liked him a lot.

Special Assets Group: where bad commercial loans go to die. With recent mergers Lawson now covered a 16-state area, and five of those were my responsibility. He reported directly to the chairman of the bank. He had worked at the bank for almost 30 years. I was in my fifth year, but with business school and two years on Wall Street at an investment bank sandwiched in between.

"Morning Sam," he said as I poked my head in the door. "Come on in. There's coffee on the sideboard there."

I poured myself a cup and sat down in front of his desk.

"Morning boss," I said. "Have a nice weekend?"

"Beautiful," he said. "How about yourself? Did you get out on the lake any?"

"Oh yes," I said. "Did a little skiing, a little fishing. Weather was a little hot but it cooled down nice in the evening."

"Catch anything?" he said.

"I got a nice catfish from right underneath my dock on Sunday morning. Had him for breakfast."

He chuckled.

"Fry him up in a little cornmeal and butter?" he asked.

"Yeah," I said. "A little bacon grease, too, to be honest."

"That sounds like the perfect breakfast," he said, "but you best watch that bacon grease or you will be taking a pill for cholesterol like I do."

Then he turned to business.

"So what do our boys down on the trading floor allow?"

Lawson had sent me there this morning. The markets were not part of my normal routine and didn't have much to do with my job. But Lawson had called me that morning at 7:00, while I was stuck in traffic on the way down to work, and told me to stop in there first.

"Well," I said, "I'm not sure."

I looked at the clock on his desk. It was a little before 9:00.

"The domestic markets aren't even open yet, so usually the floor is pretty quiet right now, but the international desk was going crazy. There appears to be some possibility of a Russian currency devaluation and a bond default. That's what Rajat, the head of the international desk, thinks, but information coming out of Russia is garbled.

"Anyway, it has spooked U.S. investors. George Lamb and the domestic corporate guys have a half-billion dollar deal that was supposed to go out for final pricing this morning. It's for a U.S. corporation, dollar-denominated, and it doesn't have anything to do with Russia. But it just tanked because of the news from Russia. The investors all pulled out at the last minute. George thinks it is just a blip, and they'll be able to get the deal out later this week. But I'm not so sure. It seems to me that there is something to this contagion idea, and that if Russia blows up then trouble could spread from there."

"Could be," said Lawson. "I don't know if you remember the Asian crisis from last year, but it started with a little ol' thing in Japan and the next thing you know it was in South Korea, Indonesia, Thailand...it affected all of Asia in about a week."

"What's all this got to do with us, Lawson?" I asked. "Since when do we get involved in this investment banking stuff? So Rajat loses some money on Russian exposure. Or George's domestic deal takes a little longer to get done. Those are public deals. SAG doesn't have a role here. There's no need for us to go in there and try to negotiate something, or work out a bankruptcy, or whatever. If the traders don't like their positions, they can just sell them and take the losses."

Lawson exhaled loudly.

"Historically, you are correct. As you know we bought this investment bank out of New York a year ago, and part of our agreement with them was that we would leave them alone to operate just like they used to. We liked the profitability of the firm, and the added services we were able to provide to our biggest customers. They liked the comfort of our big balance sheet, and cheaper funding costs.

"They compromised some, and let the headquarters come down here, which in my opinion they did just so they could bring their big New York paychecks down to Charlotte and live like kings. But nonetheless that was a big feather in our cap, to have an investment bank and a real-life trading floor here in Charlotte.

"Only things are not working out like we drew it up. Partly it's our own fault. We were so hot and bothered to get into the investment banking business, and show everyone how sophisticated we were, that we didn't do the proper due diligence. It turned out that these boys had a lot of garbage hidden on their balance sheet. We have been taking losses trying to get it cleaned up, but it seems like every time we kill a cockroach, two more come running out from under the counter.

"Our chairman, Mr. Christopher Avery, is getting tired of it. Last week he told Credit to take a much firmer hand on any new money being extended, and he told me to start digging through their portfolio so that he doesn't have any more nasty surprises come quarterly earnings time.

"And he has made some personnel decisions as well. There have been some management changes. Here is Part One."

He handed me the business section of the local paper and on the front page was the headline "Grant Meyers Leaving Citizens Union."

I sat back in my chair with a low whistle. Grant Meyers had been the president of the bank, the organization's #2, and had been the most enthusiastic proponent of buying the New York investment bank.

Meyers was in his mid-50s, a lifer. He had worked for the bank ever since graduating from college. He sat on the board and was the clear successor to Avery when he retired. I read through the article and snorted where it said "Mr. Meyers is leaving the bank to spend more time with his family." My foot. He bled the bank's colors and would have had to have been dug out of his office with a backhoe. He had been forced into early retirement.

Just then the phone rang on Lawson's desk and he answered.

"Yes, Sylvia," he said. "Of course, put him through."

He put his hand over the mouthpiece and grimaced.

"Here comes Part Two, I fear," he said. Then it was:

"Yes sir, good morning. Yes sir. I understand. Is that public information? As of right now? Yes sir..."

I could hear the voice through the phone; the man even shouted occasionally. Lawson listened for almost five minutes and jotted some notes on a legal pad. He punctuated the silence with phrases like "yes, sir," "I understand completely," and "no, sir, but we can certainly do that."

"We will handle it," said Lawson as the call was winding up. I could see sweat beading on his forehead. "My best man, sir, Samuel Wilson...he worked several years on Wall Street....yes sir, that's him, he did used to work here, then left for his MBA, then went to Wall Street for a few years and came back to us about three years ago...."

Lawson "completely understood" some more. There were a few more "yes sirs" in there, and then he hung up.

Lawson took a handkerchief out of his pocket and wiped his forehead. I put the paper down.

"That was the chairman, in case you couldn't tell," he said. "Here is Part Two of the personnel changes: Mr. Randall Clifton is no longer employed by this bank either, effective this morning. He has 'taken early retirement,' as the saying goes. He is going to work and have an office here until the end of the month, but his operational responsibilities cease today."

Clifton was the president of the investment bank we had bought. It looked like the head honchos from both the investment bank and the commercial bank had gotten the axe today.

"Mr. Avery wants the portfolio from the investment bank turned inside out and upside down. He says that if we have to take another charge against earnings, then we will take it, and we have three weeks to figure out how much it is going to be, but that will be the last charge we ever take regarding the purchase of our New York investment bank.

"He says he is tired of being lied to by people who get paid to tell him the truth and are supposed to know their asses from first base. He says he is going to have some answers, and they are going to be the right answers, and the final answers, or he is going to fire every last person at this bank and start over.

"The answers are going to come from this department. We are to start working on the portfolio immediately, with a dedicated staff of people who are doing nothing but that. I have carte blanche to use whoever I want from this bank, and to hire lawyers, accountants, consultants, private detectives and the Queen of England if I need to. He has already talked to the senior people at the investment bank to tell them of the departure of Mr. Clifton, and to inform them of our task.

"If anyone, and he means *anyone*, from the investment bank gives us any static whatsoever, we are to call him immediately and he will personally fire the person on the spot. The transition from New York to Charlotte is almost complete, but if we need to go to New York for any reason, then we are to go, and we can use the corporate jet.

"We are to provide weekly status reports that are on his desk by Monday morning at 9 a.m. 18 days from today, there will be a meeting in his office, where we will give him our final recommendations."

Lawson took a deep breath and leaned back in his chair. I sat there shell-shocked. We looked at each other for a while.

"I was not aware that Mr. Avery possessed such a temper," I finally said. I noticed I was talking like Lawson now.

"I am relieved to tell you that I have only seen it on a few occasions. As you can tell it is a powerful thing. He generally runs on a very even keel, but he does not like surprises, particularly when they have to do with the financial health of this bank."

"Lawson, I knew Grant Meyers, but what was this guy Randall Clifton like?" I asked. "I met him a grand total of once, when he made a short speech to about 300 of us after the acquisition was announced. I've seen him on the trading floor a few times but that's it."

"I thought he was pretty sharp," said Lawson, "but I didn't know him much more than you did. He dressed very nicely, older gentleman, going a little gray, probably 55 or so. He had a Rolodex with the name of every Fortune 500 CEO in it, or so they said. He was on a first name basis with all the politicians and the regulators. He hunted the big game, is what they told me: they brought him in on the biggest deals, when they had that client who needed to feel like he was talking to the man in charge. And he made a lot of money. In fact, in he and Meyers, we just fired the second- and third-highest paid men at this bank."

I waited with dread for what had to be coming. Lawson read my mind.

"Look, Sam, before you even say it, I know you don't want to do this. Who would? But I sent you down to the trading floor this morning for a reason. You understand markets better than anyone else we've got. Nobody else has your Wall Street experience. Do you see another choice here?"

"Lawson, that was years ago, and I..."

He cut me off.

"Samuel, you saw what happened after the last earnings report. Our stock was wrecked. It is only now recovering. You have stock options. Do you want them to be worth something someday?"

"Of course, but I don't see how me getting involved..."

Lawson interrupted again.

"I'll put it to you this way. Nobody else can do this job. I'm going to assign your current workload out to others, so you won't have anything to focus on except this. But for the next 18 days, this is your job, and this is how you earn your paycheck. Understand?"

"Well, you put it like that, sir, then I guess I do."

◆

I went downstairs to my office on the tenth floor. I hung up my jacket and then stared morosely out the office window to the streets of Charlotte below.

I had spent the weekend on Lake Norman, where I live, fishing and water-skiing and just lounging around. My best friend, Curtis, had been out of town but another buddy, Jeff, was in from Raleigh, and we rounded up a couple of local honeys and went up and down the lake in my boat on Saturday. The girls were both young and fun and cute in their little bikinis, and we tied up with other boats on several occasions and went swimming and drank in the summer heat.

That evening we had a fire and a cookout on my little lakefront beach, and partied some more until the bugs came out around dusk. Then we went inside for more drinking and eventually to bed, where my provision of food and drink and shelter was generously rewarded by Missy (or was it Mindy?) from Concord. The girls headed out first thing Sunday morning, with Jeff right behind them, and I drove to a newspaper shack in Statesville and bought all the Sunday papers they had. I spent that Sunday by myself, sometimes fishing off the dock, or lounging on my back porch, sipping beer and reading the news of the world. I watched the boat traffic go by and took a nap when I felt like it.

Refreshed and ready, I had breezed into work this morning only to be slammed by a shitstorm. Two of the bank's top managers unceremoniously fired. The chairman of the bank this close to a heart attack, yelling through the phone at my boss. Lawson saying "yes sir" like a private in the Army, sweating and nervous like I had never seen him. And now me, assigned to somehow work out a loan and bond portfolio that was so bad that two senior bankers had gotten themselves fired over it.

I had gotten lazy, I guess. SAG is counter-cyclical—when the economy was humming along, as it was right then, we were not that busy. There would always be contentious workouts and thieving managers and crooked attorneys to deal with, but right now the workload was far from crushing, and there was plenty of opportunity to slip off before 5:00 and hit the lake.

But now it looked like I was going back onto the firing line. So long ski boat and Lake Norman in the summer—hello office.

3

Well, there it was. Sometimes you've got a job to do, and the only thing to do is get started doing it.

Lawson wanted a complete printout of all the accounts we were managing in my five-state area of the Special Assets Group. He was determined that I would not have anything to worry about except the investment bank portfolio, so he was going to re-assign my workload to others. We were getting back together after lunch to go over that.

Meantime, I had to start thinking about a team to join me. This was bigger than a one-man project. I was going to need a couple of key people, smart and fast, if the job was going to get done in three weeks.

Before I got started on the reports, Vinnie tapped on the doorframe of my office. Vincent Ricci is one of my two lieutenants, a fast-talking Italian from New York with an omnipresent five o'clock shadow and intense blue eyes. He had been with the bank about five years, and I had plucked him off the commercial loan desk, where his Yankee manners were offending his genteel Southern clientele. I could not have cared less. We are not running a charm school in SAG; our clients needed to hear it straight and unvarnished.

"Sam? Can you sit in with me on this ECP deal? Those guys are up here and I am getting nowhere on the issues we have."

ECP, which stood for Entourage Capital Partners, was in the aircraft parts business—not the complicated pieces like the engine or the communications equipment, but things like the seats and the toilets and the food warmers. The company was initially owned by two brothers named Jonathan and Andrew Little. They sold equipment to everybody who flew big planes: the U.S. domestic airlines, the international airlines, the freight handlers, everybody. They even had a contract with the Air Force.

Three years ago, after a series of small acquisitions of companies in the same industry, ECP went public. The firm raked in over $300 million in proceeds from the IPO. Most of that went to the Little brothers, who still ran the company. They also borrowed money from our bank, some $200 million in a line of credit secured by accounts receivable. They had done a small, unsecured bond issue in the public market at the same time. And then last year they had done a big asset-backed deal, also public, that reportedly had gone well.

But in the last six months they had run into problems. The company was not consolidating all the little companies they had acquired over the years. The computer systems weren't talking to each other. Seats that were supposed to have been sold to ABC Corp. had actually been sold to XYZ Corp. An airplane that was supposed to have been outfitted with new carpet and lighting had actually been billed for new food service areas. The bank had had several meetings with the company to try to get things straightened out, but the computer problems continued.

Three months ago they missed a payment to the bank. SAG was brought in then. Vinnie was in charge and, in a series of meetings with management, he gave them three basic messages:

1) get the financial systems straightened out;

2) when you do that, we need full collateral lists for the line of credit and the asset-backed deal, and a list of any unpledged collateral, and

3) make sure the brothers are here for the next meeting.

Even though they were owners and executive officers, they still had not shown up for the meetings, and we were getting tired of browbeating the financial staff. We needed to talk to the guys with skin in the game.

"Sure," I said in response to Vinnie's request. "Have you gotten counsel on this yet?"

"No," he said. "I figured we would try this one last meeting, and if we don't get anywhere today, then we hire counsel and start game-planning a BK. I'll be honest, I am getting really frustrated with these guys. They just don't seem to listen."

"And they're here right now. Thanks for the advance notice," I said.

"Look, I'm sorry, I didn't think I would need you, but they just showed up with a half a dozen guys, and I don't have an attorney and..."

I got up and clapped him on the shoulder.

"Forget about it," I said in my best Brooklyn accent. "Let's go see those boys."

"Sam, we really need to lay down the law here, all right?" he said.

"Sounds like it. I'll let you handle it, and I'll back you up, okay?"

This was not good cop/bad cop. This was two bad cops. Vinnie and I walked into the conference room, breathing fire.

We did not even get a word out before their CFO, an accountant named David, pointed to a stack of papers two feet high on the conference room table.

"That is our bankruptcy filing," he said, doing his best to sound ominous. "In case we can't work things out in here today."

Vinnie and I sat down. Vinnie said calmly:

"It wouldn't be our first bankruptcy. In fact, it wouldn't be our first bankruptcy in Tennessee."

Vinnie looked at me.

"What is Memphis, Sam, Western District of Tennessee?"

I nodded. "Sure. We'd probably draw either Judge Rayburn or Judge Sonnenstein."

I looked at the CFO.

"You wouldn't like either one of them," I said. "Hard asses."

"You know what that means, right?" Vinnie asked. "Our first motion, as soon as we walk in that courtroom, is to fire existing management. That means all you guys get fired. You can kiss your car service and your expense accounts and your fat paychecks goodbye. You will be on the street looking for a job, and at the top of your resume you're going to list this piece-of-shit Entourage Capital Partners as your last job. Good luck with that."

One of the other finance guys tried to say something, but I cut him off.

"Do you have the list of collateral we asked you for?" I asked the CFO.

"Um...we are still working on that," he said.

"How about the financial systems? Are they up to snuff yet?" asked Vinnie.

"That process is coming along, but it is not yet complete," sniffed David, the CFO.

"And I don't see the Brothers Grimm in here," I said. "What are their names, Jonathan and Andrew Little, right? The guys who own this place, who are supposed to be running it as the president and the CEO? We told you the last time we wanted them in here. Where are they?"

"This meeting was not conducive to their schedules," David said.

"So what are we doing here?" Vinnie asked. "We gave you three things we wanted before we agreed to consider extending your current loans, and overlooking your payment default, and you have nothing for us? I don't suppose you brought your past-due interest payment, did you?"

"We are here to ask you to extend the line of credit for another year, and increase the amount $50 million. We feel that with the additional time and funds, we can get this financial systems issue..." David started.

Vinnie held up his hand.

"That's enough. Here's the deal. Our line of credit with you expires in eight days, and at that point you will also be 90 days past due on your interest payment. So you have one week to get in here with the collateral list, a fix to the financial systems, and most importantly, your two owners. We will consider an extension only—no extra money—when that occurs. If it does not occur, then eight days from now we will declare you in default of your obligations to us. You have cross-defaults in all your bonds, so your entire capital structure will go into default if that happens. We will then force you into bankruptcy. Any questions?"

"Do you have any idea how much this bank stands to lose if you do that?" said David to me.

"Do you seriously think we are trusting you with additional money when you have already spent, and cannot account for, the original $200 million we loaned you?" I asked. "Plus the $300 million you took out of the IPO? Plus the proceeds of last year's corporate and asset-backed bond issuances? You need to focus on what YOU have to lose. Namely, your job and this entire company."

I stood up. Vinnie stood up with me.

"Have a nice trip back to Memphis," said Vinnie.

We both started to walk out. I turned back to them with one last thought.

"Oh, and have some respect for our time at the next meeting. If the Little brothers aren't coming, then please have the courtesy to call us in advance."

"At which point we will cancel the meeting and put you into the bankruptcy proceeding you seem so anxious to get to," said Vinnie, waving at the stack of paper that was supposed to be the bankruptcy filing. His hand "accidentally" hit it, and half of it fell over on the table.

It was blank. Nothing but copier paper after the first five pages or so.

Vinnie held up the blank paper to the CFO. "Looks like you need to get your printer fixed," he said.

We walked back to my office.

"Can you believe that?" said Vinnie. "They were trying to bluff us!"

"That was a nice move, knocking that paper over," I said. "And you're right, that was bush league. I guess we were supposed to get all nervous and cut them a $50 million check."

Then we looked at each other grimly. Talking tough in that meeting was necessary; we had to give the company one final, unequivocal chance to get into compliance. But Vinnie and I weren't fooling each other. ECP was exactly eight days from turning very ugly for both the company and the bank.

"Loss estimates and bankruptcy counsel, I guess?" Vinnie asked.

I nodded.

"You handle the loss estimate, I'll get the attorney," I said.

Vinnie left and I turned my computer on and started hacking out the reports Lawson wanted. Mentally I shifted to the portfolio project, rifling personnel ideas through my head, trying to figure out who would get pressed into my new work gang.

4

With the last bite of a deli sandwich stuffed in my mouth, I was banging on the keyboard and printing my report out. It was almost 1 p.m. and that's when Lawson and I were getting back together. My secretary Sharon stuck her head in the door.

Sharon had been with me since I started in SAG. I used to share her with a real estate guy on the same floor, but he had been relocated to another area, and my group had grown enough so that there were now eight of us, so she was with me full-time now. She was a single mother of three, 50ish with a mop of brown hair that frequently needed a brush. But she probably could have been an air traffic controller, the way she handled the comings and goings of our group, and she knew as much about how the bank ran as I did.

"Those vultures are here," she said.

"Oh shit," I said with my mouth full. "I totally forgot about them." I looked at my watch. 1:00 on the dot.

I took a big gulp of tea and washed everything down.

"Listen, call Lawson for me, would you?" I said to Sharon. "Tell him I forgot about this meeting and I'll be up there with the report in a half hour."

"No problem," she said. "Do you want me to send them in?"

I took a last sip of tea and then threw the remains of my lunch into the trashcan.

"Yeah, send the bloodsuckers in," I said.

Which was not a particularly charitable way to describe a group of investors that the bank did business with routinely. "Vultures" are private equity funds that have large amounts of money to invest, and they like to shop for companies or investments that are in trouble, that might need new management teams, or that might offer some value to them that others can't see. They never pay 100 cents on the dollar; they are looking for a steep discount for getting involved with weak companies.

If that sounds like something the Special Assets Group worked on all the time, well, it was. From time to time I had sold problem loans to vulture funds. In those cases I had always concluded that the bank would make more selling its debt in the company rather than trying to work something out or pushing the firm into bankruptcy. If the vulture firm would pay a fair price, the bank would simply sell the note to the vultures, take the loss, wash its hands.

Into my office strode two people who could not have looked less like vultures. Both of them could have starred in one of those sexy Latino soap operas you see on the Spanish-language TV channels. He was dark-skinned, 6'3" easily, with shiny black curly hair that almost touched his broad shoulders. He looked fit and muscled without being bulky. He had on a beautiful dark gray suit that might have been silk, a white shirt and a plum-colored tie.

She was equally stunning, almost six feet tall herself, though her stiletto heels were adding several inches. She too had the classic Latina beauty: café-au-lait skin, long black hair, dark eyes. If the bronze-colored skirt she wore was an inch shorter you would probably call it underwear. She had beautiful legs and generous breasts to match, which were fairly spilling out of the tight lacy tan bodice she wore under a business jacket with rolled-up sleeves.

"Marcos Pereira," said the man. "And may I introduce to you my associate Anastasia Primo de Montez. We both work for the Santiago Capital Fund."

"Please call me Ana," she said. We shook hands all around.

"Sam Wilson," I said. We exchanged business cards and I invited them to have a seat.

They both looked at the clutter in my office.

"You are busy, Mr. Wilson?" asked Marcos. "We have caught you at a bad time?"

They did not know it, but they had caught me at a very good time...for them. The chairman wanted the problems in this portfolio cleaned up in three weeks, and vulture funds could play an important role. I maintained a handful of relationships, but was always looking to expand them, because they have one advantage that no one else has. They move fast.

"I got hit with a last minute project by the boss," I said. "You know how that is."

Ana leaned over a bit and smiled sympathetically. "I certainly do," she said, nodding her head at Marcos, and they both laughed politely. I made myself stop staring at her cleavage.

"Well, we won't keep you long," said Marcos. "We just came by to introduce ourselves and tell you a little about our firm."

They had brought a bound presentation with them, and Marcos went through it as I listened and tried not to stare at Ana's legs, which was tough because they were long and crossed and stretched out right in front of me, causing her skirt to ride up and…

Look at the pitch book, Sam.

The firm was out of Miami with over $1.4 billion in current investments and another billion on the sidelines waiting for the right opportunity. Their primary investors were wealthy Floridians, along with a handful of pension funds. They were looking to expand their business out of Florida, maybe as far as Virginia, and of course the banks in Charlotte could be an important source of leads for them. They were very fair in their valuations, had a very simple approval process and could move very quickly if time was an issue. I said "uh huh" and "I see" and several other things like that until Marcos was finished.

"Thank you for that information," I said. "We do some business with funds like yours and are always happy to expand our contacts. Tell me, is there a particular asset type you like? Or one that you don't like, that you wouldn't be interested in? It would save us both some time if I knew that."

"Well, we are good internationally," said Marcos. "So any large operating company with a lot of international exposure would be of interest."

"Particularly Latin or South America," added Ana. "We know those countries well, much better than most of our competitors."

"Does that give you a chance to get home?" I asked.

She and Marcos both laughed.

"You are very astute, Mr. Wilson. You are right, we are both from Columbia," said Marcos.

"I've never been there," I said, "but I've heard it's a beautiful place."

"You must come and visit sometime," Ana purred. "I will show you around."

"What else?" I said briskly. I didn't have time to daydream about a trip to Columbia with Anastasia Primo de Montez. Which is what I had started to do.

"We understand asset-backed securities and hybrids like CBOs, CLOs and CDOs. We also like small-to-medium sized manufacturing companies," said Marcos.

"Particularly US-based parts and equipment manufacturers," said Ana. "We have several of those in our portfolio now, and they are doing quite well."

"Anything you don't like?" I asked.

"We would not be particularly helpful on real estate right now," said Marcos. "We have enough exposure as it is."

I flipped Marcos's card over and wrote on the back:

- ABS, CDO, CLO, CBO
- Large operating co. w/ intnl. exposure
- Small/med. U.S. operating co., esp. parts/equip
- NO R/E

"Very good," I said, standing up. "I will keep you in mind as things come up. Can I best reach you at your offices in Miami?"

"We are on a bit of a roadshow right now, and we travel a lot as you can imagine," said Marcos as he and Ana stood up. "The best numbers for us are our cellphone numbers."

Marcos and I shook hands, and Ana pulled me in for a European-style cheek kiss. She smelled wonderful.

"We hope to hear from you soon, Sam," she said as she pulled away.

I watched as Marcos and Ana walked out of my office. She looked like she was giving her hips a little extra swish, and she looked back over her shoulder to see if I was watching. I was, and she smiled. When she got to the elevators, she studied herself closely in the shiny, reflective metal, and smoothed her skirt and hair down.

Sharon came in after escorting them out.

"Wow," she said. "Can I have that guy's number? He was gorgeous."

"She wasn't bad either. Here's his number and hers too." I handed her the business cards. "Put them in our vulture database and then put the cards back in my Rolodex, okay? I wrote their asset preferences on the back of his card."

"Will do," she said, looking at her watch. "It's 1:45."

"Damn," I said, grabbing my reports off the printer. "Call Lawson and tell him I'm on the elevator right now."

◆

"I'm going to need a team on this," I said to Lawson after I was seated in his office. "It's too big a job for just me."

"Of course," said Lawson. "Who do you have in mind?"

"I'm definitely going to need my lieutenants, Vinny and Earl."

Lawson frowned at this.

"Well, to be honest that is where I was going to try to put the bulk of your current work assignments. I don't think we can afford to have the your entire SAG group working this for the next three weeks."

"Lawson, you said I could…"

He held up his hand. "How about we compromise and you can have one of them but not both? I know a retired SAG guy I can call in to take up some of the slack here. He won't want to travel much, but I can give him the stuff that's being worked in North and South Carolina, and he won't have to get on a plane any. I will split the other states with whichever of your lieutenants stays put. It's only for three weeks."

"Fair enough," I said.

"Which one do you want?" asked Lawson.

I thought about my two lieutenants. Earl Waltrip was the brighter and more experienced of my subordinates, a slow-talking, deliberate Southerner. I had come to view him as my right arm.

But Earl would want to take his time and assess everything before making any decisions or even forming an opinion. Vinnie, his temperamental opposite, would dive right in and start busting up the china. I needed the latter. Plus, Vinnie would be entirely un-intimidated by New York investment bankers.

"Vinnie, I guess," I said. "Earl would do better here, watching the shop."

"Very well, Vincent it is," said Lawson. "Who else?"

"I'm going to need an analyst. But not one of mine. My impression is, this portfolio is mostly corporate, publically-issued bonds, is that right?

"Sixty percent would probably fit that bill, although don't hold me to the exact number. But there are some private placements, some loans and loan participations, some international and some asset-backeds."

"Well, I am going to need a good corporate bond analyst, and I don't have one on my staff."

"Where can you get one?" said Lawson.

"George Lamb has one on his staff," I said. "He won't want to let her go. But she's the only one in the bank I can think of. I sure don't want to go out on the street and try to hire one. We are kind of in a hurry here."

"I will handle that," said Lawson. "What's her name?"

"Melanie Bissell. They call her Mel. She grew up around here, Carolina undergrad, Michigan MBA. She's been on the bond desk for about two years. She is the go-to girl down there on pricing corporates. Plus she has some international and asset-backed experience."

"Fine," said Lawson. "I will call you first thing tomorrow morning about it. Meantime keep it under your hat. Who else?"

"What are you going to do? Call George? Because I have to tell you, Lawson, that guy..."

"Sam? I said I'll handle it. Now who else?"

"Counsel," I said. "I need a good debtor's attorney. He's going to have to be with me the whole time. Outside counsel, not in-house."

"Do you have someone in mind?"

"Yeah, I've worked with this guy several times recently, his name is Jay Podolski, his firm is Podolski and Wickham. They are new to Charlotte, the firm has only had an office here about a year, their main office is in Chicago. Jay's wicked smart. He'll be perfect."

"Are they big enough to take on a job like this?" said Lawson.

"I think so. Most importantly, though, is that they are only debtor's counsel. So they won't get conflicted out. If we go to any of the bigger Charlotte or New York firms, then there are going to be a ton of conflicts of interest, and the firms will have to bail on us in some situations because they represented someone in the portfolio. That's not going to happen much with this firm."

"Have you hired him yet?"

"No, I was waiting on you to give me the blessing."

"You are hereby blessed. Hire him. Get Legal to draw up the engagement letter.

"Then go down and give the news to your staff. Tell both Vincent and Earl to come see me at 4:00. Meantime I will get in contact with this retired guy, work on dividing out your current work and get that young lady off the bond desk. You need to go see security and the computer folks, and get access to whatever you need. Let's meet again at 9:00 tomorrow morning and see where we're at."

"Yes, sir," I said, starting to rise from my chair. Then I sat back down and said:

"You know, Lawson, these investment bankers are not going to be happy to see me. I mean, we made them this promise to buy them and leave them alone to run the business as they saw fit. And now I'm going to show up the day after their most senior guy has been fired and say, 'Hi, I'm with the commercial bankers from Charlotte, open up the books, we want to see how bad you guys have been screwing us.'"

"Sam, the losses in their portfolio were purposefully hidden from us. That's why their president got fired. Our president got fired for not noticing it. Nobody got fired because the crap was on the books; it was for the way they handled it afterwards. So the way the chairman sees it, and the way I see it, the investment bank broke the deal, not us. Now we have to fix it, and they can either help or they can get out of the way. But what they cannot do is obstruct us."

"Lots of ways to do that while appearing that you're not," I said.

"Of course," he said.

"What about this Clifton guy, the ex-president? So he's just going to be hanging around the trading floor until the end of the month?

"I doubt you will see him much, Sam. He is probably going to be out looking for a job."

Lawson studied me for a minute and could tell I was still unhappy.

"Sam, this will undoubtedly be a hard, nasty, time-consuming project. But it's got to be done, and right away. That's why I'm sending you. Now go on and take care of your business. I'll see you first thing tomorrow morning."

I turned to leave and heard him rummaging around in his desk. As I got to his door I glanced back and he had thumbed some tobacco into his pipe and was firing it up.

"And no, I don't give a damn about the smoking rules around here right now either," he said.

5

I gave myself a long look in the mirror on Thursday morning before work and, figuratively, caught my breath. The last three days had been a whirlwind and every night I had gotten home after 10 p.m.

Staring back at me was a grown man with his face darkened by the sun, as it usually was this time of year. I had a slight stubble. There was a blonde sun streak in my short brown hair and my blue eyes, which could get bloodshot on the occasion of too many beers, were clear. I was still holding my weight well and keeping myself fit with running and watersports. Fishing too—some people don't think fishing is much of a sport but then they didn't fish so what would they know? I sighed and picked up my razor.

Tuesday and Wednesday, Lawson and me had divided up my portfolio and Vinnie's between him, Earl and Lawson's re-hired retiree. Earl was excited to be left in charge; Vinnie was excited to be joining me on the investment bank project. He had to make the requisite introductions to his accounts, so he would be out of the office until Monday, when he would join me full time.

The firm of Podolski and Wickham was honored to take on the legal engagement. As I had thought, they anticipated no conflicts of interest, and with a little wordsmithing we had already negotiated and signed the engagement letter. Jay would meet me for lunch on Friday.

Lawson told me that when he called George Lamb to tell him that he needed his bond analyst Melanie Bissell for a three week special assignment, George had laughed at him and asked him who the hell he thought he was. Lawson then proceeded to show him who he was by having the chairman call George's boss. Mr. Avery told him that Melanie Bissell would be assigned to me immediately. When George's boss started to complain, Mr. Avery had told him if he didn't like it he could put his objections in writing, accompanied by his resignation letter.

Melanie Bissell would become a SAG employee and be in my office at the open of business Monday morning.

None of that was going to endear me to the various salesmen, traders and bankers who populated the investment bank.

The security folks had given me new badges for my team that basically would get us through any doors at the bank. I think we could have gotten into the main vault with them.

I got the lady who ran Information Systems on a conference call with one of her technicians. She widened my computer access to cover all the investment banking, treasury and trading systems, and did the same for Earl and Melanie. I said I also needed a trading station set up in one of my spare offices on the tenth floor. I wanted Melanie to be able to trade without going back down to the trading floor.

"That's going to take a while," said her tech. "A week at least. We're going to have to run cable from…"

"That's fine," his boss interrupted. "Sam, when do you need that set up?"

"Close of business Monday?"

"Two days?" said the tech. "Look, there is no way…"

"Sam, we got the memo," she interrupted again. "Or at least I did. We'll have it done by lunch on Monday."

"Lunch on Monday?!" the tech said incredulously.

"Lunch on Monday," she said firmly, and the tech had the sense to shut up. "What else do you need from us, Sam?"

There was nothing else for Information Systems, and I had already spoken to the investment bankers about the project. As I predicted, they didn't like the fact that their chief had been fired, that Melanie was assigned to me, or that I had been assigned to revalue their portfolio. Most of all, though, they just didn't like me.

George Lamb had ignored my greeting to him yesterday morning on the trading floor and brushed past me as if I wasn't there. His boss, the one that the chairman chewed out, saw me on the floor and told me:

"I know what you are here to do but I don't like it. I don't think you're capable of understanding the assets we have on the books, much less marking them to market. I know you've got weight with the chairman of the bank, so I am not going to get in your way. But I still have a job to do and I don't have time to be holding your hand. I want Melanie Bissell back in this department in three weeks like I was promised."

He then turned on his heel and marched off.

Rajat, the head of the international desk, was at least cordial, but he had little time for me as well. His eyes were on Russia and he did not seem to like what he saw. He probably gasped awake every night in a cold sweat, wondering about the bond positions he had taken in countries that he had neither visited nor fully understood.

Nobody from the I-bank Credit department helped either. Although they were ultimately responsible for the larger positions in the portfolio, they remembered neither specific transactions nor general portfolio parameters. Who had initially recommended a deal, that I might talk to about it? They couldn't recall. Did they sign off on it? What did they know about the company now? What kind of reporting was coming in? They would get back to me on all that. They were afraid of losing their jobs, and burrowing their heads into the sand in hopes that they wouldn't be noticed.

So where did that leave me and my crew?

"You want a friend?" said Gordon Gekko in the now-famous 1987 movie *Wall Street*. "Get a dog."

I shaved and drove into work.

The trading floor was subdued that morning, although there was still a quiet rumble at the international desk. I went up there and looked over a trader's shoulder. He had a chart of the Russian equity markets on the screen. It was a sea of red. Russian stocks were down almost 70% in the last year. Oil, Russia's biggest export and primary source of foreign currency, was down almost 25%. Bond yields were surging; those few brave souls willing to lend the Russians money were asking over 100% interest for short-term loans. I knew bookies who charged less.

I looked around and saw that most of the salesmen and traders were on their phones. I saw Rajat talking quietly into his phone, too. He looked like he was about to lose his breakfast.

But looking around at the screens and markets from the other countries, it seemed to be a normal trading day—stocks up a little here, down a little there, bonds not doing much. So far the Russian problems seemed to be contained in Russia. The U.S. market would not open for another hour or so.

I left the floor and went up to my office. Browsing around the trading floor was informative, and a good way to get a daily temperature on the markets, but I was not kidding myself. That was not where the work was going to be done. The investment bank's portfolio was causing the losses that had the chairman so exercised, and I needed to get my snout down in it.

I had two days, four counting the weekend, before my staff was fully assembled, and I needed them. Come Monday morning I had to have a plan. Last night, using my new system access, I had ordered a few programs run on the portfolio.

How big was it? How many individual positions did it hold? What were the asset types and were they liquid? This job had to be broken down into manageable parts quickly or we would never meet the three week deadline.

I logged onto my computer and as promised I had several internal emails with the analytics I had asked for. The portfolio had been subdivided up into separate asset types, six in total. I sighed and, calculator at the ready, opened up the first one.

Around lunchtime, having gotten through the whole portfolio once, I called Lawson.

"Hi Lawson, I'm going through the portfolio right now. Couple of quick questions for you."

"Shoot," he said.

"There is a fairly large repo book here. Several billion dollars. Do you want me to get involved in that?"

"Repo" stands for repurchase agreement in this case. It's a fairly standard way for banks to borrow from each other.

"No," said Lawson. "None of the losses have come from that portfolio. It seems to be fine. Leave it be."

"And you don't want me messing with the equity book, either, do you?"

"No, the stock trading operation here is fairly small, and easily marked. Leave that be too."

"What's the story on the derivatives book? I asked for information on it but the computer guys gave me nothing."

"There is none," said Lawson. "Thank the Good Lord, these boys did not do any derivatives underwriting or trading."

"Well that's good news I guess. So that leaves just the debt, right?"

"That's where the problems are," he said. "Unless I miss my guess, we have two portfolios there, Held for Sale and Own to Maturity, is that right?"

"You got it," I said. "The Held for Sale is about a billion, and the Own to Maturity is a little less than two billion. I figure the Held for Sale is the active trading book, which would change just about every day, where the Own to Maturity is more long-term investments which would be more stable."

"You'd be surprised," said Lawson, "and that is where some of the trouble has been. These traders will buy a bond to help a deal along, 'provide liquidity' as they like to say. Then, when they go to sell it, sometimes they don't like the price they get. In fact, if they took that price, they would have to take a loss in their own book. So suddenly, magically, the bond which was supposed to be a short-term holding shows up in the Own to

Maturity portfolio, and the bank is stuck with it. So we are going to have to dig into that issue pretty good."

"Okay. There is a sub-portfolio inside the trading book for international bonds. How about that?"

"Yes, we will definitely want to understand that. What else?"

"That's it for now," I said. "I am still trying to get a handle on the size of this thing, and how to work it. Is the chairman expecting a report from us on this Friday?"

"I would expect so," said Lawson. "I think he will understand if it is brief."

"I will have something to you after lunch on Friday, is that all right?"

"Sure. And Sam? Let's keep this report close to the vest, please. Send the email to the chairman, with a copy to me, make sure you have a copy in your files, and that's it, okay?"

"Yes, sir," I said, and we hung up.

$3 billion, give or take a few million, and believe me a few million is a rounding error when you are playing in this big a park. I could fret about the size of the thing, I guess, but in truth Lawson had cut my job down significantly. Not having to worry about the repo book or the stock portfolio was a big weight off. And no derivatives book! It could take three weeks just to value that. Now, at least, I was dealing with one general asset—debt—that I knew pretty well.

I closed the door to my office, forwarded my phone to Sharon, and pulled up to my computer keyboard. It was time to dive a little deeper.

Around 7:00 that evening I turned the computer off and rubbed my bleary eyes. I had a start on it, but I was tired now and making simple mistakes with formulas and programming. It would still be there tomorrow.

As I headed for the elevator my cellphone rang.

"Hello, Sam? Hi, it's Ana," said a woman's voice.

"Who?"

"Ana. Anastasia Primo de Montez. Remember we met in your office a few days ago? I am with Santiago Capital. I was with my associate Marcos."

Oh, that Ana, I thought. The *columbiana* with beautiful skin, long, shiny hair, a model's legs and tits like halves of a cantaloupe.

"Oh, of course," I said. "How are you?"

"I'm fine," she said. "I have caught you in the middle of something?"

"No, in fact I was just about to leave work and head home," I said. "I thought you and Marcos were on a roadshow up north somewhere."

"Well, we were just in Richmond, Virginia, but I received a call that I am needed back in Miami tomorrow. I could not find a direct flight; the only one that I could get connected in Charlotte. So I am staying here in Charlotte tonight. My flight doesn't leave until the morning. I was hoping I could buy you a drink?"

I hesitated. I was tired. If it was her associate Marcos making the same call, then I probably would have begged off. I wasn't really up for a wine-and-dine listening to all the great reasons why my bank should sell assets to Santiago Capital.

But it wasn't Marcos, was it? It was a beautiful, single lady all alone in the big city of Charlotte. And I was a Southerner, wasn't I? We must be hospitable to our foreign guests.

"That would be great," I said. "Why don't we meet at Ri Ra's? It's an Irish pub just a few blocks from the bank." She told me her hotel and I gave her directions. I told her I would be there in 10 minutes.

"Fantastic!" she said. "I just need to change clothes and I will be right there."

I swung by the bathroom, washed my hands and face, took off my jacket and tie and stuffed them in my briefcase. I unbuttoned a button on my shirt, and ran some water over my hair. Best I could do. I took the elevator down to the street and walked a half a block to the bar.

I was staring at the remnants of a pint of beer when Ana walked in. Or made an entrance, would be a better description. She had on a short silk summer dress, spaghetti straps, sandals and not much else. You can tell a woman is gorgeous when not only the men but the women stare at her.

She saw me at the bar and gave me a long hug, pushing her breasts against my chest. In flat shoes she stared me right in the eye, which made her right about 5'10". She smelled like an exotic incense. She stayed in touch with me—her breasts, her arm, her hip—until she was seated next to me.

"You look wonderful," I said. "And you smell so nice."

"Thank you," she said as she pulled her bar stool closer. "And thank you for meeting me on such short notice. It is so nice to have a friend in an unfamiliar city."

The bartender approached and stood at a polite distance. She saw I was drinking beer and wrinkled her nose. She was not a beer girl.

"What kind of rum do you have?" she asked.

The bartender ran down the list of rums they carried. Nothing appealed to her.

"What about tequila?" she said, and as he was running down that list she stopped him at one she liked.

"I will have that," she said, "on the rocks with a lime, and salt the rim please."

The bartender looked impressed and then nodded at me. "Another beer, sir?"

"You know, I think I'll have what she's having," I said.

"Excellent," he said.

She smiled and squeezed my arm.

"You like tequila, Sam?" she said.

"I do," I said. "It's not something I order often."

"I prefer rum,' she said, "but in Miami you can find the best rums, and here is just average. But this is very good tequila."

The drinks came. She licked the salt on the rim of the glass and then squeezed the lime into the drink and took a large sip.

"See?" she said. "Just like to have a shot!"

I followed suit. The tequila was smooth and strong and I felt my face flush slightly. Take it easy, here, ace: tonight is a school night. We have to be able to function in the morning.

I chatted with Ana. She said they had covered the Charlotte banks and had spoken with two firms in Richmond, with plans to see a couple of others, but she had been called back to Miami to deal with a troublesome client. Marcos would have to finish the roadshow on his own.

We ordered another drink. I told her that we might have a chance to do some business together soon, that I was looking at the investment bank's portfolio and was not sure what I would find. She said she had seen the news about the head guys in the papers in the last few days, and was that related? I said it was and told her a little of the background behind the firings and the portfolio problems.

We finished our second drinks.

"Well it would be wonderful if we could do some business together, but that is not why I called you tonight." Then she leaned over, put her hand behind my neck, and gave me a long slow kiss right on the mouth, slipping her tongue in at the last second and then disengaging before I could get my hands around her.

"Excuse me to go to the ladies' room," she said, and giving me another brush with her soft breasts, she pushed past me and walked toward the restrooms.

The bartender raised his eyebrows at me. I probably looked shell-shocked. She came back in a few minutes and asked for the check. I tried to get it but she said, no, no, she had asked me to drinks, she was buying.

"You would like to have another drink at my hotel?" she asked as she settled the bill. The bartender's eyes bulged—if I wasn't going, he seemed to be saying, he was.

"Uh, sure," I said.

In twenty minutes we were in her hotel room.

In the gloaming of the evening, outlined against a slatted window that looked out onto downtown Charlotte, Anastasia Primo de Montez slid out of her silk dress and revealed her stunning figure in French-cut white silk panties that were high on her hip, and a matching low-cut bra. I was sitting on the bed and I reached for her but she pushed my hands away.

"No, you are too eager, just watch," she said.

She reached around to undo her bra clasp. As she did she leaned over so that her cleavage was about two inches from my nose. Again I reached for her but she evaded my clutch, turned back around and let the bra fall to the floor. She cupped her breasts with her back to me, looked over her shoulder and smiled.

My Johnson was so hard I could have drilled for diamonds with it.

Still with her back to me, she started to pull her underwear down over her ass. She let me see a little of it, then pretended to by shy and pulled them back up slightly.

"Don't look, you are too fast," she said coyly.

But I had seen enough of the strip tease. I grabbed her and threw her on the bed. I pulled her panties down quickly and threw them across the room. She squealed and said:

"No, not yet!"

I pushed myself on top of her. She pretended to struggle but I kissed her hard and she kissed back while working on getting my belt and pants off. Foreplay was over. I got her bra off and her tits had large, dark aureoles. Her underwear was next; she had blacker-than-ink pubic hair. I separated her legs slightly and plunged in.

She cried out. She was so moist as to be slippery. The strip tease had turned her on as much as me. I took her nipple in my mouth and caressed it with my tongue.

"Bite it," she said.

I gave it a little tug with my teeth.

"Harder," she demanded.

I bit down on it and she moaned.

"*Otra,*" she said, pushing my face to her other breast, and I gave the other one the same treatment.

I wanted to take it slowly, to pay her back for the striptease, but now she was the eager one. She clutched at my back and said things in Spanish that I couldn't understand. She came quickly, arching her back and going strangely silent at the top, then letting out a low guttural moan. For a moment we lay entwined on the bed as she caught her breath. Finally she said:

"I have been a bad girl. Selfish in love. You must punish me for it."

She turned over and pushed her ass up in the air.

"Spank me," she said.

I laughed and lightly slapped her on the butt.

"No!" she said. She grabbed my pants off the floor and pulled the belt out from them. "Use this!"

I gave a slight slap to her butt with my belt.

"*Mas fuerte!*" she said.

I strapped her a couple of good ones. She wriggled slightly on the bed.

"Yes, like that, again," she whispered.

I gave her another slap or two with the belt, then I rubbed myself against her from behind. She raised her hips and I put my weight on her and slapped her with the belt again. She bucked and I shoved deeply into her and we both cried out. I alternated belt slaps with deep pushes into her, and in a few minutes we both came wildly together, clawing and grasping.

For Act 3, she had me use the belt to tie her hands to the headboard. She was still on her stomach. I noticed, as she instructed me, that she was looking in the mirror above the bed, but not at me or the action. She was looking at herself. Maybe she just liked to watch.

"Treat me like your slave," she said. "Do whatever you want to me."

So I did.

◆

I came awake quietly, as I usually do. Ana was sleeping next to me.

My loins ached. The bed was destroyed. The room was darkened, although there was a light on in the bathroom that cast dimly throughout the room. I looked at the clock. 6:08, it blinked back at me.

I looked at Ana lying rumpled on the bed next to me. She was sleeping face down, naked, with her hair halfway off the bed and my belt still partially roped around one of her arms. Last night while we made love, I had caught her looking in the mirror next to the bed several times. At first I thought, well maybe she just likes to watch, but gradually I noticed that she wasn't looking at me. She was looking at herself.

I nudged her awake.

"What time did you say your flight was?" I asked.

"Mmmm...hey baby...7:30 I think."

"It's after 6 a.m.," I said. "We better get going."

She quickly showered and dressed, and I put my clothes on from the night before. As we were gathering our things and getting ready to walk out the door, she accidentally knocked my wallet off the credenza.

"I got it," I said, and reached down to scoop it up.

"*Lo siento,*" she said. "I am so sleepy."

We walked to my car, and I drover her to the airport. When we got to the airport, she gave me a long kiss, and I said something about enjoying it, and she did too, and we would talk soon. And then she took her suitcase and her briefcase and was gone, striding quickly and beautifully across the sidewalk and into the airport.

I left the airport and got back on the interstate. I had to drive home, shower, change clothes and then drive right back to work.

After I got home I cleaned out all my pockets and put my belongings on the kitchen counter. Then I showered and put another suit and tie on. I went back in the kitchen, put on my watch, and went to pick up my wallet and car keys. When I had tossed my wallet on the counter after coming in, it had hinged open, and I stared at it now as if it didn't belong to me.

I'm not obsessive-compulsive. My house is kind of messy. Underneath it's clean. I have a housekeeper in once a week, but there are a lot of things scattered around, suit jackets draped over chairs, books here and there, music and movie discs lying all over. I have one drawer for socks, and a different drawer for underwear, but I just throw the stuff in there. It's not all folded up neatly by color, or into perfect geometrical squares, or anything like that. I have a shoe rack in my closet, but I frequently have to go browsing through the house to figure out where I last left the pair I was looking for.

I am, however, fussy about my money. What can I say? I'm a banker. My checkbook is balanced to the penny. I rarely carry a credit card balance, but when I do I know exactly how much it is and what I spent it on. I pay my bills promptly; nothing drives me crazier than a $2 late fee.

And my wallet is organized, too. The money is in order from lowest to highest denominations. In the slips in the wallet, I keep my driver's license in the front, and then a credit card, a gas card, my medical insurance card and a library card. In that order. Because that's about the order of their usage.

Only, as I stared at my wallet on the counter, the cards weren't in order. The library card was in front, the credit card was in the middle, and the license was in the back.

I picked it up, pulled the cash out and counted it. It was a little over $200, which was right. Nothing missing. I looked at the outside. Nothing strange. I looked at the cards again. They were jumbled up, in the wrong order.

I remembered Ana knocking the wallet to the ground accidentally in the hotel room. I had picked it up. But nothing had spilled out. I didn't re-arrange anything. It was just the wallet on the floor.

Well, maybe it was that demon tequila that Ana had served me. Probably the cards had dropped out somewhere along the way, and I just didn't remember putting them back in. I re-arranged them in my wallet and put it in my coat. I looked at the time and thought, shit, I've got to get to work.

6

I swung by the trading floor first. It was a little after 8:00 and most of the traders were at their stations and the salesmen were trickling in. Again the floor was pretty quiet, with the exception of the international desk. Rajat was up there staring at a screen. I walked over.

"Morning Rajat," I said. "How's Russia?"

"Sam," he nodded. "Russia is not good. In fact, financially it's on the verge of total collapse. Basically no one is lending to them right now, and I don't know if they can make it to the weekend."

"Anything else being affected yet? Emerging markets or anything?"

"South America and Europe seem to be hanging in there. Asia is fine. But credit spreads are widening across the board. There's a massive flight into Treasuries; everyone is fleeing for a safe haven at the same time. If we can get through the weekend, and not have Russia spread to anywhere else, we should be fine. If not..." he left the rest unsaid.

"Good luck," I said. I made to leave and then turned back.

"Oh by the way, do you know if that deal George was working on ever got done? What was it, Seletrex or something like that?"

Rajat shook his head.

"It's still hung," he said. "Nothing's getting done right now. Until Russia settles out, everyone is on the sidelines."

Stay away from George Lamb and the corporate bond guys today, I thought. I turned away and headed for my office. As I passed the break room I glanced in and saw the strangest thing.

George was in there with Melanie Bissell, the bond analyst who was joining me on Monday. He had her cornered. His back was to me, and one arm was outstretched against a wall so that Melanie was penned in.

Melanie is a cute Carolina blonde with fine features and a nice figure. I would have guessed her age as 27 or so; she had been out of business school for a couple of years. I did not know here that well, but liked what I knew, and she had a reputation on the floor as a "quant," a math whiz who was very quick at the complicated business of pricing bonds.

Melanie is also petite, very small. George towered over her. She was facing me and had a look on her face that was part angry and part fearful. George was bent over and his face was very close to her, too close for a professional situation. With his other hand he was stroking a scarf that she had on. I was too far away to hear the conversation.

I decided to ignore my own advice. I went into the break room.

"George," I said. "Melanie. Good morning."

George turned around, upset at being interrupted and then looking even more aggravated when he saw it was me. He picked up his cup of coffee from a nearby table and brushed by me, again without speaking.

"Sorry if I interrupted something," I said.

Melanie snorted, and turned her back to me to fill a cup with ice. Was there a tear in her eye? Did I hear a sniffle as the ice from the machine cascaded into the cup?

Maybe I was imagining things. She filled her cup with soda, and when she turned back to me, she was perfectly composed.

"So I hear I'm working for you for the next few weeks, starting Monday," she said brightly.

"Yeah, I'm looking forward to it. I have been meaning to call you, but things have been a little busy lately."

"Tell me about it," she said. "With this mess in Russia, we've been spending all our time trying to settle our own customers down. And trying not to buy their bond portfolios."

"I'll fill you in on everything on Monday morning in my office, okay?" I said. "It's a very important project, it's going to be a lot of work, but you'll do a great job with it and I guarantee it will help your career down the road."

"My career," she grumbled softly to herself. Then she brightened again and said:

"Sounds good. I'll see you first thing Monday morning."

She walked out of the break room. I took the elevator up to my office, and after hanging up my coat, I stared out the window for a few minutes.

The political correctness police were everywhere at my bank, just like every other large corporation. I had already attended several seminars on sexual harassment, inter-office romance, what was and was not appropriate behavior toward the opposite sex, etc...

I had never sexually harassed anyone, so here is the effect all that lecturing had on me: I never complimented a woman again on how she looked at work; could be misconstrued. I never traveled alone with a woman; too easy for a misunderstanding to occur. I did not date anyone who worked at the bank, or even flirt with anyone; rumors might get started. And except for a handshake, I never, ever touched a woman again at work for any reason, not even an old-fashioned pat on the back. The rules of the game had been made clear, and I would surely follow them. But I wasn't going to pretend I believed that sexual harassment was rampant, or even common. It was an hysterical over-reaction drummed up by Personnel and Legal to justify their big salaries, was what I figured.

And then you see something like what I had just seen. Unless I missed my guess, that was nothing but an old-fashioned coercive sexual pass. George was propositioning Melanie and he wasn't being particularly subtle about it. And he was her direct supervisor. And she didn't appear to like it at all.

Melanie's reputation as a bond analyst was outstanding. It was why I knew of her, and why I picked her to join this project. But several of the people I had talked to mentioned one minor *caveat* about her: she should have been trading her own book by now. The bank's general career path for traders was, out of business school you are an analyst or a trader's assistant for a year or so, and then they give you your own book and your own client base to develop. Melanie had been out two years now, but was still working as an analyst for George and other traders.

The folks who told me that hurried to add that George appeared to really like her, and had resisted several attempts from other departments to poach her away from his group. But he had not promoted her, and no one really knew why.

Maybe I did, now. Maybe Melanie wasn't doing everything George required.

I sighed and sat down at my desk. If that was true I felt bad for Melanie, but it was not my little red wagon. My little red wagon consisted of a $3 billion portfolio that I still knew very little about. I turned my computer on.

For the next four hours I sliced and diced the investment bank's portfolio. Just before lunch I took some sheets off the printer, laid them on my desk, and studied what I had done.

After everything that Lawson had eliminated for me, there were three different asset classes remaining: standard bank loans, corporate bonds both domestic and international, and a catch-all I had labeled "exotics" because they really didn't fit anywhere else. In that basket went debt like asset-backed securities, collateralized bond obligations, private placements, etc...

It was a good start, but I needed to whittle it down some more before it became a manageable project.

Just then Sharon stuck her head in the door.

"You have lunch in ten minutes with Jay Podolski," she said.

"Thanks," I said. I picked up my jacket, and walked down to my favorite local restaurant, Mert's Heart and Soul, to meet with the principals of Podolski and Wickham.

Jay met me at the door with his partner, David Wickham. Jay was a slender man, about my height, with dark, thinning hair and a ready smile. David was older, a fleshy white-haired man who apparently lent *gravitas* when it was needed.

We were seated and after ordering, I laid out for the attorneys the task we had in front of us, and the time frame. They studied on that for a minute and then Jay asked:

"So are we selling the whole portfolio, or what?"

"Not the whole portfolio," I said, "this is more of a mark-to-market project. But we will undoubtedly have a problem marking assets, or find some positions that we really don't want to keep, so we might have to sell selectively."

"So what exactly do you want us to do?" asked David. "Of course we are glad to help anyway we can, but I don't imagine that you need attorneys telling you the value of corporate bonds or asset-backed securities."

"There are sure to be problem loans in the portfolio," I said. "We might have to get you involved in some quick workouts or restructurings. I don't anticipate being able to clean up a big bankruptcy candidate in three weeks, but we may in fact take someone BK, in which case we will need you as counsel until it is resolved. And we will need you for research purposes. I've already had a good look at the portfolio, and there are a bunch of names I don't recognize. I need some help from you guys figuring out who these corporations and the principals are."

Both Jay and David nodded their heads

"So when do we get started?" asked Jay.

"Right now," I said. I handed Jay a piece of paper and he read it aloud.

"Marcos Pereira, Anastasia Primo de Montez. Santiago Capital. Miami, Florida. Jonathan and Andrew Little. Entourage Capital Partners. Memphis, Tennessee. Who are these people?" he said.

"The first, Santiago Capital, is a vulture fund that called on me earlier this week. I want you to check them out. They gave me a pitchbook and they look pretty good. I want you to do a quick background check on them, who owns them, how long they have been in business, assets under management, that kind of thing."

"Are we going to be selling assets to vulture funds?" asked David.

"Almost certainly," I said. "You might as well pull out whatever forms you've got on note sales and purchases, and brush those up if they need it. We will have to move fast when the time comes.

"The second on that list, Entourage Capital Partners, is rapidly heading toward bankruptcy. We have millions out to them and have been trying to work something out for the last three months, with no success. You will meet my lieutenant Vinnie on Monday, he is handling this and will fill you in.

"The main thing I want you to work on right now is, where the hell are the Little brothers? They own the company, ran it when it was private and took it public, and they have so far refused to show up to any bank meetings. They seem to have disappeared from the face of the earth. They are unreachable. They are not at work, at home, or at any of their usual hangouts. And they almost always travel together.

"I don't want to take this company into bankruptcy without at least talking to them and telling them what's going to happen if we don't start getting some cooperation. So I need you to find these guys, so we can have a conversation with them."

"I can try," said Jay. "Now, on these principals at Santiago Capital, Marcos Pereira and Anastasia Primo de Montez. Do you want me to get into their personal backgrounds any?"

"Just make sure they exist," I said. "Right now I just want to make sure that Santiago Capital is who they say they are, and they can write a check as big as they say they can."

"How big a check do they say they can write?" Jay asked.

"A couple hundred million," I said.

"Got it," said Jay, scribbling some notes on the paper. "What else?"

"The kickoff party is in my office Monday at 9 am. I'll introduce you to the rest of the crew then. By then I should also have the portfolio broken down and a plan to address the problems."

"How soon do you need this information on the Little brothers and Santiago Capital?" asked Jay.

"Yesterday," I said.

David laughed. "That's how this whole thing is going to go, isn't it?"

"Yep," I said. "Sorry, but this deadline is very real, and I hired you guys because I figured you can move quickly when you need to."

"We can," David promised. "And we will."

Our lunches came, mine fried chicken of course, and after we ate I thanked them and told Jay I would see him first thing Monday. In the heat of the August afternoon I walked back to my office to do more work on the portfolio.

Around 4:00, eyes bleary from staring at computer screens and printouts, I left the portfolio alone and typed out a brief memo to Lawson and the chairman, describing the size of the portfolio and the team I had assembled. I also mentioned the disruption in the markets being caused by the Russian situation, but could not predict where that would go. Given where I was, there wasn't much else to say. I sent the email out, then I shut down everything and stuffed the portfolio papers and my laptop in my briefcase.

"Sharon, I'm going to swing by the trading floor, and then I am heading home. I'll be working this weekend, so if anyone needs me have them call my cell. I'll be checking voicemail and email all weekend."

"OK, have a great weekend, see you Monday," she said.

"You too," I said, and took the elevator down to the trading floor for one last glimpse at the markets before I left.

I was greeted on the trading floor that afternoon, with fewer than 10 minutes before the market closed, by an almost supernatural quiet. I didn't see George or Rajat anywhere. I saw a bond trader I knew who was sitting by himself at a row of trade stations, glumly staring at his computer screen. The rest of the floor was almost deserted.

"How did the market trade today?" I asked.

He barely glanced up.

"Equities and bonds both down," he said. "This Russia shit is really starting to spill over. I spent all day talking to clients who were trying to sell not just Russia, but anything that remotely has to do with Russia: oil, energy in general, commodities. I mean *nobody* wants to go home this weekend with any exposure to them."

Just then a computerized voice came over the intercom and announced that American markets were now closed.

The trader turned off his screen and picked his jacket up off his chair.

"And Elvis, having done what he can do, is now leaving the building," he said.

I followed him toward the door, planning to leave myself. As I walked toward the exit, I happened to look up.

There is a suite of offices for the big shots, like George and ex-president Randall Clifton, on one side of the trading floor. They actually are on the second floor—the trading floor has probably a 40-foot ceiling, and the offices are elevated above the pit on one side of it. There are four or five offices, a secretary guarding the stairs and elevator to them, and a catwalk around the offices that lets the chiefs come out and look down on the action on the floor.

Randall Clifton, the former head of the investment bank working a two-week notice, was doing that now, leaning up against the guardrail around the catwalk and looking down into the pit. My movement toward the exit must have caught his eye, and he stared at me for a long time. I had stopped walking and was looking back at him, wandering what he was doing. We stared at each other for a while, neither of us saying a word, until finally he broke eye contact with me, walked back into his office, and quietly shut the door.

Weird. I walked out the door to the elevator and went home.

◆

As I pulled into my driveway, I noticed that my bushes had been trimmed, my lawn cut and my flower beds cleared. Curtis's crew had been there that day. Pulling up to my house, I saw a big black pickup truck in the driveway, which meant that Curtis himself was probably on the property.

Curtis Plyler was my best friend, a six foot tall, powerfully-built black man whom I had grown up with and who lived two coves over on the lake. He had spent eight years in the Army, including five in Special Forces, and now owned a landscaping company that did residential and small commercial work all around Lake Norman. He employed maybe 30 people, and the business was profitable and well-run, not the least because Curtis had the discipline that his master-sergeant father and the Army had taught him. His customers included me and my land and a 40-year old A-frame on Lake Norman.

The lake was different now. Back when Curtis and I were kids, it was just a big body of water surrounded by fields and woods. We would hunt small game with .22 rifles and fish with hardly a care in the world, camping out on summer nights wherever we felt like staking our tent and eating what we killed. We would take a canoe and go back into the creeks, or if it got too hot we knew where there was a swimming hole with a tire swing. Our parents did not worry about us; they knew we were together and knew our way home.

Those farm fields are housing developments now. Staking a tent around the lake would get you run off before you could get it raised. When's the last time anybody from Lake Norman ate a rabbit? Much less shooting a .22 rifle—you could probably get thrown in jail for that.

Huge powerboats, some of them ocean-worthy, zoom up and down the water. You didn't want to be in a canoe when one of those things goes by. And anyway every kid over the age of 10 is now electronically tied to Mama's apron with a cellphone, and the idea of baiting a hook and catching a fish is as foreign to them as France. In fact, half of them don't even like the outdoors; video games are a lot more fun. Curtis and I still lived in the houses we had grown up in, but the life we had lived as kids was almost gone.

Curtis was taking his boots off on my front porch. "Come on in the house," I said, "let's get out of this heat." I opened the front door.

"What's up Sammy? Damn that air-conditioning feels good, doesn't it? You don't feel like doing any fishing tonight, do you?" He had a six pack of tall boys, minus one which was in his hand.

"No," I said. "I'm beat. I will entertain one of your friends there, though."

Curtis nodded and handed me a beer. He sat down at the kitchen table.

"Me too," he said. "I just ain't as young as I used to be. Working in this damn heat takes a toll."

I threw my jacket on the couch, took off my shoes and my tie, and joined him at the table. I cracked the beer. It was perfectly cold and I took down about half of it in one long slug.

"I see you know your way around a can of Budweiser," he said.

"Not my first rodeo, as they say," I said. We both then finished our beers at about the same time, crushed the cans, and got two new ones.

Curtis looked at me closely.

"You know, you do look beat. You got some serious bags under your eyes. You getting any sleep?"

I belched, then told him about the week at work, the guys getting fired, and me getting the portfolio job from the chairman.

"I saw that news about your president in the paper," Curtis said. "But hey, you have to feel good about the assignment. I mean, if the four-star is calling for your unit, he must have a lot of trust in you."

"I don't know if it's that, or they just don't have anyone else," I said.

Curtis shrugged.

"Same thing," he said. "You got the call because you're the best man for the job."

I then told him about my tryst with Ana Primo de Montez.

"Whoa!" he said. "Liked a little ass-spanking, did she?"

"She was a freak," I said. "And gorgeous too. You should see the body on that woman."

"We need to see if she has a sister or something," he said.

His eyes wandered to the couch, where there was a hardback book I was reading. He went over and picked it up.

"You reading this?" he said.

It was *Grant Takes Command,* a military history of the Civil War after Lincoln got tired of his wimpy generals and put Ulysses S. Grant in charge. It was supposed to be a classic.

"I started it, but haven't had much time for it lately," I said. "Have you read it?"

"Yes," said Curtis, "it was part of the curriculum in college."

"Is it any good?" I asked.

"Yeah, it is. Grant has taken a lot of flack over the years for being a butcher, just throwing his troops into the Confederate maw. And being a drunk and an anti-Semite and a bunch of other crap. But the man won. He accepted the surrender of three different Confederate armies. He saved the union, no question."

He tossed the book back on the couch.

"And," he continued, "that book is a good study of command. It's funny that you're reading it right now, right when you have this new project at the bank. There are some lessons in there that would be good for you to study on."

"I'm not fighting a war, Curtis," I said.

"You always say that," he said, "but leadership is leadership, and there is a lot to be learned from studying how commanders lead in battle. Grant came into a situation where everyone else—Winfield Scott, George Mclellan, Henry Halleck—had all failed. The one thing that Grant made clear to everyone was, they were going to fight. There weren't going to be any more 'tactical retreats.' The North had numerical and weapons superiority over the South, and had cut off most of its supply lines. But that only mattered if they fought. So Grant said, we are going to fight them wherever we find them, wherever they will sit still long enough for a fight. And he got everyone on board with that. And that's what leaders do."

Our second tallboys were finished.

"What say we take your boat up to Bill's for some 'cue?" said Curtis.

"Let me change my clothes. And don't start on that last beer either. Save it for the ride up."

We rode 20 minutes up the lake to Bill's Barbecue, and stuffed ourselves with barbecue sandwiches, hush puppies and pitchers of draft beer. Then we settled up our tab, drifted back down the lake, naming constellations in the crystal clear starlight above our heads. Curtis got in his truck and went home, and I laid down on the couch and turned on the TV. I awoke around 2 a.m. to the sounds of an old Bruce Lee movie, turned off the TV and stumbled into bed.

7

In 1998, the size of the U.S. stock market was a little north of $11 trillion. The U.S. bond market, including federal and municipal government debt, was roughly the same size. For some reason most everyone has heard about stocks, but not many know about bonds.

Corporate bonds are simply debt issued by corporations and funded by the investment community. Say you are BigCorp. You need money to build a new plant? You sell $500 million in the public market; professional investors provide the money. You pay them back over time, with interest, just like a loan. The big thing about bonds is, they are publically traded, just like stocks. You have a bond from BigCorp that you want to sell? You can get a quote from your broker in 10 minutes.

Corporate loans are for SmallCorp. Loans come from banks. You are a family-owned business, with a nice track record of profitability, but you only need $2 million for your building expansion? You go see your local banker; he gives you the $2 million. The big thing about loans is, they are not publically traded. They are illiquid. If you are a bank that wants to sell your loan to SmallCorp, you can't go to your broker. It's tougher to sell.

"Exotics" like asset-backed securities, private placements, loan participations, all these things are hybrids, some combination of loans and bonds. They might be liquid, they might not.

On Saturday morning I got out of bed and, feeling guilty about a lunch of fried chicken followed by a dinner of barbecue, went for a long run. After showering up and eating breakfast, I went into the spare bedroom that doubled as my office, and hooked up my laptop.

My main goal that weekend was to organize the job. I had already subdivided what was left into three portfolios: loans, bonds and exotics. Now I wanted to find all the good assets within those three sub-portfolios, so that when I handed out the list on Monday, we wouldn't waste our time on good assets. The only thing we would be working on would be a) bad assets and b) assets we didn't know much about yet.

I logged onto the bank's information system, and also onto the rating agencies' sites. Rating agencies are public companies that theoretically provide objective information on bonds; they are far from perfect, but one more piece of data about bond quality certainly would not hurt. I then began the laborious task of figuring out which assets were good. If I could separate the good from the bad and unknown, then the job might become do-able in three weeks.

For all day Saturday, and most of Sunday, I didn't answer the phone or talk to anyone. I ate tuna fish out of the can and leftovers from the fridge. I drank water and sun tea that I made out on the porch. Finally, late Sunday evening I printed the results of my work out on my printer, and shut everything down.

I had basically cut the job in half. Starting with a $3B portfolio, I had identified $1.7 billion in assets that were fine. They were either known to the bank through previous relationships, and were highly regarded, or were publicly rated "investment grade" or better by the rating agencies. All of them were current, making whatever payment they were supposed to make.

That left $1.3 billion, slightly more than 150 different assets, that were either clearly in trouble, or that I just didn't know anything about. The assets were distributed about equally through the bank loans, the bonds, and the exotics, although as I had noted earlier there were a troubling number of small exotic positions: $5 million here, $6 million there, with either no ratings or very low ratings from the rating agencies. The New York investment bank had a policy of not buying any junk bonds. But there were a suspicious number of BBB-positions, which is just one step above junk, and more than a few securities that were not rated at all.

I yawned and rubbed my eyes. The answers would come soon enough. I threw the papers and the laptop into my briefcase and went to bed.

◆

Monday morning at 9:00 the troops gathered in the conference room next to my office. I introduced Jay Podolski to the bankers, then introduced Vinnie to Melanie. We all sat down.

"OK, here's the deal. You are all aware of the personnel moves that were made at the bank last week. The primary reason for both of those guys leaving was the big losses in the portfolio that the investment bank brought to the merger. The chairman has tasked our boss, Lawson McCoy, to dig into this portfolio and mark it to market. Lawson has asked me to do the work, and I have picked you to help.

"Vinnie, you have the loan book. This week I broke it down for you into good assets, bad assets and unknowns."

I slid some papers across to him.

"The good assets I verified through the rating agencies and the bank's internal system. Don't spend any time on those. What I need is your read on the bad assets and the unknowns. There are 42 total transactions totaling about $330 million in your loan portfolio."

Vinnie was nodding vigorously. He was ready to go.

"I have widened everyone's computer access to cover treasury systems and investment banking systems. Here are your access codes and your new badges, which will get you pretty much anywhere you need to go in the bank."

"Sounds perfect," Vinnie said.

I turned to Melanie.

"Melanie, you are on corporate bonds. Most of your portfolio is domestic but you've got some internationals too. I did the same analysis for you that I did for Vinnie. You have a lot of rated transactions. According to my math your bad/unknowns total 56 transactions and $650 million. The policy of your investment bank, as you know, was not to buy any junk, but that doesn't mean there isn't any in there."

"Oh, there's some in there, all right," she said. "If you buy a BBB- bond and it gets downgraded, then just like that you have a junk bond on your hands."

"Okay, anyway, you're job is the same as Vinnie's. I need to know how much garbage we have and what specifically it is."

"Got it," said Melanie.

"And that leaves me with the exotics," I said. "There are 54 transactions and $320 million in outstandings. It's mostly asset-backeds: cars, mortgages, credit cards, CBOs and all that. There are a few loan participations and a few other odds and ends. There's a lot of small stuff in this book, and I expect some of it is related to the other two books, so we need to stay in close contact about the problem assets we find. I don't want to be working a $5 million asset-backed stub only to find out that it's part of larger relationship in the loan book that I didn't know about."

Everyone nodded.

"I've arranged offices for Jay and Melanie up here for the next three weeks. Jay is available for any legal issue that comes up. Melanie, you'll have a trade station up before lunchtime today. Sharon will gather up everyone's extensions and cell phone numbers and print out a list so we can all reach each other at any time. And we work this thing 24/7 until it is fixed, okay? It is number one on the chairman's to-do list, which makes it number one on ours. Any questions?"

"Are we selling bad positions, or do we just want a better estimate of the loss?" asked Mel.

"We have to be careful of bank relationships here. I want to sell anything we don't like, but we don't want to upset an important client if we can help it. Obviously we can sell one-off transactions, or orphan credits, where there is no customer relationship and the bank was just trying to make some money. Most of those will be in the bond book or the exotics. Long-term problems will mostly occur in the loan book, and we will treat those like any other workout: meet with the client, try to remediate the situation, move it to an appropriate risk grade, and estimate the loss. But nobody disposes of anything until talking to me, okay?

Nods all around.

"Okay," I said, "let's get to it."

♦

While Sharon was showing Jay and Mel their offices, and collecting phone numbers and emails, I took a quick ride down to the trading floor to check out the international desk.

This time the domestic markets were open, so the floor was buzzing, but the international desk was once again the center of attention. Guys were yelling into phones again, staring at computer screens and muttering at the TV. Rajat was in a quiet and tense conversation with his boss off in one corner.

I saw "Elvis," the guy who had left the building with me on Friday, and asked him what was up.

"Today's special is currency devaluation!" he said in the tone of a game show host. "Yes, friends, the Kremlin has officially announced it is defaulting on all ruble-denominated debt and will no longer allow the ruble to float against other currencies. And what is behind Door Number Two, you might ask? Perhaps Brazilian default? We'll be right back after this important commercial message from our sponsor."

Traders come in all flavors; this one was apparently a comedian in his spare time. His phone rang, and I left his desk and took a few steps forward to hear an exchange between one of the traders and Rajat.

"Rajat, Jimmy over at Radar Capital will give us 12 cents on that Russian oil position, what is it, Gasprom?" The trader was holding the phone away and covering up the mouthpiece.

"We have $10 million bonds?"

The trader nodded.

"Sell it," said Rajat without hesitation.

The trader nodded and got back on the phone.

"You're going to take an $8.8 million loss on a $10 million bond?" Rajat's boss asked.

Rajat shrugged.

"You said get us out of Russia. This is what it's going to cost."

I tiptoed away. It was going to be a bad day on the international desk. The question that remained, as Elvis had so succinctly put it, was what was behind Door Number Two? Would the contagion in Russia spread? Was this permission for other countries to throw in the towel on their debt?

I was rounding the corner to the elevator when I literally bumped into someone who had just gotten off. Of course it had to be George Lamb.

"What are you doing down here now?" he asked. He shook his black curls as if they weren't arranged properly on his shoulders. His eyes were bloodshot and his nose looked irritated, like he had a cold or something.

"My job," I said.

"Your office is upstairs with the other HOSOBs," he said through stuffed-up naval cavities. "You don't have any business on the trading floor."

HOSOBs translates to Home Office Sons of Bitches.

"My job is wherever I decide it is," I said. "And just now I decided it was on the trading floor."

George's face reddened and he stared at me with icy blue eyes.

"You Southerners crack me up," he said. "We kicked your ass in the Civil War and here we are, 150 years later, and you still act like you didn't lose."

You know whenever a Yankee brings up the Civil War you are getting under his skin...or he is trying to get under yours.

"Why don't you call the chairman and tell him that?" I said. "He's from Charleston. I'm sure he would love to talk to you about the Civil War."

"Whatever," he said. "I know you and the chairman of the bank are tight. I could not care less."

Then he kind of crowded me and poked his finger into my chest.

"But this is my trading floor. If you keep putting your nose into my business, I am going to burn you down like Sherman did Atlanta."

I went to slap his hand away, but he spun and gave me a little shove and I fell back into the wall. Then he walked off, leaving me waving into thin air. I got on the elevator and angrily punched the button for my floor. As the doors closed, I looked back into the lobby, and saw that there were two security cameras up in the ceiling. Bank security had just gotten that on tape.

In my offices I found Mel getting situated in at her new desk. She was powering up her trading computers when I put my head in.

"I was just down on the international desk. Russia has defaulted on its international debt and devalued the ruble."

"Shit!" said Mel. "Come on, dammit," she said, banging on the side of her trade station as it slowly powered up.

"Rajat just sold $10 million Russian oil bonds for 12 cents on the dollar," I said.

"Really? That must be the Russian oil company. It needed to go. He's lucky to get 12 cents on the dollar for it."

"Apparently his boss has told him to get out of Russia," I said.

"Wow," said Mel. "It's the right call, but it's going to cost them. Russian bonds will be worthless by the end of the day.

The question is, what about other countries?   Kazahkstan is dead. Same for all of Russia's neighbors. Could this spread to Venezuela? Brazil? We could be looking at defaults for half of South America this week. Was there any word on that down there?"

"Nothing except speculation," I said.

"Well, I will get on it as soon as this trading station wakes up," she said, slapping the side again.

"All right," I said, "I will leave you to it. Let me know if it starts to look like it's spreading."

"You got it, boss," she said, and then her eyes lit up as the trade station screen finally came to life. She immediately started hacking away at her keyboard.

Vinnie was in his office with his face about three inches from the computer screen.

"Heads up," I said.   "Russia just defaulted on its international debt and devalued the ruble. I'm not sure if that affects anything you guys have, but there it is."

"OK, thanks, I will let you know if I see anything in here related to Russia," said Vinnie.

I gave the news to Jay Podolski, who was getting his office set up a door down from mine.

"What's that mean for us?" he said.

"Not sure yet. The international traders are selling out of all Russian exposure, and Vinnie and Mel are checking their books for any the traders might miss. I doubt there is much in our portfolio, but you never know, so we need to check through it. And if it spreads…"

"'If it spreads?'" said Jay. "How can it spread?"

"Well, if the market loses confidence in Russia, which it will clearly do, then people could start looking around to see who might be next. Where is the next weakest country? And if they start to pull funding from, say, Venezuela, then it can go on for weeks. And anyone owning stocks or bonds in those countries is going to get punished."

8

At about 7:30 that night I went through the offices and called a halt to business for the day. Mel and one of Jay's lawyers sat side by side at her computer screen; Vinnie and Jay had a stack of documents three feet tall on Vinnie's desk that they were going through.

"That's enough for today," I said. "I'm buying drinks across the street. Let's go."

We gathered at a darkened Irish bar called Connolly's, and after we got the drink orders in I asked Vinnie what he had found so far in the loan book.

"First glance, it's not too bad, but there are still some large loans that I don't know much about yet. There is definitely crossover in the portfolios. I've seen a lot of loans and then found related debt in the bond portfolio or in your 'exotics.' So you were right, we need to keep an eye on that."

I asked Melanie what she had found. She put down her drink to respond.

"I was mostly watching Russia today. Rajat sold everything he had before lunch. He took some big losses, but you know the old saying: first loss is best loss. In addition to Russia, I'm checking our emerging markets exposure, places like Venezuela, Brazil, Argentina, Mexico. I figure if Russia is going to spread, that's where it's going. Asia had its turn with this a few years ago, so they are probably not going to be vulnerable this time. Europe will hold on.

"In business school they teach you all about 'rational markets' and 'strong-form efficiency,' but when something this big hits everyone panics and all of these so-called professional investors turn into one big cattle stampede. When? Who knows, but if it's going to happen I think it will be pretty soon."

We had a second round. After my second beer I stood up and said I had to go. I encouraged them all to stay, telling them Jay had insisted on paying and it wasn't often that we would get into the wallet of Podolski and Wickham. This brought a laugh and a call to the bartender. Melanie pulled me aside while the drinks were coming.

"What time are you getting in tomorrow, Sam?" she asked.

"I don't know, I usually get here about 7:30. Why?

"I'm not sure yet," she said, "but I think Rajat bailing on Russia signals bad news ahead. We might ought to get out of some other emerging markets debt too."

"Okay," I said. "How much do we have?"

"It's over $100 million bonds," she said.

I looked at her with surprise.

"You want to sell $100 million of emerging market debt tomorrow?"

"Well, Rajat won't like it, but look, this Russia thing could spread really quickly. I mean, in 12 hours. So if we're going to get out, we need to go ahead and get out. It's about managing our loss right now."

"Let me sleep on it," I said. "What time do you want to get together?"

"Say 7:00? By then I will know how much we've got for sure, and I can start rounding up pricing information before the markets open."

"I'll see you in your office at 7:00 tomorrow," I said.

Jay walked with me to the door of the bar.

"I checked out Santiago Capital," he said. "They seem to be who they say they are. They've been in business for 25 years in Miami. Lots of rich Latino investors, particularly ex-pat Cubans. Not illegals, second- or third-generation families. My guy says a couple hundred million would be no problem for them. Pereira and Primo de Montez are listed in the employee directory. It all looks legit."

"Great," I said. "I'm going to get them on the phone with Vinnie and Mel tomorrow, get them introduced."

"I've got a guy working on those two brothers in Memphis, a private eye. Vinnie filled me in earlier on the company. I guess we are formally retained as counsel on that deal?"

"Yes," I said. "Like I told you, I really want to brace those brothers before we drive this thing BK. If they don't show, then we'll do what we have to do, but I want to make sure we have done everything we can to contact them and get them engaged."

"What is your gut on what is going on here?" Jay asked, leaning against the entrance to the bar. "Why are these two brothers ignoring the issue?"

"Best guess, they know exactly what the situation is and think it's hopeless, so they're staying away," I said. "But it could be anything. Maybe they are getting bad advice from their lawyers. Or maybe management is trying to pretend like they are working things out with us, and there is no reason for them to be involved. I tell you one thing, when they get the subpoena from the bankruptcy court judge, they will start paying attention. But the normal communication channels are not working right now, and I want to make sure we have exhausted every effort to talk to them before we put their company in bankruptcy."

"All right," said Jay, "I will let you know as soon as I hear from my man in Memphis."

◆

I sat on my deck that night. A front had come through and it was cooler than usual, no bugs. The lake was placid and still. There weren't many boats out on a Monday night, and except for the occasional splash of a fish or hoot of an owl, I seemed to have the place to myself.

Dozens of academic studies have been done on the difference between professional and retail, Mom-and-Pop investors. It turns out that, in managing profitable positions, the two are remarkably similar. Whether the pro or the individual bought a stock at $100, and watched it go to $125, they both rode it up intelligently, occasionally added to their positions, and generally knew when it was time to get out. Nobody was perfect at selling at the highest possible price, but both pros and retail investors knew when to take profits.

But there was a huge difference between the two in managing loss positions. When a pro bought a stock at $100, and watched it fall to $75, he would simply sell the stock and take his loss. His mentality was, I got that one wrong. Time to move on.

But the retail investor finds it impossible to admit that to himself. He stays with the stock as it falls further and further, even to $0 and bankruptcy, rather than take his medicine. Cold-eyed realism governs his winners, but unreasonable optimism and stubbornness rule his losers.

Melanie, I realized, was acting like a pro. We had losses in the bond portfolio. She was trying to keep them from getting worse. It's exactly what I would have done in the loan book, if it was liquid like the bonds.

And with that, I went to bed. Tomorrow, when we sold $100 million out from under the trading desk, I would need full body armor to deal with the backlash. But that night, I shut off the air-conditioning, turned on the ceiling fans, opened the windows and the screen doors, and fell asleep to the sound of the breeze softly blowing through the tops of the Carolina pines that surround my house.

◆

I met Melanie at 7 a.m. that Tuesday morning in her office. Her trade station was up and whirring. She looked at me expectantly.

"We have $126 million in emerging market debt," she said. "Brazil and Venezuela make up most of the Latin American stuff. There's $14 million in Asia, mostly South Korea. We've got nothing in Russia's neighbors, like Kazahkstan or Moravia."

"And you want to sell it all?" I said. "Is that going to move the market?"

"No," she said. "If people get the idea that we're selling, then they might try to drive us down on the price some. But I can mitigate that to a certain extent."

"How much are we going to lose?"

"Hard to say for sure, but I would say we would get at least 90 cents on the dollar on average, maybe as high as 95. So call it $6-12 million total."

"Okay," I said. "I'll tell Lawson. The guys on the trading floor aren't going to like it, but it's our call now."

"It's the right thing to do," she said.

"Have at it," I said. She turned to her trade station and her fingers started dancing across the keyboard. I punched her speakerphone on so she could hear the call, and dialed Lawson. He picked up on the first ring.

"We're selling all emerging market debt as we speak," I said. "It's over $100 million."

"I see," he said.

"Rajat doesn't know about it yet but he will not like it when he hears about it. None of the traders will. I need you to tell them that they cannot reinvest the proceeds in emerging markets. I'm afraid their going to go out and buy more risky debt with the cash we get today."

"I'll take care of it," said Lawson. "When will the traders figure out what is going on?"

"Soon," I said. "A matter of hours. They are likely to come at us like a screaming horde."

Lawson scoffed. "That is what they told Lee at First Manassas. But they did not reckon on my fellow Virginian Thomas Jackson. You and Melanie do what you need to do; I will protect our flanks."

He hung up. Melanie looked at me.

"First Manassas? Thomas Jackson?" she said.

"It was a Civil War battle. The Union called it Bull Run. It was the first major Confederate victory. Thomas Jackson earned the nickname 'Stonewall' there."

"I didn't realize we were so into Civil War history here at the bank," she said.

"I've worked here for five years and never heard it mentioned," I said. "Now it's been mentioned twice in two days. That's not a good sign."

She raised her eyebrows, but said nothing, and I left her to her trading station. Later that morning I swung back by her office and eavesdropped while she was on the phone.

"Hi Matt. Listen, we are doing a little rebalancing in the international portfolio. I've got a few bonds for sale. Interested in anything from Latin America? Brazil, maybe, Venezuela, Mexico?"

She listened then looked over her list and rattled off some CUSIP numbers, which identified specific bonds.

She waited some more and then said.

"$5 million here, $10 million there. How much you want?"

She acted outraged at the response.

"93? 93 cents on the dollar for a bond with this coupon? I was thinking more like 102." She saw me at the door and winked at me.

"95 huh? For $10 million Brazil '08s? 97 sounds a little more like it. No? 96? Okay, it's a deal."

She rattled off the details, and then got some operations people on the line to settle the trade and hung up.

"How's it going?" I asked.

"About like that," she said. "We are getting decent prices, but I am not selling any big chunks and am talking to anyone who will listen. I've been turning down anything under 94, but Venezuela is not moving and I might have to take lower for them pretty soon. We're averaging 95 right now."

95 cents on the dollar spread over a $126 million portfolio meant about a $6 million loss. Which might be stupid...or it might be brilliant. We would find out soon enough.

I went back to my office. Sharon was waiting on me.

"Hi Sammy," she said. "Those vultures are queuing up on the conference lines. It's almost 11:00."

"Right," I said. "Call everyone and ask them to come into the conference room."

When Mel, Vinnie and Jay Podolski had all gathered I said:

"Okay, as per my email yesterday, we are going to talk to three vulture capital funds right now. They are each getting five minutes; this whole thing will take 15. Just names, numbers, and emails, okay? I just wanted to make an introduction so you could hear their voices."

The phone rang and I punched it into speaker mode. Sharon said:

"Hi, Santiago Capital? This is Sharon at Citizens Union. Sam Wilson is on the line, go ahead."

The musical voice of Anastasia Primo de Montez came over the line.

"Hi Sammy!" she said. "Thanks for giving us a few minutes."

"Hi Ana," I said. "Is Marcos there with you?"

"Hi Sam, yes I am here," he said. "How are you?"

"Busy," I said. "I just wanted you to meet some folks. I think I told you last time we were together that we might have some assets for sale because of..." I borrowed a phrase from Melanie..."some portfolio rebalancing that we are doing. I have a couple of key people here, and I wanted you all to connect. I'll let my folks introduce themselves."

Vinnie went first, as usual speaking so fast that he had to take a deep breath when he was done. Melanie went next, and then Jay. Ana and Marcos then did the same thing. I then asked them to explain what Santiago Capital was looking for in assets.

"As we told you earlier, Sam, we are interested in anything with Latin American exposure," said Marcos.

Mel jumped in quickly.

"Does that mean sovereigns too?" she said.

There was a pause then. Ana and Marcos seemed to have put us on mute. Why? It was a simple question. Melanie looked at me with a question in her eyes. Then Marcos came back on the line.

"I'm sorry, can you explain the term 'sovereigns?'" he said.

Mel and I looked at each other again. What the hell? It was like you were supposed to be talking to a baseball umpire, but he didn't know what the phrase "foul ball" meant.

"Sovereigns," Mel said. "Direct obligations of a sovereign government. You know, like Mexican government bonds or Brazilian government bonds."

"Oh, of course," Ana said quickly. "I'm sorry, we were having a little translation problem with that. No, we don't like sovereigns. Here is what we do like."

And then she went through the list they had told me before: US corporations with international exposure, small and medium-sized domestic manufacturing companies, maybe asset-backeds, and no real estate.

"All right," I said. "Everyone can exchange contact information through emails. We've got to run now, thanks for calling in."

We did that drill twice more, with two other firms. We didn't find any more takers for sovereigns, but we had covered just about anything else that might exist in the portfolio. After we hung up with the third firm, I said:

"Okay, maybe if we need it, we can get a bid on some of this junk from the vultures. There are more in the database than these three; Sharon can help with that. I just chose these because they have been in contact recently expressing an appetite. Let's get back to it."

We were all clearing out of the conference room when Sharon nodded me over to her desk and said:

"Lawson called. He wants you up there right away. He asked that you bring Melanie."

Melanie and I looked at each other, then hopped the elevator up to Lawson's office.

"What do you think this is about?" she asked.

"Selling those bonds," I said, and sure enough in his conference room were Lawson, George, Rajat, and the big, baldheaded boss of the trading floor. He was the guy who tried to keep Melanie from her temporary assignment to SAG, and as a result got his ass chewed off by the chairman. He was also the one who had braced me on the trading floor and told me I wasn't qualified to understand his bonds.

"What's that guy's name?" I whispered to Mel as we approached the conference room. "Somebody told me once but I forgot."

"Brad Meunster. They call him The Monster sometimes. He's famous for making really large bets in the market. He's George's boss, he doesn't trade often but when he does it's always a really large position. He runs the entire sales and trading operation. Pretty aggressive personality. Very Type A."

Great. Me, Mel and the genteel Virginian Mr. Lawson McCoy against The Monster and his minions.

But I had again under-rated the steel in my boss.

Everyone was seated except Meunster, who said he preferred to stand. Rajat looked fairly calm, but George looked inflamed and irritated again. He blew his nose on a handkerchief.

"Sorry," he said. "Allergies."

"All right, everyone is here as you requested, Mr. Meunster," said Lawson. "Now what is the problem?"

"Our problem," said Mr. Meunster, "is simple. Your two people here are stepping all over our trading strategy. We simply cannot have people issuing sell orders outside our purview. *We* run the trading operation. *We* make buy and sell decisions for publically traded assets. I understand that there is some concern about quality issues inside our book, but you should be discussing those with *us*, because *we* are the experts. I don't intend any offense to anyone, and I am sure you are all experts in your fields, but you are not experts in trading bonds. With the exception of Melanie of course, who is still young to be making multi-million dollar trading decisions.

"We absolutely cannot accept restrictions on re-investing trading proceeds. You have to understand, that will bring our international trading operation to a screeching halt. We might as well all go home if we can't trade."

Lawson answered in an even tone:

"I'm sorry for these changes, and I hope as we all do that they are temporary. But they are irrevocable. Sam here, with Melanie's assistance, is making decisions on this portfolio for the time being, and if they give a sell order, then the bond will be sold. They have no plans to purchase anything, so the money will sit in our cash accounts for the time being. That's the end of that story.

"As to trading restrictions, all of the restrictions you have right now are in emerging market economies. You are free to continue trading in other markets."

"Sir, with respect, there isn't much money trading German or Swiss bonds these days. They trade pretty tightly," said Rajat. "To make any decent profit, we must be able to trade in emerging markets. And the problems in Russia do not appear to be spreading right now. It is premature to take losses on non-Russian positions; there just isn't any evidence in the market that they are going to be affected."

"And not to be disrespectful to you, sir, but you haven't made a decent profit trading in emerging markets in quite some time," said Lawson. "In fact, you've lost a sizable amount. Which is one reason that control of this portfolio has been temporarily removed from your hands."

Rajat took the rebuke like a man. But George charged in.

"I hope this doesn't mean you are planning to mess around in my book," he said.

"I'm not sure what you mean by 'mess around,'" said Lawson, "but it is indeed being subjected to the same scrutiny as the international portfolio, and we might very well sell some bonds from there, or place restrictions on your trading positions."

George stood up angrily and gestured at Melanie and me. "How in the world can you put a $1 billion worth of assets under the control of these two children? I can tell you one thing, I am not going to be held responsible for the damage they do to my trading operation."

"Mr. Lamb," said Lawson, "you will forgive me if I am a lot more concerned about the damage to our bank than I am 'your' trading operation. As for your accountability, the people responsible for this...situation...no longer work here. But that does not mean that everyone can rest easy in his job security. This problem is ongoing, and so is the evaluation of the personnel involved in it. If you catch my meaning."

George had a furious look in his eye, but he didn't seem to have the appetite for taking on Lawson. I thought he would come after me, but instead he turned to Melanie and raised a finger at her. He started to speak but Lawson cut him off.

"Mr. Lamb, I understand this might be an emotional issue for you, but please behave as a professional. None of us is particularly excited to be in this position, but we all have a job to do, and we all work for the same bank."

George lowered his hand but continued to glare at Melanie.

Mel was in a lousy spot. She worked for us, temporarily, but eventually she would have to go back to the trading floor to face George's wrath. She looked at the table, her face emotionless, and said nothing.

"Mr. Meunster, please see that everyone in your operation complies with the instructions you have been given. Is there anything else?"

Meunster was red-faced and angry but he nodded his head. They got up and filed out.

Lawson looked at me meaningfully but said nothing.

Melanie and I went back downstairs. She was silent as she went back to her trade station. I wanted to give her some comfort but couldn't think of anything to say. I went back to my office.

Later that afternoon there was a tap on the doorframe. I looked up and the whole crew was there. Vinnie, Mel and Jay.

"We have a problem," said Vinnie. "Conference room?"

I got up and started for the conference room. Vinnie said: "You might want to bring your exotics portfolio."

I grabbed the list and we all got seated in the conference room.

"It's Entourage Capital," said Vinnie.

"The guys we just met with? With the expiring line of credit and the no-show owners from Memphis? What's the problem?" I said.

"We have more exposure to them than we thought," said Vinnie.

I put my arms on the table and then laid my head on them.

"Oh no," I said. "Don't tell me there is something in the exotics book from them."

Melanie nodded.

"And," she said, "we have some exposure in the corporate bond book, too."

I closed my eyes. "How much?" I said without picking my head up.

"Well, you knew about the line at $200 million," said Vinnie. "We have $20 million of the corporate bond issue they did a few years ago. And we have another $40 million in your exotics portfolio."

"$40 million!" I shouted, raising my head up. "How could we have $40 million in asset-backeds?!" I grabbed my sheet and started looking through it.

"They did an asset-backed deal a few years back, but couldn't sell the lower tranches. So George bought them off the desk, and then put them in Hold-to-Maturity."

"Where is it?," I asked, looking through my list. "I don't see anything with ECP's name on it."

Vinnie pointed it out to me. "Obion ABS Trust #1. We've got half of the single As and all of the triple Bs."

"What the hell is Obion?" I said.

"Um...I think it's a river in Tennessee," said lawyer Jay.

"Great," I said. "So the asset-backeds are secured by receivables, obviously. Is the corporate bond secured?"

Jay shook his head.

"We are pulling all the docs now, but the most I have been able to find is a negative pledge on assets. It is probably unsecured."

I let out a big sigh.

"OK, we have $260 million, not $200 million. That's not a disaster."

"Well...." said Vinnie.

"What?"

"This confusion over collateral is starting to look like bad news for the line of credit," he said. "There was a collateral release done in association with the asset-backed deals. That would be typical—the line of credit has the receivables, and then they are released from the line to use as collateral in the ABS deal. The line is then paid down with the proceeds of the ABS deal. Standard stuff. But...well, we're not sure the line got paid down that much."

"You're telling me our whole line of credit has no collateral?" I said incredulously.

"No, no," said Vinnie quickly. "It's just...we're not sure. There seems to be some double-pledging of collateral. Receivables are listed as securing both the line of credit and the asset-backed bonds. We're cross-checking everything now."

I felt a rising sense of panic. I tried to calm down.

"OK. Vinnie, you work the line of credit. Call the company and scream at them for current information. It probably won't work, but try. If we have a shortfall of collateral on the line, we need to know how big it is immediately.

"Mel, check our seniority on the corporates. If we have to go into bankruptcy owning those things, we need to know where we stand in line to get paid. And after you figure that out, we need a bid on the corporates and the asset-backed bonds. Real bad. Get on the phone and see what you can come up with."

"Jay, we have got to find those two brothers from Memphis. Use whatever resources you've got. I need you on that full-time."

Jay nodded, and everyone rose to leave.

Melanie stopped on the way out.

"Oh by the way, Sam, I've sold all the emerging markets bonds. Averaged about 92 cents on the dollar. They kept beating me down on the Venezuelan stuff."

"Still, good work," I said. "Any sign of contagion yet?"

"No," she said. "It's honestly pretty calm out there. Maybe this won't spread after all. We might have jumped the gun a little."

"Too late to think like that," I said. "That train has left the station. Let's move on."

She nodded and left. She seemed worried, and we were now in the position of hoping something really bad *did* happen in the markets, to justify our trades. Not a good attitude to have.

But we were supposed to be pros. Yesterday's trade was yesterday. In fact, the trade from ten minutes ago was also forgotten. Right now, we needed a new trade.

A few hours later I looked at my watch and realized it was almost 9 p.m. I had been on the job non-stop for 14 hours.

I typed an old trader's saying out on my computer, printed it out, and taped it to Melanie's screen before I left. It said:

"A ship in port is safe. But that is not what ships are for."

Then I drove home.

At my kitchen table I loosened my tie and cleaned out all of my pockets. There was a stack of mail there that I hadn't looked at in a week, and I started thumbing through it. As I did I happened to notice the light on my cellphone was blinking, which meant I had a voicemail. I checked it and it was from Ana.

"Please check your work e-mail, Sam. I have sent you something important."

I went into my office and hooked my laptop into the phone lines and dialed up the bank's server. After a few minutes I was into my email, and found a large file from Ana.

I opened it. It said, "Is this what you are missing, *guapo*?"

There was a file attached. She had taken a picture of herself in a big mirror. She was dressed in skimpy underwear, smoke gray in color, with boy-short panties and a bra that she had unsnapped. She was leaning into the mirror to show me her breasts, but was holding them inside the bra so I couldn't see them all. Her long black hair spilled out behind her and I could see the barest wisp of pubic hair from her undies. She had a smile on her face and along with her arched eyebrows was saying, "come and get it."

What a tease, I thought. I called her cellphone but she did not pick up. I did not leave a message.

I went to bed, but took a while to get to sleep, with the image of Ana Prima de Montez in her smoke gray lingerie bouncing around in my libido.

9

Wednesday morning I stopped in on Melanie tapping away on her trade station; one of Jay's young lawyers was at a side table reading through a document stack the size of three phonebooks.

"Anything going on in the emerging markets?" I asked Melanie.

She shook her head.

"Everything's quiet. Trading is normal. It looks like we might shake off this Russia default."

Then she smiled at me and nodded to the saying I had taped to her computer screen.

"Thanks for that. It's nice to see that you know the game too. But don't worry about me, okay?"

"I don't," I said. "I just want you to know I'm with you. Anything on the ECP corporates, or the asset-backeds?"

Again she shook her head. "Working on it, but no bids so far."

I went to my office. Jay came in to say there was still nothing from Memphis on the whereabouts of the Littles, and he would let me know as soon as he heard something.

Vinnie came in several times, worried like I was about the true loss on ECP.

"How bad do you think this could get?" he asked during one visit.

"You tell me, partner," I said. "I tell you this much, I bet it is a lot more than the $20 million we first thought."

He nodded his head. "Oh yeah, it's a lot worse than that," he said.

"We need to adjust the risk ratings and the loss estimates, as soon as we have some idea what it's going to be. Lawson needs to know about this, but there is no point in telling him until we can estimate how big the loss is."

"'Adjust the loss estimates,'" he repeated. "The Memphis profit center is going to love that."

"Yeah," I said. "And the losses on the corporates and the ABS will get allocated to the trading floor. Right after they've taken it in the shorts from Russia. When George Lamb hears about this his head is probably going to pop off his neck."

I hacked through the exotics portfolio, sizing up positions, marking bonds as "safe" or "sell" or "loss" as I could. That went on most of the day, and I decided to take an early day and go home at a decent hour for a change.

I swung by Melanie's office on my way out but she wasn't there. I clicked through her trading screens to check the domestic and emerging markets. Nothing—a choppy trading day, but no sign of panicked selling or freezing of financial markets. Everything looked normal.

When I got home, I changed clothes, then grabbed a six-pack and walked through the woods two coves over to Curtis's place. He has an old ranch-style house that sits up on a point overlooking both the main channel of the lake and a small cove, where he has a dock and keeps his fishing boat. His whole property was probably 5 acres or so, and his work office and warehouse are there, too. I found him in the workshop, fiddling around with a lawnmower engine.

"'Bout time to knock off, ain't it?" I said. I waved the six-pack at him.

"Yes it is," he said, wiping his hands off on a shop towel and then accepting a beer. "Let's go sit on the deck."

He locked up the workshop and we went to his deck a few yards away, a multi-level affair that looked out on his cove. There were some bream popping down by the dock, and across the water a small party of about 20 college-aged kids was pumping music and dancing on the lawn of a ramshackle red-roofed cottage. There was plenty of drinking and hollering going on too.

"Sonny Grainger's place," said Curtis. "He only lives there in the summer. Looks like his daughter Rachel has it for the week again. Those kids will have me up half the damn night."

"Call the cops on 'em," I said.

Curtis laughed. "I'll call Sonny on 'em if it gets too bad. He'll come screeching tires down here from Statesville and those kids will wish it was the law. Anyway, I know Rachel. I can always just call over there and ask her to settle things down. She will. She doesn't want her daddy riled up. He's got a heart condition."

I told him what the last few days had been like at work. He stopped me in mid-sentence.

"Slow down on the jargon a little. What is 'BK?'"

"Shorthand for bankrupt," I said.

"What is 'mark-to-market?'"

"Nothing more than establishing a current price for an asset. Like if you have 100 shares of Microsoft, and you wonder what it's worth, you go get the stock tables from the paper and look up the price. It's as easy as that for stocks and some bonds, harder for less-liquid positions."

"Now I know what stocks and bonds are," he said, "but what is this asset-backed thing you keep talking about?"

"It's a type of a bond," I said. "Say you've got a car loan, okay?"

"Sure," he said, nodding to his big black pickup truck parked in the driveway. "That's $400 a month and I've got about a year left on it."

"Right. Well, the bank that loaned you the money for that has a bunch of car loans just like it. Thousands. So they have $400 a month coming in on thousands of car loans. They package those loans up, and sell the big package to investors."

"Why?" asked Curtis.

"Well, three reasons. One is, the investors will give them the money pretty cheap. What are you paying on that car loan, about 10%? So all those car loans that the bank packaged up into one big bond are paying 10%. But the bond investors will only charge, say, 6% for the loans. So the bank gets to keep the difference, 4%.

"The second reason is, there is enough money in the deal for the investment bank to make some fat fees packaging up the loans and selling them. Millions.

"And the third reason is, it's another source of funding for the bank. They don't just have to rely on deposits. If they can securitize their loans, and sell them to the market place, then that diversifies their funding base, and makes them a little safer. That's the theory, anyway."

Curtis shook his head.

"None of that makes any sense to me," he said.

"Okay, I'll give you a simpler answer," I said. "The bank securitizes for profit. How's that?"

"That I understand."

The bream down at the waterline had gotten more active as the sun started to set. Curtis got us a couple of light rods and we went down to see what we could catch from his dock. We hadn't been there five minutes, nor caught a fish, when Curtis suddenly recoiled and said:

"Oh my God, look at that."

Roiling through the water, first above it and then just below the surface, about the size of a soccer ball, was a nest of baby snakes.

"Oh, shit!" I said. "Copperheads!"

We both watched with disgust as the snakes slithered and slimed their way back and forth in the water in front of Curtis's dock. Finally Curtis said:

"We've got to do something about this. I don't want a bunch of copperheads nesting under my boat dock."

He went up to the house and came back with two shotguns, an old Remington .410 and a newer Beretta .12 gauge. He had two boxes of shells. He gave me the Remington, and we loaded up and commenced to shooting shotgun shells into the snake nest. After about ten minutes, we had thinned the nest down considerably, but it was still there, dipping out of sight underneath the water and then popping up 10 yards away a minute later. The cellphone on Curtis's belt rang. He picked it up while I cracked my shotgun open and stood at ease.

"Oh, hi Rachel," he said. I looked up and could see her standing about 50 yards away on the other side of the cove, with a cellphone in her ear.

"What's with the shotguns?" Curtis said into the phone. "Well, there is a nest of baby snakes over here, and they are the poisonous kind, and we are killing them."

I could hear Rachel say "Eww, snakes!" from across the water, and I watched her whole party collectively take about three steps back from the water.

"Yeah, I wouldn't go swimming for a while," Curtis told her. "But we'll have this taken care of in another 20 minutes or so."

And so we did. We shotgunned every last one of them. Then we had the rest of the beer, and a little after dark, I went home and had a couple more. But I still had a hard time getting to sleep, waking up several times that night from nightmares about water-skiing into a nest of copperheads. In my dreams the nest was much bigger than a soccer ball, more the size of swimming pool, and unidentifiable human faces were on many of the snakes.

The next morning I stopped at the trading floor before going to my office. George was not around. I saw Meunster prowling around in the offices above the floor, looking anxiously at the action at different trading areas.

Rajat and his crew watched their screens with a studied indifference. I looked at the screens from markets around the world and realized that, finally, the Russian default was spreading. Most Latin American stocks and bonds were getting pummeled. In 48 hours Melanie and I had gone from naïve dopes to prescient geniuses, but it was going to be anything but pleasant for the bank. The domestic guys looked anxiously at the international screens, wondering if they were next in the barrel.

I wouldn't be getting any pats on the back from either set of traders. But I wanted to congratulate Melanie for saving the bank a lot of money, so I went upstairs to her office. She was staring at her keyboard.

"Looks like Latin America is getting hammered," I said.

"It is," she said. "Sovereign debt from several different countries is down 20-25%. I guess we did the right thing."

"Yeah, you made a good call on that, even if It was looking iffy there for a few days," I said.

She smiled.

"I never had any doubt," she said.

I smiled and headed back for my office, but Vinnie called to me as I passed his door.

"Sam? Got a second?"

I went into his office. Jay was sitting in there with him. I sat down.

"What's up?" I said.

"The ECP guys are coming back in tomorrow," Vinnie said. "They said they've got a collateral list and some progress on the financial systems."

Then he waited for the drum roll.

"And they're going to bring the brothers with them," he said with a smile.

"Whoa-ho!" I said. "Looks like the Vin-man finally got through somebody's thick skull. Way to go!"

He basked in the accomplishment for a minute. Then he said:

"Who do we want in there?" he asked.

I thought about it.

"Me, you and Jay. My instinct is to leave Melanie out of it until we get an idea of whether we can sell those bonds to someone, and if so for how much. Plus we don't want them arguing that Melanie is getting private information while managing public bonds. They could sue us for that."

"Have you thought about Santiago Capital on this one?" he asked.

"Um…well, yes, but to be honest I was trying to figure out how to sell them some asset-backed bonds. What were you thinking?"

"I was thinking about selling them the whole damn shooting match. They said on that conference call that they liked small, domestic manufacturing companies. That's what ECP is. You and I both know these loans are not going to turn out well, even if we do succeed in getting the attention of the Little brothers. The bank is heading for a big loss on that line of credit. Why not get Santiago Capital involved and see if they want to make a bid for the whole company? Can't hurt. Even if it turns out all they want is some asset-backeds, then, well obviously we can sell them those."

And that, I thought, is why I always try to hire the best.

"I like it. Good thinking. When is the meeting?" I said.

"10:00 tomorrow, here at the bank," he said. "Santiago will have to move fast to get somebody up here by then."

"That's what they get paid for," I said. "I'll call them and let you know."

"Ok," said Vinnie. "I guess we can put the collateral valuation on hold until we get their collateral list?"

"Sure, no point spinning our wheels on that until we get more current information," I said.

I rose to leave, and asked Jay for a private word. We stood in the hallway outside Vinnie's office.

"This investigative firm you've been using in Memphis, to try to find the brothers. Are they a one-man operation, or is it a bigger shop?" I asked.

"They're regional," he said. "Southeast mostly. Miami, Atlanta, Richmond, Nashville, Little Rock. And here in Charlotte. Raleigh too."

He looked at me quizzically for a second then said:

"You want to put a tail on the brothers, don't you?"

I nodded.

"Very astute, Counselor. Yes, I do. It looks like a great opportunity to me to figure out where their nest is. I figure we can pick them up at the airport, or even coming out of the bank, and follow them home. With one guy in Charlotte and the other waiting for them in Memphis, we've got a good chance of tracking them to their base."

"Very good," said Jay. "I'll get it set up."

At lunchtime I left the office to get a sandwich, and after I finished I went back to my office and called Ana's cellphone. She picked up.

"Hi, Sam. It's a nice surprise to hear from you. Did you like the email I sent you?"

"I did. It was very...inviting. But why do you want to tease me like that?"

She laughed.

"I don't want to tease you. It is, how do you say, *un apertivo*?"

"An appetizer," I said.

"Yes, well that was an appetizer, but the meal is here for you."

"Maybe sooner than you think," I said. "Are you folks familiar with Entourage Capital Partners?"

"ECP?" she said. "That is so funny that you should mention them. I was thinking of bringing them up to you. I found out the other day that you are their agent bank, and...well, we have been following their troubles for some time. We track their financials and their asset-backed deals in the market."

"We are having a meeting with them tomorrow at 10:00," I said. "It would be a good time to introduce you to them, if you are interested. I have to tell you, things are not going well between us, so if you are interested you will need to move fast."

"But of course, that is what we do. I guess it will just be the financial guys?"

"No, the Little brothers are supposed to be here too."

"Wow," she said. "I heard they were almost hermits. How did you find them?"

"It hasn't been easy getting them here, I can tell you that."

"Well, good. I will definitely be there. Marcos is traveling, he will be sad that he missed it, but it is a good opportunity for us so I will be there. I will come in tonight. Maybe we can have dinner?"

"Sure," I said, "call me when you get a flight and you know what time you will be here. Are you going to bring that grey lingerie?"

She laughed.

"No, I will have a different surprise for you," she said.

"That sounds great. I look forward to seeing you tonight."

"Ok, I will see you soon, *guapo*," she said, and hung up.

I found myself gazing at the wall, daydreaming, and roused myself to start thinking again. I sent an email out to the team telling them that Ana was going to be joining us, and not to introduce her. ECP could just assume she was with the bank. I sent another one to Jay asking him to get with our Legal department and get a confidentiality agreement for Ana to sign. I would get her in the meeting, but I didn't want her talking about it publically.

I was feeling good, so naturally I decided to go back down to the trading floor. The international desk was deserted. The place was quiet; traders stared glumly at their screens or the financial news programs on the TVs. The only action seemed to be in domestic equities. I sidled up to the desk and overheard a conversation between the head equity traders and his troops.

"This thing is spreading," he said. "Don't kid yourselves. It is going to roll through South and Central America, then go back to Europe and Japan, and then it is coming here. You need to think long and hard about any position you have going into this weekend."

"Have you seen the prices?" asked one of his traders. "How can we sell into the teeth of this? It's the exact opposite of buying low and selling high. We'd be selling at the low point."

"What makes you think this is the low point?" another trader countered. "Our market hasn't been hit that hard. We could be down another 500 points easy next week."

"They're your books," said the head guy. "You can make the call. But I am seriously advising you that anything you take into this weekend needs to be blue-chip, gold-plated and bullet-proof. The bears are coming next week and they are hungry."

He turned around to leave and saw me.

"What the fuck are you doing here?" he said. "Why don't you go hover over somebody else's station? This place has gone to shit ever since you walked in the door. You're haunting us like a God-damned ghost."

He brushed past me angrily. I could feel my face getting hot and turning red. The rest of the traders eyeballed me with no expression. I left.

Ana called that night after she had gotten in from the airport. She had already eaten, and wanted to meet for a drink. She was at a different hotel than the last time, it had a nice bar, why didn't I meet her there for a drink? So around 8:00 I left the office and walked down to the hotel bar where she was staying. She wasn't there yet, and I had a beer as I waited.

After about ten minutes a hotel bellman came up and handed me a note. It said:

Come on up to room 318. Ana.

I settled up with the bartender and took the elevator up three floors and knocked on the door of 318. Ana opened the door and invited me in.

She was dressed like a Catholic schoolgirl. She had on a tartan mini-skirt with a shiny black patent leather belt. Her top was white and tied off at her stomach; she had on a simple white bra that peeked out through the top of the shirt. I doubt there were many Catholic schoolgirls with that kind of cleavage. She had on white knee socks and black leather shoes to match her belt. She had pulled her hair back into a simple ponytail.

"Do you like my school uniform?" she asked me.

"It's very nice," I said. "Why don't you come over here and sit next to me on the bed, little school girl?"

I patted the bed next to me. She came over and sat down. She crossed her legs primly.

"I am very shy," she said. "Normally I would not sit this close to a boy, but you are very cute. I make an exception for you."

"I thought we were going to have a drink at the bar," I said.

"I am not allowed to go to bars," she said. "My parents forbid it."

I leaned over and tried to kiss her. She put her hand on my chest and held me off.

"No, I am not supposed to kiss boys, either," she said.

This little act was making me hornier than I already was. I slid closer to her and persisted.

"Just one little kiss couldn't hurt," I said. At the same time I probed with one hand to her midriff and got ahold of the little knot that kept her top tied together.

"Well, one little kiss…" she said, and when I pulled her face closer she greedily put her tongue in my mouth. I kissed her back hard and managed to get the knot loose so that her shirt fell open and I could see her bra.

She pushed me off again and tried to get her shirt tails back together.

"No, you can't see my bra like this!" she said. "What would the nuns say?"

I hand wrestled with her a little and got ahold of the clasp in the middle of the bra. I flipped it open and her breasts spilled out. She tried to cover them up. I pushed her arms aside and squeezed her breasts. I took one of her nipples in my mouth. She gasped and grabbed my hair.

"Did the nuns tell you about this?" I asked. I slid my hand under her skirt and felt her. I pulled her cotton white underwear off and slid my fingers into her moistness. She moaned.

"No, I cannot let you touch me there," she said. "Papi said that I would go to hell if I let a man touch me there."

I stood up and pulled my clothes off, and then fell on top of her on the bed.

"There are some things your daddy didn't tell you about. Let me show you."

◆

Later that night I slipped from the room while Ana was snoring softly on the bed. She still had her little tartan skirt on but was otherwise naked, sprawled on the bed. I made sure the lock clicked shut and then headed for home. I could not afford another sleepless night with her; there was too much work to do tomorrow.

I walked back to my car, smiling at the thought of her lovemaking. It had been fun, no question, but like the first time, I had caught her looking in the mirror at herself while we were in the middle of things. It had made me feel a little bit like a prop, and that she would have been just as happy to be alone with herself and her striking beauty.

Women. I drove home, slept, and then got up and came right back into work. I got off the elevator heading for my office, and then I pulled up short and stared at my conference room.

Lawson was sitting in there. Next to him was Sherman Ellis, an outside attorney the bank hired to put out big fires. He and I were old friends. They both had very serious expressions on their faces.

Standing at the windows, gazing into the streets below, were two plainclothes police detectives. They both had .45 side-arms and badges on their belts. One was black, the other white, both of them big men. They looked like locals.

I walked in.

"Sam, there you are," said Lawson. He pushed out a chair for me. "Have a seat."

"Sherman," I said.

"Hi, Sam," he said.

The two detectives turned to look at me with hawk eyes.

"Sam," said Sherman, "this is Detective Young, and this other gentleman is Detective Jeffries. They're with the Charlotte-Mecklenburg Police."

Both men nodded, but neither offered to shake hands.

"Look, Sam, there's no way to give this to you gently, so I'm just going to give it to you straight," said Lawson. "George Lamb is dead. He was shot yesterday in a parking garage about three blocks from here."

10

"Mr. Wilson, we have to ask this," said the black cop, I think he was Jeffries. "Where were you yesterday afternoon around 5:00?"

"What!" I said. "Am I a suspect? That's insane and…"

"Sam," said Sherman. "Calm down, okay? They're just doing their job. They have to ask."

I took a deep breath and tried to gather my wits.

"Yesterday afternoon? Well, I was here at work. Vinnie and Jay and I were working on a credit, Entourage Capital. We were here until, I don't know, 8:00 or 8:30, something like that.

"Did you go out at all?" Young asked. "You know, coffee break or grab some dinner?"

"No," I said.

"Where was your car parked?"

"In the bank's parking deck, where it always is, the one attached to this building."

"And Vinnie and Jay were the only folks you saw?" said Young, the white guy.

"No," I said, "I was on the trading floor some. The traders on the equity desk certainly saw me. Sharon, my secretary, was here until about 6:00. She saw me."

"And you left the bank at 8:00 or 8:30 or so, and went home?"

"Yeah," I fudged a little. "I had a drink with a friend at a hotel bar, then went home."

They asked for names and phone numbers for the people who saw me while I was at work, but didn't ask anymore about Ana. I gave the information to them. Then Detective Jeffries said:

"Mr. Wilson, we are just trying to figure out what happened to Mr. Lamb. This appears to be just a random mugging. His wallet and watch were both missing. But anything you can tell us about him, anything at all, would be a big help. His personal life, what you guys might have been working on here at the bank, anything."

"Well, I didn't know George very well. Our paths crossed every now and then for work reasons. We're not working on anything together right now."

"Your boss here was explaining this portfolio revaluation project of yours. Wasn't he involved in that?" said Detective Young.

"Not really," I said. "I mean, we kept him informed, obviously, and we also had to borrow one of his bond analysts, Melanie Bissell, for a few weeks. But in terms of an active role in any of that, there wasn't one for George."

"Is there anything else you two were working on?" the other detective, Jeffries, asked. He seemed to have something in mind, so I thought carefully before answering.

"Well, the only thing that comes to mind is this company I've been working on called ECP. That's a client that he brought into the bank, and they are close to being bankrupt, so they are my responsibility now. His group managed some bond sales for them over the last few years. But again, there was no active role for him in it.

"How about personally?" said Detective Young. "You guys buddies? Hang out together, go out for a few beers, that kind of thing?"

"Not really," I said.

"You were friends, though?" said Young.

"We had a cordial, professional relationship," I said. "We did not see each other socially."

"'Cordial, professional relationship,'" said Jeffries, mimicking my tone. "Are you sure that's how you want to play it?"

Sherman shot me a warning glance but he didn't need to; I could sense Jeffries' animosity well enough.

I didn't answer.

"If it was so cordial and professional, maybe you can explain why bank security has a video of George pushing you into the elevator banks a couple of days ago," said Detective Jeffries.

"And pointing his finger in your face," added Young.

I looked over at Lawson. He raised his eyebrows but said nothing.

"Oh. That," I said. "Well, George didn't like seeing me down on the trading floor that often. He felt like that was a space for the sales and trading folks only."

"So you got some new access to the floor because of this portfolio project, and you were down there lording it over the traders, is that it?"

"No," I said, "that's not it. I have always had access to the trading floor. I just didn't have much reason to be down there, so I didn't go that often. But there has been a lot of trouble in the markets lately, which could affect our decision to keep or sell some of these bonds, so I was down there more often, and George didn't like it."

"He didn't like you taking his bond analyst, this Melanie lady, from him either, did he?"

"I wasn't taking her from him at all. It was for three weeks. He wasn't happy about it, but I think he was professional enough to understand it was only temporary."

The two detectives smoked on that a while, then seemed to accept it.

"Did George have any problems here at work that you know about?" asked Jeffries. "Trouble with anybody? Somebody he didn't like, somebody didn't like him?"

That question I wasn't able to brush off that easily. In fact, it froze me. I immediately thought of Melanie and that scene from the break room.

"Mr. Wilson?" said Jeffries, smelling blood and looking at me with renewed interest.

"Um...can I have a moment with Sherman?" I asked.

The two detectives stared at me, then looked at each other.

"Mr. Wilson, if there is something you know..."

Sherman held up his hand.

"Hang on a second, Detective. He's asked to talk to his attorney. Can't you just give us a minute?"

The two detectives looked at him with veiled hostility, then Young nodded his assent and they both walked outside the conference room and closed the door. They lounged outside the door within view.

"What is it, Sam?" said Sherman.

I told him and Lawson about the scene with Melanie, and my suspicion about George harassing her. Lawson sighed loudly.

"Go ahead and tell it to them," Sherman said. "Keep it brief and don't embellish—just what you saw, what you thought might be occurring, that's it."

We called the detectives back in and I told them what I had seen in the break room, and what I suspected. They looked at each other meaningfully.

"Stroking her scarf, huh?" said Young. "Crouched over her. Did he touch her anywhere else?"

"Not that I could see," I said.

"She didn't slap him or tell him to leave her alone or anything?"

"No, it was just what I told you," I said.

"And you and George weren't pals?" said Jeffries. "Didn't hang out after work?"

"No," I said, "but I certainly didn't wish him dead."

The two detectives both looked at me suspiciously. Detective Young sat down in the chair next to me.

"You use drugs, Mr. Wilson?" he asked.

"Come on, Detective!" said Sherman.

"Of course not," I said. "I take a drink every now and then, that's all."

"How about George? Did George Lamb use drugs?"

"I have no idea," I said.

"He seem excitable to you?" said Young. "Talk a lot, mood swings, happy then depressed, that kind of thing?"

"He's a bond salesman," I said. "Or he was, I guess I should say. All those guys are chatty and excitable in my opinion."

"And you never saw George Lamb use drugs? Smoke pot, maybe do a couple lines of coke off the bathroom counter?"

"Detective…" said Sherman with exasperation.

"What?" said Detective Young. "We're all adults here. I'm not accusing your client of anything, just asking him what he saw."

"The bank obviously wants to cooperate in the death of one of its employees. But I will not countenance a fishing expedition," said Sherman.

"To answer your question, Detective, no, I never saw George Lamb use any drugs."

"Did Melanie ever tell you that George was bothering her? Ever say that she felt pressured to have sex with him?"

"No," I said.

The detectives paused then, looking back and forth from each other to me. Finally Young said:

"We pulled the phone numbers, both dialed and received, from George's cellphone, and also from his phone here at the bank. Can you look through these and see if anything strikes you as unusual?"

I looked through the numbers on the cellphone first. Most of them were local; I didn't recognize any of the numbers.

"I don't see anything I recognize here," I said.

Then I looked at the long-distance calls. There were a lot of 212 area codes: New York. Other area codes like 217, 305, and 404 were all big cities, too.

"A lot of these are probably work-related," I said. "These are all big cities, where money managers tend to be: New York, Atlanta, Miami. George was a bond salesman, and the big cities are where his clients work. That's about all I could tell you from just this."

Young stood up, pulled out a business card and handed it to me.

111

"If you think of anything else that would be a help, please call," he said.

"Now if you wouldn't mind giving us a few minutes alone with your attorney and your boss," said Young, effectively dismissing me from my own conference room.

◆

I sat in my office in a daze for some unknown period of time, wondering why George Lamb would have been killed. A random mugging? Something personal? Something work related? I had no clue and the cops had been careful not to give me one. As I sat there perambulating on George's history with the bank, Melanie walked in. Her eyes were red and puffy; she had clearly been crying.

"I guess you heard about George?" she said, sitting down in front of my desk.

"Yes," I said, "shocking. I just got through talking to the Charlotte police who are investigating."

She shook her head, looked down, and started to sniffle. I kept a box of tissues on my desk and handed her one.

"I just can't believe it," she said after she composed herself. "I worked with the guy for two years, and for someone to just kill him in cold blood on the streets, in the middle of the day...I just can't believe it."

She started to cry again and I handed her another tissue. When she had settled down again, I knew it was time to tell her.

"Listen, Melanie, the cops asked me if I had any knowledge of anyone who might have had cause to dislike George. I told them about what I saw with you and him in the breakroom. I know it was probably nothing, but I had to tell them. I'm sorry."

She looked at me sharply, then seemed to reconsider, and sighed.

"Well, that was just George being George. He kept bugging me to go on this party cruise with him and his friends. He said Mr. Clifton went on some of those trips, and I could get some good face time with the big boss if I would go. He said they were clients of the bank and the bank would pick up the tab. Champagne, gambling, hot tubs and a wild weekend. Maybe flying to Vegas or Miami or New York.

"That's the kind of thing some salesmen do, and call it client entertainment, but I didn't want to be around that. You...well, George at least, didn't understand, but there is no way a woman can do that kind of thing and the next day be respected as a professional. Guys can get away with it, but as soon as a woman does something like that in this business, she's a slut. And anyway I didn't *want* to do it. I didn't want to socialize with George and Mr. Clifton and their high-rolling clients.

"What I want, what I have always wanted, is to be a trader. I knew that from my first day in finance class at Carolina. When I got assigned to George I knew it was going to be tough. He has...had...a certain reputation. They said he was a womanizer and a sexist and all that. I didn't care. I was going to be a trader and no one was going to stop me. And that's still true. I'm sorry for George and his family, but I am still going back to that floor and doing what I have always wanted to do. Trade."

She said it with a certain fierceness that brooked no argument.

"Well, that might be something that the police need to know, I mean stuff about George," I said. "Have you talked to them yet?"

"No," she said.

"Well, they surely will want to talk to you," I said. "You might want to think about what you need to tell them."

She nodded, resigned, then looked at me with alarm.

"What?" I asked.

She didn't respond, looking down at her feet with confusion on her face.

"What is it, Mel?" I said again.

"I was in a meeting," she finally said, "two, three weeks ago. Me, George, The Monster, and Mr. Clifton. Mr. Clifton was running the meeting. This was before he got fired. Anyway, there was a huge argument going on about a mark I put on some bonds. George had given me a handful of bonds, 10 or 12, and asked me to mark them to market. After I was done, he said send it out to those two guys, Meunster and Clifton. I guess George was busy or something, but he didn't pay any attention to my work, and when he finally did, in that meeting, he didn't like it. He said it wasn't indicative of what the bonds were really worth. He told everyone that the markets were tight because of Russia and this Long-Term Capital thing, but that was only temporary, and there was no need to panic and sell the bonds today.

"Clifton was killing him—'your own people did the mark, now you're telling me it's not any good? What kind of show are you running?' And anyway, I was thinking, what do you think mark-to-market means? It means…'"

"It means what can you get for the bonds today," I interrupted. "Not when the Russian situation gets sorted out. Not when Long-Term Capital stabilizes…"

"…not when the equity markets are trading up and interest rates are going down and all the birds are singing in the trees," Melanie finished for me. "It means today, right now, what can we sell those bonds for, what price could I guarantee we could get? So when it came around to me, that's all I said—you asked me to mark the bonds to market, to find out what I could get if I had to sell them today, and so that's what I did. If you want me to use a different set of assumptions, then I would probably give you a different number, but right now, that's the number. And it's the right number. I can sell those bonds for that number today."

"OK, you marked the bonds to market, and nobody was particularly happy about the price. That happens all the time. So what's the big deal?"

"The big deal is, Mr. Clifton blew a head gasket. He started screaming at Meunster and George about how this was going to cost him his job, and he was not going out without taking them both with him, and they were a pair of incompetent idiots and God knows why he hadn't fired them earlier."

"Oh," I said.

"Yeah. Like that. George started to get up, saying he didn't need to take this kind of shit, and Mr. Clifton shoved him...slammed him, really, right back into his chair. 'Sit the fuck down and don't fucking move until I tell you to!' George is a pretty big man, but he was definitely intimidated, and he sat down and shut up. It scared me pretty good, too."

"Oh, boy," I said.

"It went on like that for a few more minutes, and then Mr. Clifton looked at me and told me I could leave. So I did."

"What happened after that?" I asked.

"I don't know," she said. "I left and went back to my trading station. Mr. Clifton was still yelling, you could hear it all the way down the hallway even though the door was closed. George came back to the floor about a half hour later. I didn't see Meunster again that day, or Mr. Clifton. And then a few weeks later, Mr. Clifton got fired."

As if on cue, Sherman stuck his head in.

"Hi," he said with a smile. "My name is Sherman Ellis. I don't think we've met."

They shook hands, and I explained to Melanie that Sherman was legal counsel hired by the bank to represent it in any and all issues related to George's death. She could trust him to look out for her, too.

"Nice to meet you, Mr. Ellis," Melanie said.

"Likewise," he said. "And please call me Sherman. I wonder if you might have a few minutes to talk to these Charlotte police detectives about George?"

"I guess so," she said, and started to get up.

"You might tell Sherman what you just told me," I said. "Before you go in there with the cops."

So she sat back down and told Sherman the same story she had just finished with me. About halfway through her story, Sherman eased all the way into the office and closed the door behind him.

When she finished, Sherman said:

"So Mr. Clifton was really angry? Actually put his hands on George?"

"Yes, sir," she said. "Pretty much slammed him back into his chair."

"Don't call me sir," Sherman said with a smile. "It makes me start looking around for my Dad. Now this was when?"

"A few weeks ago," she said.

"Did you see any interaction between Mr. Clifton and George after that?"

"No s...no, Sherman," she said. "In fact I don't remember seeing Mr. Clifton again until the day he announced to the trading floor that he was leaving the bank."

Sherman drummed his fingers on the window sill where he was sitting, gazing out across the center of Charlotte.

"Well, I reckon we need to tell it to the police. Let's go along there and you tell it just like you told it to me. Short and sweet, and no editorializing, okay? Just the facts, ma'am."

They left, and in the silence that remained I reviewed what I knew about The Monster and Mr. Randall Clifton. Not much, was the answer.

My only interactions with Meunster had been when he braced me on the trading floor, and later in that meeting with Lawson where he complained about the trading restrictions we had placed on him. Of Clifton, I knew even less. A few days ago he had stared at me from the catwalk above the trading pit; other than that there had only been that speech on the day the acquisition was announced. That was it. Otherwise I knew absolutely nothing about either man.

Could Clifton have been involved in George's death? It seemed impossible. Even if those bonds were responsible for him getting fired, and even if George was the one who bought the bonds, you wouldn't kill a man over that. Clifton probably had plenty of other opportunities for employment back in New York. For that matter, he probably didn't even need a job; surely he had made millions when his bank was sold. No, despite what appeared to be an explosive temper, it would be hard to imagine him killing George in broad daylight on the streets of Charlotte.

But who would? And why? George was a pompous ass, in my view, but he certainly didn't deserve to get shot. If the cops really thought it was a random mugging, why were they investigating the murder like it was work-related? Weren't most murders domestic-related? Didn't something like two-thirds of the victims know their killers? Maybe this came out of George's personal life and not his work.

I mulled this over some more, then there was a knock on my door and Lawson came in.

"They just finished with Melanie," he said. "I think they are going to start talking to the guys on the trading floor now. You ought to go on home. I know this is a shock to you, but the police have it now."

"I need to tell my staff," I said.

"I've already taken care of that," said Lawson.

"Has anyone notified George's family?" I asked.

"The police are handling that, Sam."

"What was all that about George and drugs?," I asked.

"I think the cops heard from somebody that George was always suffering from head colds or allergies," said Lawson. "He was blowing his nose a lot and his sinus cavities were clogged up. Sherman tells me that frequent nasal irritation can be a sign of cocaine use. He says if you snort cocaine a lot, your nasal passages eventually just fall apart. If a person also demonstrates mood swings then you might be looking at a habitual drug user. Or so the police seem to suspect."

"This just makes me sick," I said.

"I know," said Lawson. "It does me too. Why don't you go on home?"

"Lawson, how can I go home? This Russian thing is spreading to Europe. Every bond in our portfolio could get hammered. Plus, ECP's management is here tomorrow at 10:00 and we are about a week from a free-fall, $260 million bankruptcy with those guys. No, I don't think I can go home."

Lawson put his arm on my shoulder.

"Sam? Nobody expects you to work miracles here. You made a good call selling the emerging market debt. That saved us a lot of money. Nobody is going to hold you responsible if the markets fall in the next few weeks because of Russia. You can't do anything right now anyway. The markets are closed. Go on home. Get a good night's sleep, and come in tomorrow and deal with ECP. One thing at a time here, Samuel. Let's don't try to be Superman."

So I got my jacket and left. As I went past the conference room, I saw Sherman and the two police detectives in there, with some guy from the trading floor.

◆

I drove home, but was restless, pacing around the house. Eventually I got in my boat and drove south on the lake to The Green Room. It is an old-fashioned pool hall located near the 150 bridge close to the town limits of Mooresville. And ex-cop an old friend named Bill Ritchie owned and ran the place. I had worked there in college, bussing tables, serving beers, racking pool balls.

There was only one boat slip available, the farthest one down, and I eased into it and walked in through the back porch. There were a few folks taking it easy on the rocking chairs, looking out over the lake. Of the dozen regulation-sized pool tables there, only two were empty, but being early in the evening it was a quiet crowd, older folks talking calmly and laughing amid the click of pool balls. The overhead fans were going and Bill Ritchie was jawing with someone up front when I came in. I waved to him and had a seat at one of the booths on the wall. In a few minutes he brought me a long neck and had a seat.

"How you been, Sammy?" he said, reaching across to give me a firm handshake.

Bill was a friend and someone I could confide in, but George's death was too fresh. I didn't feel like talking about it.

"I'm good," I said, "busy at work as usual. Looks like you're doing pretty well."

"Can't complain," he said. "It's been pretty busy this summer. Probably get busy tonight. Nice mix of crowd—some older folks, retirees and such come in early, and then later on we usually get a younger crowd, couples from Charlotte and the lake. You going to play any?"

"I don't think so," I said. "I just came in to have a beer or two."

"Pea-head over there is looking for a gin game, quarter a point."

I looked over to the card table and there was indeed a man with a tall, broad-shouldered frame and a shrunken head that, on his frame, looked like a pea.

"I'm not playing cards with Pea-head," I said. "He cheats."

"Yeah he does," said Bill. "I tell him that's why no one wants to play with him, but he acts like he doesn't understand English when I say that."

He looked at me quizzically.

"You sure you're okay?" he said.

"I'm fine," I said. "Just a little tired."

"Well, I've got to get up front. Let me know if you need anything else. That first one is on the house. Good to see you again."

I sat there and drank a few beers, turning over in my mind what had just happened, how it would affect George's family, who had done it and why, what his loss meant for the bank. I was lost in thought when I heard a deep voice behind me.

"Wyatt? That you?"

Anyone who called me Wyatt, my middle name, was old enough to have known my father. He went by Sam too, and when I was a kid I went by Wyatt. In college I started being called Sam again, which is what most people call me now, except for the older folks who live around the lake.

And I knew that baritone well. I turned around and shook hands with the largest man I had ever known, Maxwell Darius Buford.

Big Max was probably 60 years old, 6'8" tall and weighed 300 pounds. But he was not fat; he had a huge barrel chest, arms like an orangutan, a weathered face with a white burr haircut, and massive hands. He owned a used-car dealership in Troutman, not far from my house, and I was one of the few people who knew he didn't really need it. He had inherited a bunch of money, and the car business was just a hobby for him. Although I do have to say, he was a good car man and knew his stuff. He hung around The Green Room a lot. He and Bill were old buddies from way back, I think they even went to high school together. More than once when I was working at The Green Room in college, he had helped us close the place up after midnight.

"Hi Max," I said. "Long time no see."

"You look good, Wyatt. How's things down at the bank?"

"Busy as usual," I said. "How's the car business?"

"Beating them off with a stick," he smiled. "Hey, a fellow came by my place yesterday looking for you. Or your house, more particular."

"What? Why?"

"He said you was a pal of his, and you had a place around here, and he just wanted to drop by and say hello. I didn't believe him a lick. It was just after lunchtime. Any friend of yours woulda knowed you was at work."

"What'd you tell him?"

Max guffawed and slapped his leg.

"I sent him on a snipe hunt out Brawley School Road. He's probably still out there looking for you."

Max was still smiling at the thought of that trick when I said:

"What'd he look like, Max? Big fellah?"

As soon as I said that, I wished I could have phrased the question differently. "Big" was a concept that Max understood much differently than most people. I know he considered me a "little feller," and Curtis was "kinda on the skinny side."

Max stroked his chin.

"Well he had some size on him I reckon. Long black hair he kept petting at. Nice suit. Drove a brand new BMW, one of those 5-series with the big engine, the M-Class, shiny black. That's a beautiful car right there, probably $80,000 fresh off the lot. When he drove up in that I thought, if he wants to trade it to me, it has got to be stolen. You know old Max don't hardly get a shot at any fancy foreign cars. But he wasn't interested in trading cars. Just your address."

He slapped me on the shoulder hard enough to rattle my molars.

"Well, good to see you, Wyatt. Are you still driving that old wood-paneled Jeep?"

"The Woodrow is still running," I said.

"I know you're attached to it, but when she gives out, come see me and I'll put you in something you'll like a lot better. You know, with air conditioning."

He laughed at another one of his own jokes and strolled off to the card table where Pea-head sat. Pea-head suddenly looked sick to his stomach—it would take a pair of stones to cheat Big Max at cards.

I settled up my tab, got in my boat and drifted on back to the house as the sun set, wondering if this it what is was like to be on the rack during the Spanish Inquisition.

Boss gives you an impossible job.

Crank.   Your hands and feet start to feel a little uncomfortable.

People on the trading floor express hostility to you and your new job.

Crank.

You make a controversial call on the markets. The traders think you're an idiot.

Crank. A different deal, ECP, blows up, and suddenly you have a bunch of balls in the air. While you're trying to manage that, someone kills of one of the bank's employees.

Crank. Crank. Crank.

The police question you.   The victim turns out to apparently be a cokehead and a sexual predator whom you work with and who hates your guts. And you find out that some guy matching his description was looking for your house a few days ago.

Crank, crank, crank.

You begin to notice, after all those cranks, that everything hurts now, not just your hands and feet. Your eyeballs are about to pop out of their sockets. Your shoulders and hips are screaming, your arms and legs are about to break, and your lungs are so stretched out that you can barely breath.

And then The Grand Inquisitor himself, Fray Tomás de Torquemada, leans into your vision and smiles, and asks if you've had enough.

Or would you like to try the Fifth Degree?

11

In the morning I parked in my usual spot in the bank's parking garage, but instead of going inside to the bank, I walked up and around in the parking lot and made a slow tour of the garage, looking at all the cars. The BMW M5 is a killer—faster than just about any street-model car, with six-on-the-floor and a top speed of 155 mph. It can go 0-60 in fewer than 6 seconds. You had to have a big checkbook and a sizeable need to be the fastest guy on the street to own an M5.

The top four levels of the garage were where the investment bankers parked. There were Porsches there, Mercedes, Land Rovers, Audis and a panorama of BMWs. But they were all either regular 3-, 5-, or 7-series. No shiny brand new M-Classes.

I went inside to the trading floor.

There was turbulence on every desk. Contagion had swept through Europe and was on the doorstep of the US, eager to get in.   Rajat was at his normal station, as was The Monster, prowling the offices above the floor. He looked agitated.

The equity traders were on the phones, looking at the ticker, and shouting at each other. The market had 15 minutes before trading began and futures markets were indicating a large drop on open.   Stocks were bracing for a full frontal barrage. I wasn't happy about that, and I was set to leave, but then I caught the eye of the head trader who had cursed me yesterday. I stared at him for five seconds, leaning against his trading station. He didn't say a word and after the first glance would not even look at me.

Kid games. I was disgusted with myself, and I left for the elevator and my office. I was going to leave the traders alone for a while. Unless I missed my guess, they were in for a very bad ride. There was no need for me to be taunting them about it too. It was childish.   And I could get whatever market intelligence I needed from Melanie.

In my office I had a voicemail from Lawson. The police had told him that, for now, they were still treating George's death as a mugging gone bad. His family had been notified as had the bank's chairman, and the flags at all our branches were to be flown at half-mast today in his honor. There would be no local funeral; George was not married and had no children, and the body was being shipped to his family home in New York.

I hung up after that and shook my head.   Poor George. Shot to death in downtown Charlotte in broad daylight, all over what was probably $50 in his wallet. I thought the flags were a nice touch. I sent an email out to my team giving them the news.

What was there to do but go back to work?   I started reviewing our materials for the ECP meeting. At 9:30 Sharon rung me on the phone and said "Ana from Santiago Capital is in the lobby. Everyone else is in the small conference room. You want me to bring her there?"

"Take her in and introduce her to Jay first. He has a confidentiality agreement she needs to sign. I will meet them at the conference room in 10 minutes," I said.

Jay and Ana were waiting for me outside the small conference room when I got there ten minutes later. Ana behaved very professionally and I got a handshake to go along with the European-style kiss on both cheeks. She gave no indication that we had slept together the night before and I played it the same way. It was work, after all. She was again dressed in a short skirt, high heels and a tight top and jacket. I took her in and introduced her to Vinnie. I explained what was going to happen.

"So we are not going to introduce her in the meeting as being with a different firm?" said Vinnie.

"We're not going to introduce her or anyone else. I'll tell them that we have retained counsel, and that should explain why there are four people in the room now instead of just me and you. They can make their own assumptions after that. You okay with that, Ana?"

She nodded. "*Claro*. We can make the introduction later, if we decide to get involved."

"So how are we going to play this?" asked Vinnie.

"Let's just wait and see what they have to say," I said. "They know what we want. We'll react to what we hear."

"Under what terms or conditions would we be willing to extend this line?" said Vinny. "I mean, today is Friday. It expires on Tuesday. What are they going to say that is going to makes us comfortable in extending the line, even short-term?"

"If they're making progress on the systems issues, and they can give us a clear collateral list, delineating what the line has versus what was pledged to the asset-backeds, and the line was covered, then we might be willing to extend it for a while," I said.

"It would be nice to get brought current on interest," Vinnie said.

"Do you think they've got the money for that?" I said.

And so it went, back and forth, with no real decisions made because everything was hypothetical. At 10:00 Sharon stuck her head in.

"ECP is here," she said. "Five of them."

"Okay," I said, "put them in the big conference room up front. We're on our way."

As the group filed out, Jay Podolski buttonholed me.

"Sam, a word in private?" he said.

"Sure," I said, and we stepped back into the now-empty conference room and closed the door.

"Listen, I'm really sorry about George. I'm still kind of in shock over it," he said.

"Yeah, me too," I said.

"Yeah...well, that P.I. firm I hired? To find those brothers? They got on their tail last night in Memphis. The brothers flew down here on a private plane. They're staying at a hotel over near the Civic Center, under assumed names."

"Great!" I said. "So after they leave here, we can find them back in Memphis?"

"If they go there, yeah, we should be able to. But here's the thing. Last night they had dinner at one of those fancy steakhouses. The P.I. got into the bar area ahead of them, and had a partial view of their table. He's also pretty sneaky with a little camera he's got, and he snapped a couple shots.

"I know what the Little brothers look like, Jay. I've met them before."

"Did you know they were having dinner with this guy?"

And he handed me a picture of three guys eating dinner in a nice restaurant. The older brother, the slightly tubby Jonathan Little, was closest in the frame. The tubbier, younger Andrew Little was set off to the right, only partially in the shot. The photo was centered on a nattily attired, 50ish gentleman, tall with pallid skin, a receding hairline in front and silver wire-rimmed glasses.

Whom I had last seen staring down on me from the offices above our trading pit. Formerly president of our investment bank, now working a two-week notice. Name of Randall Clifton.

I took a minute to process the fact that Clifton was having dinner with customers who 1) had been virtually impossible for me to find for the last three months and 2) owned a company that was on the rocks and very close to bankrupt. And it had been, what, three days since he had been fired? There he sat as if he still represented the bank, drinking fine wine and chewing on the best steak in town.

"What the fuck is Randall Clifton doing having dinner with the Little Brothers?" I asked.

"That's not all," said Jay. He handed me another picture. In the photo Clifton was handing a manila-sized envelope to the older Little.

"The P.I. says that Clifton gave them an envelope. He couldn't see much more than that."

I looked at the photo closely.

"That's not a stack of money, that's for sure," I said. "It doesn't look like there's much in that envelope. Plus, Clifton is giving it to them. If there were some kind of bribe going on, they would be giving it to Clifton. Do you or the P.I. have any ideas on what this is?"

"No," said my attorney.

But we would find out soon. And we would not like it. Not at all.

We went into the conference room. ECP was there: the Little brothers, who nodded at me but didn't speak; the CFO and one of his minions; and their attorney.

"We have now retained counsel in this matter," I said, nodding vaguely toward Jay and Ana. ECP had no reaction to the news. Ana slid unobtrusively into a chair and tried, I guess, to look like a lawyer. The rest of us sat down.

"So," I said, "what's the situation on the financial systems?"

This got us 20 minutes from the CFO and his staff. Concentrated efforts on systems integration. Identification of key problem nodes and joint teams of financial and information systems professionals. Consultants hired to work on financial reporting quality control. Banking jargon flew thick and fast and finally Vinnie called a time out.

"So can you now give us a true and correct list of the collateral on the line and the collateral on the asset-backed deals?" he asked.

The CFO slid a few sheets of paper and a diskette across the table.

"Here is a list of the collateral for both the line and the asset-backed securities, and the diskette has it in computerized spreadsheet form," he said.

We all thumbed through the copies.

"What is this "Market Value" for the receivables?" Vinnie asked. "It says here that the market value of collateral for the line is $248 million."

"Well, we based those marks on the proceeds from our asset-backed deal from last year," said the CFO. "As you know

Stan Meihaus

we received significantly more than 100 cents on the dollar for the …"

Vinnie interrupted. "What's this column here, Amortized Cost? This says the collateral value of the line is only $161 million."

"That's actually our cost on the receivables, less the payments that have been made. We don't consider that the most realistic number; we think Market Value is a better indication of the true collateral value."

"That's not what our agreement calls for," said Vinnie, his voice rising. "Collateral is measured on a cost basis, not as some ginned-up market value. The line is fully drawn at $200 million, and we only have $161 million in collateral. So we have a $39 million shortfall, is what you're telling us?"

"Again, we don't look at cost basis as being the most realistic value…"

This time I interrupted.

"With all due respect, sir, no one cares what the 'market value' of the receivables is. And unless you can come up with another $40 million in collateral pretty quick, we are going to have a hard time extending the maturity of the line."

"Mr. Wilson, every single asset that the company owns is pledged to one debt instrument or another," the CFO said. "We have nothing else to give."

"How about the Littles?" I asked, looking at the brothers, who had so far been sitting at the conference table like fat stone Buddhas. "Perhaps they've got some personal assets that could stand in?"

Both of them stirred in their chairs, and the older brother said:

"I don't think we have any personal assets we would want to pledge to the line of credit," he said.

130

"Then I don't think we're going to be able to extend the line," I said.

The brothers looked at each other like they were confused.

"Extend the line? But the bank has already agreed to a 30-day extension, to give us more time to work on the financial systems, and perhaps to find some additional investors."

I actually laughed.

"Vinnie, did you extend the line?" I said.

He laughed too.

"I was going to ask you the same thing," he said. "Because I sure haven't signed anything."

"Neither have I. So I'm not sure what 'agreement' you're referring to, but none of the bank officers in this room has agreed to an extension of any kind."

Jonathan Little then reached into a manila envelope and slid a piece of paper across the desk to me. I recognized it instantly; it was a standard maturity extension agreement on my bank's letterhead.   ECP's line was properly identified, and the maturity date was extended for another 30 days.

"OK, you've gotten our standard document filled out," I said. "That doesn't mean we're signing it."

Jonathan again pretended to be confused.

"But the bank has already signed it. Turn it over. You will see where Managing Director Randall Clifton placed his signature."

◆

That wiped the smile off my face in a hurry. I turned it over and sure enough, Clifton had signed the document. I slid it over to Vinnie. He looked at it and his face turned dark. Jay reached over and took the agreement from Vinnie, and started to study it.

"Randall Clifton was the head of our capital markets group," I said angrily. "He is no longer an employee of the bank, as I'm sure you know, and even if he was he has no authority to sign this agreement."

Andrew Little shrugged.

"He told us he was employed until the end of the month. As far as his authority, listen, he's the head of the investment bank and a bank officer, right?" he said. "I mean, he told us he could sign for the bank. How are we to know whether he can or not?"

"He is distinctly not a bank officer," I said. "The bank and the investment bank are entirely separate. Officers of the investment bank..."

But Jay Podolski had placed his hand on my arm.

"We're going to discuss this among ourselves for a few minutes, all right, gentlemen?"

"Sam," Jay said when we had adjourned into a separate room, "they've got us."

"What do you mean, they've got us?" I said. "Randall Clifton resigned last week. And he was never an officer of the bank. He was an officer of the separate capital markets subsidiary. He never should have signed that extension, and he knows it, because legally speaking he does not have the proper authority."

"Legally speaking," said Jay, "the Littles are probably right. I read the press release on Clifton—technically he is still an employee of the bank until the end of the month. The Littles know Randall Clifton to be a senior officer of this institution. They don't know—or at least, they can credibly claim that they don't know—about the different subsidiaries and divisions of the bank."

"That's a crock!" I said. "Clifton pulled this little stunt to get back at me for selling bonds from the investment bank's portfolio! He knows he doesn't have the authority to sign this!"

Vinnie was bouncing off the walls.

"That God-damned geezer! With his comb-over and his shiny fucking cuff links!? I swear I will go down to the trading floor and choke him out right now! Who the fuck does he think he is, sticking his nose into my deal?"

Jay put his hands out, palms down.

"Let's all relax, okay? What I am telling you is this: Clifton signed that extension. That's not a point of contention. The form of the extension, on the bank's letterhead, is also legitimate. I read it.

"That leaves solely the issue of whether or not Clifton was authorized to sign it. Believe me, you do not want to take that issue in front of a judge. ECP will say that of course they assumed Clifton was authorized. He was the head of the investment bank, obviously a very senior person, and when he said he could sign the line extension, why would they doubt him? And they will win that argument 10 times out of 10."

"So what's the bottom line?" said Vinnie. "I mean, that was our hook. We were using the potential default of the line to force these guys to get their financial systems squared away, to get the collateral shortfall fixed, everything."

"The bottom line is, the bank just extended the maturity of the line another 30 days," said Jay. "So you don't have that hook any more. Randall Clifton took it away from you."

◆

We went back into the conference room with ECP, and I bellied up to a plateful of crow.

We are going to respect the line extension that Clifton signed, I said. They were hereby notified, with all parties as witness, that Clifton was not authorized to sign anything else ever again for the bank. But this one time, we would accept his signature. The line was extended an additional 30 days.

The brothers nodded solemnly. The CFO tried but was not quite able to hide a smile. The words had tasted very sour coming out of my mouth, and the smug looks between the brothers and the CFO made it worse.

We wanted solutions to the collateral shortfall. It was up to them to come up with them. We wanted the financial systems up to snuff. At the end of the day, nothing much had changed. They just had 30 more days to get it done.

The brothers nodded some more. We discussed financial systems and collateral options and a whole bunch of other stuff, and then about an hour later they got up and left. I handed the line extension form to Vinnie.

"Get me a copy of this for Lawson," I said. "Then book it."

Vinnie looked like I had asked him to eat a box of broken glass, but he took it.

"And stay away from Randall Clifton and the trading floor," I said.

Vinnie and Jay left, leaving me with just Ana.

"I guess that does not happen so often?" she said. "I have heard of Randall Clifton, but he was not supposed to sign this?"

"No," I said. "He's the head of the investment bank—or he was, until he decided to take early retirement a few days ago. He knows ECP, his group led their public bond deals. He knows he shouldn't have signed that form but...well, it's political."

"So what will you do?" she asked?

"Well, if we can't find any other way to default them, or unless we get cross-defaulted by another deal, then I don't think there is much we can do except wait."

"Cross-defaulted?" asked Ana.

"Yeah, you know, if the asset-backed deal goes into default, then our deal automatically does, too. Cross-default."

"Oh, of course."

"What are you going to do?" I said. "Are you interested in this deal or not?"

"Oh, definitely," she said. "I think the problem here might be management. If we could replace them, then perhaps things would be much better."

"Are you sure? I mean even with the discount you'd get from us, it's going to take a pretty big check to buy the debt of this company," I said.

"Oh, it's not about the money, Sam. Believe me, we have plenty of money. It's more about...how do you say... the fit? Can we absorb this operation into our existing businesses, that is the issue," she said.

"What other information do you need from us?"

"Let me call my office," she said. "I will get back with you after lunch."

"Okay," I said. "You can use an office here if you want."

"Ummm...I have my cellphone and a portable fax in my car. I think I will just call from there." She stood up to leave.

"Are you okay, Sam?" she said. "You seem sad."

"It's nothing," I said, "just a tough couple of days."

She trailed her fingers across my shoulders as she rose to leave.

"Maybe I can make you more happy later, *guapo*." she said.

I allowed myself a brief review of two nights ago, and thought that maybe there was another night like that to come.

But ah...the day was young.

◆

I had lunch with Lawson at a local deli. I told him what had happened at ECP, how we were furious that Randall Clifton had just handed the company a get-out-of-jail-free card, at least for the next 30 days. I described what the shortfall looked like now, and handed him a copy of the extension with Clifton's signature on it.

Lawson stroked one of his chins.

"Well...I gather that this is payback to us for interfering in the investment banking operation?" he said.

"I think so," I said. "I think he's saying, if you stick a finger in my eye, I can stick one in yours. Plus maybe it's a parting gift for us, while he goes on to pursue personal fulfillment in early retirement."

"It would be nice if Mr. Clifton would consider the larger picture here, wouldn't it?"

"What does he care?" I asked. "He doesn't work here anymore. Or he won't in two weeks."

Lawson nodded sourly.

"Yes, one of the more foolish aspects of allowing someone to stick around after you have shown them the door. You would hope that the severance package would help him go quietly, but obviously it didn't in this case. I will speak to our chairman about it, but that won't do any good either."

"And I guess we have no choice but to accept the extension?"

Lawson ruminated over his roast beef sandwich momentarily, then said:

"I am in agreement with Lawyer Jay on that. Unfortunately, we have no choice. I will make sure that Mr. Clifton understands he is not to sign anything else related to bank matters. But I don't think we will pursue it any further than that, and we will just have to live with the 30 days."

◆

I went back to my office to find my whole crowd, absent Ana, gathered in the small conference room. Vinnie, Jay, two of Jay's associates and even Sharon were intensely reading a single sheet of paper.

I went in.

"What in the world is going on?" I said

"Hey Sam," said Sharon. "This came in on the fax machine about an hour ago. I read it and thought I better get it out to everyone quickly. I hope you don't mind but it seemed urgent."

She handed me a copy of a single spaced letter on plain white paper, no letterhead or address. It had the fax line descriptors on the top of it.

I sat down in a chair and read it. It said:

To Whom It May Concern:

For about three years, I worked at Entourage Capital Partners in Memphis, in the finance unit. My responsibilities included reporting on the company's asset-backed and corporate bonds, and also reporting regularly to its bank, Citizens Union.

During that time, a partnership called Wolf River LLP came to my attention. Wolf River bought defaulted receivables that served as collateral for both the bank line of credit and the asset-backed securities. Whenever someone stopped paying on an account, Wolf River would buy it for 70-80% of its value, and the proceeds of that "sale" were reported as collections.

The "purchases" from Wolf River, however, were not in cash. ECP accepted a note payable from Wolf River, and, in violation of both the bank and the ABS agreement, considered the notes as cash.

I now know these purchases to be fraudulent. The accounts sold to Wolf River are from companies that are bankrupt, and they will never pay. Neither will Wolf River; it has no cash that I know of. It is fully owned by Jonathan and Andrew Little of ECP.

ECP is essentially bankrupt, and the bank and the ABS deal have large amounts of worthless collateral.

I could not be part of this any longer. These facts as I have stated them can be easily verified by checking the asset-backed reports with the trustee, and the collateral reports for the bank.

It was signed "Anonymous." The distribution list for the letter included myself and several bankers in the

Memphis office, George Lamb, Randall Clifton, and the trustee for the asset-backed securities.

And...oh yeah. The Securities and Exchange Commission, the Federal Bureau of Investigation, the Office of the Comptroller of the Currency, and the Federal Deposit Insurance Corporation. Each and every federal regulator who had anything to do with banks or securities had received the letter.

"Oh shit," I said, rubbing my eyebrows. I put my forehead down on the cold table top.

I looked up after a minute. The faces of Vinnie and Jay looked as bad as I felt.

"Well, Vin-man, what have we got here?" I asked.

"What we have here is a rhinoceros dick right up our ass," he said.

That made both Jay and me laugh, and made me feel a little better. You could always count on a memorable image from Vinnie.

"Well, I didn't see Lawson on the distribution list. I better go tell him. Before he tells the chairman, he's going to need a loss estimate. So I guess you better start going through the line of credit and the asset-backed monthly reports, and try to figure how much real, actual cash is available, and how much is bullshit."

"I'm just having a hard time believing this is a coincidence," said Jay. "I mean, ECP was just in here, and they found a very sneaky, unethical way to get a 30-day extension on the line. And a few hours after they leave, this comes over the fax? That sure seems like unusual timing."

"You're saying you think they knew this was coming?" asked Vinnie. "And they came in to get the line extension before the shit hit the fan?"

I shook my head.

"I think the opposite is true—that just like us, they had no idea this was coming. I mean, why come in here and go through all that hoopla for a 30-day extension, if you know this letter is coming? Because this letter is an event of default, right? There are all kinds of clauses that require 'truthfulness and accuracy of information' in our line of credit agreement. Hell, every month the CFO has to sign a collateral certificate for both us and the asset-backed deal, and right underneath the signature line it says 'certified true and accurate to the best of my abilities.'"

Jay nodded. "I see your point—if the letter is true."

"If the letter is true, then their whole capital structure is in default," said Vinnie. "The asset-backed and corporate bonds surely have the same type of wording in their agreements. And even if they don't, when the bank defaults them, the ABS trustee will cross-default them."

There was a moment of silence while we all considered that. Vinnie spoke first.

"If the letter is true," he said, "the company has no source of cash for operations. And they have virtually no cash on hand. This show is over. These guys are functionally bankrupt."

"If you're ECP, why even ask for 30 days?" said Jay. "I mean, if you know you're out of money, and there is no way to continue your business because you don't have any cash, why not just throw in the towel and file?"

"I know one reason," I said, after thinking about it for a moment.

"What?" said Vinnie.

"To get yourselves 30 more days to steal the bank's collateral, and turn it into some personal cash for yourself."

12

We gathered in Lawson's office. He read the letter twice, slowly. He put it down on his desk and looked at us balefully.

"Who is the author of this fine piece of writing?" he asked.

I shook my head.

"I have no idea. It has a ring of truth to it, but it could be a prank. Finding out who *might* have written it would take weeks. We just don't have that time."

"But we don't need it," said Vinnie. "I've got the line of credit reports and the asset backed reports for the last year, and I just got off the phone with the asset-backed trustee. There is a line on both reports called "Miscellaneous Other Collections." That's where we think the Wolf River collections are listed. In the last year, they have quintupled, from $500,000 a month last year to over $2.6 million last month. That's 20% of total collections. There should be millions in their cash accounts, but I checked, and they have a few hundred thousand in there. These collections are all bogus. There is no cash from the Wolf River purchases."

"So both our line of credit and the asset-backed bonds have been underwater for at least a year? Because if these Wolf River 'purchases' are in fact fraudulent, and there was no cash paid for those defaulted receivables, then the collections shortfall would have tripped all kinds of triggers in both deals," said Lawson.

"Correct," I said.

"And the Little Brothers are doing this why?" said Lawson.

I shrugged.

"They're trying to keep this show going as long as they can. They are milking ECP for all its worth. It's just straight-up fraud now. Every day they are in business is another day where the bank's collateral disappears, and our loss gets bigger. Every day."

Lawson exhaled loudly and took out his pipe, which he stuck in his mouth and chewed on but didn't light.

"How much?" he said.

"We have a new loss estimate," I said.

"Updated from two hours ago?" Lawson asked a little sarcastically.

Vinnie handed over his loss estimate. Lawson read it out loud.

"Estimated line of credit loss: $70 million. Estimated corporate bond loss: $18 million. Estimated asset-backed securities loss: $15 million. Total loss estimate: $103 million."

He put the paper down on top of the letter.

"So a $103 million loss on $260 million in exposure. Works out to about 40%, doesn't it?"

"Yes sir," said Vinnie. "39.6%, to be exact."

"39.6%. We are now looking at losing over $100 million on ECP. Where the average loss on senior secured debt is supposed to be less than half that," Lawson said ruminatively.

He chewed on his pipe some more.

"Well, put them into Chapter 11 first thing," he finally said. "The Good Lord knows how we are going to keep them from moving this collateral on us. Receivable payments flowing into company-owned bank accounts? We're going to have to ask the court to freeze those accounts immediately; if they won't, ECP could walk off with 60 days worth of collections before we could even turn around."

He reached into his desk and pulled out a pouch of tobacco. He started stuffing his pipe.

"Well, best get to it," he said. "I will call the chairman, and then start calling these regulators."

He looked at his watch.

"4:00 on Friday afternoon. Not a single one of those govvies will be in his office. They are all in the Blue Ridge mountains or at the Outer Banks by now. Well, at least the message will be stamped before the close of business. But nothing will happen on this until Monday."

He lit his pipe and picked up the phone, and that was our signal to leave. But then he paused and said:

"But on Monday, we are getting hit with a Category 5 hurricane. There will be three vans full of Feds here by 9 am. So get ready."

◆

I prepared my weekly chairman's report, and sent it out. I imagined the chairman would find that default letter joyful reading indeed.

After that I talked through the bankruptcy filing with Jay. Vinnie had joined us and we started going through what we would need in detail—subsidiaries, account freeze orders, secured and unsecured creditor lists, pension plan information—it was a mammoth job, and it had to be done by Monday morning.

Jay and Vinnie finally adjourned to an office to continue working on the petition. I went to Melanie's office to take one last look at what the markets were doing. She wasn't in there. The U.S. stock market had fluctuated wildly on the Russian contagion, down almost 300 points at one time but then getting back to even before the close. A wild ride for not much reason, it seemed. The other international markets, both stocks and bonds, had been down, with the international bond market again taking a beating.

I don't know why I am doing this, I thought suddenly. It's too late to sell anything now. We'd be just as well off holding it and riding out the storm as to sell into a market where no one wanted to buy. We were holding what we had. This was now a simple valuation job.

The whole idea depressed me. I changed the topic in my head and started to think of ordering dinner somewhere, because it was looking like a long night. Right then my cellphone rang. I looked at it; it was a Charlotte number I didn't recognize. I answered.

"Sam? Is this Sam Wilson with Citizen's Union?" said a male voice with a Texas twang on the other end.

"It is," I said.

"This here is Augustus Harvey with Collins Investigative Service. We haven't met yet, but Jay Podolski hired me on a certain matter. Does that ring a bell?"

"Of course," I said. "What can I do for you?"

"Well, I tried Jay's number, but he's not picking up, so I thought I'd call you. As I think you know from that photograph I took last night of the two brothers and their guest at dinner, I am here in Charlotte. Actually, I'm at the Charlotte airport, in the private section. I thought you might want to come down here and take a look at something. Maybe bring Lawyer Jay with you."

I contemplated that for a minute.

"Well, Augustus, we are kind of busy up here. The kind of busy where you work all night. So can this wait? Or can you tell me about it on the phone?"

"Sir, I know you surely must be busy, but this is something I just cannot describe, and if we wait it might be gone soon. I promise you I would not ask over something trivial."

I sighed.

"All right. Jay has to stay here, but I can come myself. Where are you?"

"I'm sitting in the parking lot of the main private terminal at the Charlotte airport. Do you know how to get here?"

I did. He described his car. And so at 6:30 that night, with the sun beginning to set and the Friday after-work traffic thinning down, and with the body of George Lamb probably being prepared for burial, and the bank fixing to force a client into Chapter 11, I drove out to the private plane terminal at the Charlotte airport.

I had been there twice before, both times hitching a ride on the bank's plane to somewhere. In the parking lot of the terminal was a gray four-door Ford parked facing the private hangar. I parked next to it and got into the passenger's seat.

The man in the driver's seat reached over and offered me his hand. He was older, 60 maybe, with a face that had earned every one of those years, but he was fit. His hair was cut short and he had a gray-and-black speckled mustache. Both he and his car smelled like stale cigarette smoke. There were coffee cups and fast food bags littering the back floorboard. A pair of binoculars and a small camera were on the dashboard in front of him.

"Augustus Harvey. Folks call me Auggie. I'm with Collins Investigative Services. I understand you're the paying client. Thank you for the business."

"Sam Wilson, Citizen's Union," I said. "You're welcome. Now what are we doing here?"

"Well, Sam, it's like this. I've been following these Little boys since they got here last night. Little boys, that's a good one, huh? Because they are both fatsos. Anyway, this morning, after the meeting you folks had at the bank, I was back onto their tail, with them walking back to their hotel and me walking along a ways back. To be honest I wasn't paying enough attention and I crowded up on them until I was really too close.

"Right about then we got to the hotel and I was damn near in their back pockets, and I heard one of them say to their pilot, who was outside the hotel waiting on them, to 'get the plane ready for later tonight.' I walked on around them, because I really had no choice. Stopping or turning around would have been stupid. So I walked right to my car and came out here.

"See, when they first touched down, I was sitting right here, knowing they were coming in on a private plane because my partner in Memphis had told me. But he hadn't been able to get the tail number, and they got that darn plane into a hangar so fast that I didn't get a chance to look at it either.

"So after I overheard the instructions to the pilot, I figured they would be heading this way eventually. Sure enough the pilot got dropped off by a cab in about 45 minutes. I heard the terminal folks give him the gate code, and I saw the hangar he went into. I sat here for a piece, and in about an hour a van pulls up and goes through the gate with the same code. The driver pulled up to the hangar and started loading a bunch of boxes into the hangar. Food and drink, is what I was thinking, but there was a lot of it, especially if all they were going to do was go back to Memphis."

He looked at his watch.

"About an hour ago, the van left and the pilot was in the passenger's seat. So I called you to come on down. What I was thinking was, we'd punch in the gate code, and get into that hangar, and have a look at that plane. Plus I would really like to get that tail number, it would make it a lot easier to track."

"You called me down here to see a plane?" I said. "I've seen planes before. There's a lot of work I've got back at the office that..."

"Oh, what we've got here is a lot more than just a plane. I've been asking around some, to the runway workers and such," said Auggie. "What we got here is a pleasure palace. That's why I thought you might want to see her."

I looked at him, not really understanding.

"Game?" he said. "Great. This will only take 15 minutes and then you can get on back to work. I'm not sure how much time we got, so let's move pretty quick-like. I'm going to swing the car around to the other side of the hangar, where we can't be seen from the gate. There is a side entrance, we'll go in there."

Auggie pulled the car up to the gate and punched in a 4-digit code. The gate slowly slid open and we went through. We were on the back side of the airport, across the runways from the main commercial terminal. We drove down through the private hangar area and pulled up to a large, gray, sheet-metal hangar. We got out and Auggie walked up to the door and pulled out a leather sleeve of tools.

I watched while Auggie jimmied the lock and opened the door in no time flat.

"Product of a misspent youth," he whispered to me. He held the door open and I walked quickly into the hangar. It was dimly lit, and Auggie came in behind me touched me on the shoulder.

"Let's just hold quiet here for a second and make sure we don't have any company."

After a minute he gestured us forward and pointed.

The only plane in the hangar was the size of a commercial airliner.

"Where's the Little brothers' plane?" I asked.

"That is the Little brothers' plane," he said.

"What? That's a 747!" I said.

"757," Auggie corrected me.

The door to the plane was open and a rolling stairway had been pulled up to the door. The area was spot-lit, as if a superstar or a politician was about to emerge from the plane.

"Let's go look inside," said Auggie, and we proceeded across the hangar to the stairs. I went up first.

"Holy shit," I said, when I finally got into the plane. Auggie was right behind me and he gasped when he saw it too.

The whole interior of the plane had been refitted. The rows of seats you normally see on a plane that size had all been ripped out. In their place there was a movie viewing area with large leather couches and a floor-to-ceiling screen, and a large mirrored bar fully stocked with liquor, wine, beer, champagne and mixers. I opened up a stainless steel cabinet that felt warm. Food, and a lot of it: sandwiches, barbecue, fried chicken. Another refrigerated drawer held quarts of slaw and potato salad and beans, trays of brownies and cupcakes.

I closed the doors and walked past the lounge and the theater. Auggie was opening and closing drawers as I passed by.

"Check this out," he said.

I looked into a drawer he had opened and there were several hand mirrors in there with razor blades on them, and on one of them there was also the remnants of a fine white powder.

"Coke mirrors," I said.

"Yep," said Auggie.

I kept walking back into the plane. There were several sleeping cabins, with queen-sized beds on either wall next to the windows. The beds had been made up with black sheets; I ran my hand along them as I walked by. Silk.

In the back, though, was the *pièce de résistance:* an 8-person, sunken hot tub surrounded by mirrors on all sides and the ceiling. I reached down and felt the water. It was still heating up, according to the digital read out, on its way to a perfect 103 degrees. "Getting the plane ready" obviously had a totally different meaning for the Little brothers than just gassing up.

"Can you imagine the expense of flying this much water around?" said Auggie.

I could only shake my head. I had seen opulence before, but this was way past opulence or even bad taste. This was decadence.

I opened the doors on either side of the hot tub. One was a bathroom, although about three times as big as a normal airplane bathroom. The other was a large shower, again with mirrored walls. Plenty of room for two in there.

Auggie was busy snapping photos of the whole thing, being careful not to include me. He finally said we should leave, and we filed down the stairs and headed for the door with Auggie taking one last snap of the tail number of the plane.

We were in his car and starting to ease out when we saw headlights coming from a long way away, at the gate. Auggie accelerated forward and we went another terminal down, on the runway side, then swung around where we could have a view of the hangar's main door without being seen. He had never turned his headlights on.

"That's the same van that dropped off all the food and drink a while back. Let's wait here a minute and see what we can see," said Auggie.

This time the pilot was driving and a co-pilot was in the seat next to them; or that's what I figured them for, they had matching uniforms. They pulled up to the main door, got out, and slid open the passenger door of the van.

First out was Andrew Little, then his brother, and then three very attractive young ladies in short tight skirts and high heels got out.

"Pros," whispered Auggie.

And last man out? With his custom-made suit, his perfect white pocket square, and his silver cufflinks that matched his silver glasses? Mr. Randall Clifton, head of the Citizen's Union Capital Markets Group, until a few days ago.

They all filed into the hangar. A towing vehicle showed up, the front door of the hangar was raised, and in about ten minutes the plane had been towed to the taxi area and the engines fired up. It taxied out of the hangar space toward the runway. It sat there for several minutes, apparently waiting for tower approval to take off, and eventually it moved to the end of the runway and the pilot hit the burners. We watched it until it was a speck in the sky heading north.

I sat there and rubbed my eyebrows and looked at the runway. Auggie rolled the front windows down and lit a cigarette.

"Can you explain to me what I just saw?" I said.

"Before I answer that, let me ask you this," Auggie said. "I know the two brothers, and I saw the pilots the first time around. The girls were probably hired here in Charlotte. But how about the gentleman with the silver glasses? He's the same fellow I took a photo of last night, in the restaurant with the brothers. Do you know him?"

"Yes, I know him," I said. "His name is Randall Clifton. He used to work at the same bank that I do. He announced his early retirement last week, but in reality I think he was fired."

Auggie whipped his head sideways and looked at me.

"Some bank you boys are running down there," he said.

"Tell me about it," I said.

"Did his firing have any thing to do with those Little brothers and their company?"

"Not directly," I said.

He turned to face the front again.

"Well, I tell you what all this looks like to me, strange as it may seem," he said. "I think they're having a party. I think those three girls were hookers. And I think those boys are just going to fly around tonight and get drunk and stoned and bang those hookers in the hot tub."

"Why do you think that?" I said. "I mean, I think the girls were hookers too, but maybe they are just going back to Memphis with them."

"Did you see the booze in there? In that plane you could be in Memphis in an hour. Do you need a case of champagne for that? Or six bottles of premium vodka? Or enough food to feed eight people for three days? Plus there are plenty of hookers in Memphis. You don't need to import them from Charlotte."

"But why would you do that? Why?"

"Because you can," Auggie said. "Because it impresses the girls, and all your friends, when you tell them about it. 'Yeah, we just flew around the country all night and snorted coke and got drunk with naked strippers! In a hot tub! On a plane!' No chance of your party getting busted up by the cops, either."

I just shook my head.

"The Little brothers are in the airplane parts business," I said. "I guess I can see outfitting a showpiece of some kind, you know, a really fancy plane, to show potential buyers what you're really capable of. But actually flying the thing around? With hookers and coke and a set of pilots? That is just beyond expensive. You could get the same effect with a fiberglass body on a showroom floor."

"I don't mean to pry, but are you saying that your bank is paying for all this?" said Auggie.

I didn't answer. I didn't want to even know the answer.

Auggie finished his cigarette, flipped it out the window and put the car in gear. As we drove slowly back to the gate, he said:

"If they fly that plane back to Memphis, my partner will have them soon as they hit the airport. I'll call you or Jay, and let you know if that happens. But I wouldn't be expecting my call, and if you don't hear from me in two hours, then they probably didn't land in Memphis.

"And if they don't, then I am going to get a line on that tail number, and probably end up camping out here for the next couple of days. If that fellow that works at the bank lives here in Charlotte, and those whores are locals, then after the party is over the plane will stop back here to drop them off. Who knows when, but the coke and the booze will wear off after a while, and they will get tired of each other. Maybe late

Saturday or early Sunday. Anyway, Old Auggie will be sitting here waiting for them."

We were through the gate and back to my car in the parking lot. I started to get out and Auggie put his arm on me.

"One other thing you need to know," he said. "There is another tail on these guys. I don't think he's seen me, but I saw him this morning here and then later, down close to your bank."

"Who is it?" I said.

Auggie shrugged.

"I don't know. I didn't get any kind of a look at him. He's pretty good, he's done this kind of work before, I can tell you that. He knows how to get lost in traffic, disappear in a crowd. He's just made one mistake: he's got a gorgeous car. Really stands out. You see what I'm driving, a gray Ford sedan.? Normal, right? Average. Most people don't even notice this thing.

"This guy's driving around in a big black M-series BMW with platinum wheels on it. I mean, it's great if you want to race, but it's too distinctive for surveillance work."

"Any ideas on who it is?" I asked.

"No," he said. "I'll keep an eye out though."

I thanked him for his work, got in my car and left.

13

The best form of corporate bankruptcy, if there is such a thing, is called an "11 pre-pack," which stands for pre-packaged bankruptcy under Chapter 11 of the federal bankruptcy laws. In this form, the bank and the company agree beforehand not only that the firm will file bankruptcy, but in general terms on what the firm will look like as it emerges from bankruptcy: who will be managing it, how big it will be, what products it will sell, etc... Pre-pack Chapter 11s are still bankruptcies: jobs are lost and so is a lot of the bank's money, and equity holders get wiped out as per usual. But many times the firm can emerge as a smaller, leaner version of itself, and get back in business.

At the dead-ass bottom of the totem pole, the worst form of bankruptcy, is what Jay and Vinnie and I had started working on that Friday: an involuntary free-fall. While still inside Chapter 11, there would be no agreement between the bank and the borrower. The bank would just go straight to federal court and insist that the borrower was broke and had to file bankruptcy. It was risky. The company could object and so could the judge. And free-fall is just what it sounds like. Even if the judge agrees, and forces the company into Chapter 11, the bank has no idea what it will discover post-bankruptcy. There is no common analysis of the company's financial condition and no agreement with its managers on who will run it. And at the end of a free-fall, there is the loud thump of a dead company. Free-falls almost never emerge from Chapter 11; they go straight to liquidation.

Pre-pack is infinitely more attractive than free-fall because it is reliable. It is consistent, orderly. Losses can be estimated; worried bank executives could be assuaged; plans can be made. Free-fall is like walking into the jungle at night without a flashlight.

But the letter from the former employee of ECP had left us no choice. If the company was committing fraud right under our noses, we had to act fast to preserve whatever collateral we had left. And if there was any doubt at all about the wisdom of that choice, all I had to do was conjure up a vision of the flying 757 Love Boat, and the hot tub and the coke mirrors and the hookers. And the fat Little brothers and their stocked-up booze cruise in the air. And feel the knot in my throat over the very real possibility that they were stealing from the bank every day to pay for it all.

And Randall Clifton was aiding and abetting.

Back at the bank, it was now about 9:00 and Vinnie, Jay and two of our analysts were working on the bankruptcy filing. I decided that right then I was a fifth wheel, and things would move faster if I just got out of the way. So I got in the car and headed for home, and was halfway there when my cellphone rang.

"Sam? Hi, it's Ana, how are you?"

In all the excitement I had totally forgotten about her and Santiago Capital. I had last seen her late yesterday morning, when she was leaving to huddle with her partners.

"Oh, hi, Ana. I'm glad to hear from you. I was wondering if you would call."

"We are still quite interested, if that is what you are worried about. In fact we brought a team into Charlotte today to work on it here. I apologize for it taking so long. You know how the bureaucracy can be, I'm sure. Anyway, I was hoping we could get together tonight, if it is not too late. We could talk about ECP and...you know, catch up a little." There was a clear invitation in her voice and I was not slow to take it.

"That sounds great. I am almost home, though. Would you like to come up to the lake somewhere?"

"Yes! I have not seen the Lake Norman area, I have heard it is beautiful. Would you like me to come up to your house?"

Something gave me pause right then. Had I ever told her that I lived on the lake? I couldn't remember. And there was that earlier thing with my wallet, and the guy who asked Max where I lived. And her tone seemed a little too eager, like she really wanted to see where I lived. Anyway, for whatever reason, I demurred.

"Well...there is a nice pool hall up here that I go to sometimes, they have some rocking chairs out back overlooking the lake. It can be a fun place on a Saturday night. I don't know if you like pool, though..."

"That sounds very nice. I love pool, we used to have a snooker table when I was growing up. I am...how do you say...a shark?"

"A pool shark," I said. "Good, we can play some then if you like."

"*Muy bien*," she said. "Maybe we can go to your house later."

I gave her directions to the Green Room and she promised to meet me in 45 minutes or so. I went to the house, changed and showered quickly, and then took the boat down.

She was sitting outside in a rocking chair when I pulled into the boat slip. She had on the usual mini skirt and low-cut blouse, but in a change from her work uniform, she wore a pair of long leather boots that went tightly up to her knee. Her hair was pulled back in the same simple ponytail she had worn with her schoolgirl outfit.

She watched me dock and tie off and then I hopped out and walked up the stairs to give her the European double-kiss.

"Wow, you have a boat?" she said. "That is very nice. You must live on the lake?"

"Yes," I said, taking the chair next to her. "I'm sorry to keep you waiting. I have a small house about 20 minutes from here by boat. It's a little farther by car."

She was holding a brown bag of something in her lap, which she handed to me.

"Here, I brought you a present."

I opened the bag. It was a bottle of Havana Club rum, straight from Cuba.

"Havana Club," I said, impressed. "You can't get this around here. Have you been to Cuba since yesterday morning?"

She laughed and put her hand on my arm.

"I have my sources," she said. "We were talking about rums the other night, so I thought you might appreciate the best one. You drink rum, yes?"

"I don't usually, but as you say, this is the best. Why don't we go inside and have a little?"

"Do you think they will let us have the rum in there? I don't know if that is legal here. In Miami usually is not."

"I am friends with the owner here, I don't think he will mind...but we might have to give him a little taste of the rum."

"Ha, you have *la mordida* here too, I see! It means 'the little bite,' like a small bribe. In Mexico and some other countries, is very common."

"I guess it happens here too," I said. "Greases the wheels a little."

We went inside and I saw Bill Ritchie up front. We walked up to him and I introduced Ana, then explained the rum.

"Sure, let me handle it up here, okay?" he said. "I'll just put it under the counter and pour it for you. What do you want to mix it with?"

"Just some ice for me," said Ana.

"Me too," I said. "And pour yourself one if you like. You don't get a chance at Havana Club around here too often."

He whistled and looked into the bag.

"No, you don't. That's a $100 bottle of rum."

"Not so much if you have contacts," Ana said.

"Oh, excuse me," Bill said, smiling. "I didn't realize I was talking to a woman of influence as well as beauty."

Ana smiled glitteringly back at him, and then asked after the ladies' room and walked off. She gave us an extra little hip swing to admire, which we both did.

"She's a knockout," Bill said, handing me a drink and taking a sip of the one he had poured himself. "Man, that's good. So where have you been hiding that lovely lady?"

"I just met her," I said. "She's in the finance business too. Works down in Miami. She's from Columbia originally. She's up here on business."

"Is it serious?"

"What, the business?"

"Don't play dumb with me. You know what I mean."

"It's early for that," I said.

"Well, I advise you to get busy. You are not getting any younger."

I scanned the room and saw there were a few empty tables, and the crowd was mostly my age, and couples. I also saw Big Max playing pool at the end of the room, with someone I didn't recognize.

"Can we get a table?" I asked. "And how about sending Big Max a couple of fingers of that rum?"

Ana returned from the bathroom. Bill gave us a nice table close to the back door, where we could feel the evening breeze a little. Big Max was a few tables away and gave me a wink and a salute with the rum I had sent him. I racked up a standard eight-ball set and asked Ana if she knew the game.

"Of course," she said. "Solids and stripes, except for the eight, which is the last one down. I will break?"

She had a nice snap on her break and a solid went down. She then proceeded to almost run the table. She had all the shots: short cuts, banks, long diagonals.

She was not kidding when she said she was a shark. In about thirty minutes she was leaning over the table, on one leg, reaching as far as she could for a shot on the eight ball and her third win. She looked back over her shoulder at me before she hit the shot.

"There is something you would like to do to my form?" she asked with a smile.

I had to laugh. She laughed too and then slammed the eight ball home.

"Maybe is not your lucky day," she said.

Bill Ritchie had watched the last game and was laughing into his shirt.

"What's that, three in a row for Ana?" he asked. "Maybe we ought to set you up on the checkers board over there, Sam."

He and Ana both laughed, there were a few more comments about finding a game more my speed, then I said:

"How about a little nine-ball?"

In nine-ball, the only balls on the table are balls one through nine. You sink them in order, but if you can get a combination on the nine, and it goes down, you win and the game is over. It's a much faster and open game than nine-ball and requires a little more imagination.

Ana agreed and knew the game. In twenty minutes, I was up four games to none on nine-ball. I smiled and asked if she would like a nice game of checkers instead.

I got a little glimpse of the famous Latino passion as she prepared to respond, but just then her cellphone rang. She glanced at it, excused herself, and took it outside.

I went up front and got Bill to pour me a little more rum. It was going down very well, and I was starting to think of squeezing Ana into my boat and hustling her back to the house when she came back in frowning.

"What's the matter?" I asked.

"That was Marcos. I have to return to work."

"What? At 9:30 on Friday night? Are you going back to Miami?"

"No, no, we have a conference room in our hotel, we are in Charlotte working on this ECP deal, as I told you. There are some problems with our analysis and I have to go straighten them out."

I must have looked upset. She put her mouth to my ear and whispered:

"I am so sorry, *guapo*. You know how this business is. I promise it won't be long when we are together again."

"I understand," I said, swallowing my disappointment. "Let me walk you out to your car."

I hadn't told her about ECP's pending bankruptcy, and I wasn't going to. If they were interested in the company, they could still get it out of bankruptcy. And if they weren't, then it wouldn't matter to them.

In the parking lot she hugged me tight to her breasts and then gave me a long, slow kiss.

"I will call you when I can," she said.

She got into her car, and left. I stood there, stunned.

Not because I was shocked at the quick departure, although that was certainly deflating.

And not because of the things she promised in her kiss, though that was plenty to divert a man's attention.

No, what had me speechless that fine evening with its disappointing ending was her car.

She had squealed out of the parking lot in a four-door BMW. There was no mistaking the sound of that big engine either. It was the M5. And it was shiny black and had big silver wheels.

It was the car that Max identified when he said a guy was looking for my house, and the one Auggie the P.I. said was tailing the Little brothers.

◆

I went back inside, closed out my table, and sat in one of the booths, lost in thought.

"Did your girl just leave?" said Bill.

"Yeah, she had to go back to work."

"Work? At this time of night? You said she was in banking, right? What kind of banker goes to work at 9:30 on a Friday night?"

I didn't want to tell him that I did all the time. People have images of bankers as 9-to-5 types, and some of them are, but the part of banking I was in required you to be on the job whenever the job needed doing.

He took my moroseness to mean I was bummed about Ana leaving, and he brought me two more fingers of the Havana Club on ice. The bottle was halfway done—half-empty would seem the way to look at it now.

Because, between the thing with my wallet, and her fumbling around with common finance terms, and now this whole deal with the car, it was becoming clear to me that she was not who she said she was. I couldn't figure out what angle she and Marcos might be working, but I was wondering if they even represented a vulture fund.

Was I being played? For what? Inside information on ECP? What good would that do them? I could see a short-seller maybe benefiting from knowledge that the company was in financial trouble, but ECP's stock price was already in the pennies. The market was well aware of the fact that ECP was on the verge of bankruptcy. When the news of the disgruntled employee letter hit the street next week, it would be over, and anyway Monday the company was going into bankruptcy before the market opened. There was no play there.

Red lights were flashing and alarm bells were ringing in my head, but I sat there until midnight and got nowhere on "why." I drove home slowly in the boat. It was pitch dark, a moonless night, and it would be easy to hit a piece of driftwood and put a hole in the hull. When I finally got home, I went to bed.

I was jarred awake by my cellphone. I opened the phone and the face was blinking 5:35 A.M Saturday morning.

"Hello," I said groggily.

"Is this Sam Wilson?" said a man on the other end. "From Citizens Union?"

"Yes," I said, "who is this?"

"It's Augustus Harvey. Auggie. We met last night."

At the private plane terminal at the Charlotte Airport, I thought. But he didn't say that. He had taken us on the tour of the 757, but he didn't say that either. His voice sounded shaky but determined.

"Yes," I said.

"I'm leaving Charlotte, okay? I'll be out of touch for a while. I'd appreciate it if you don't mention my name, or the name of my company, to anyone else. It won't help matters."

"What? What 'matters?' What's going on?"

"I'll keep an eye on this, and if it looks like you are going to need me, I'll get back in touch. Meantime, you don't know me and this call never happened, okay? This phone is untraceable, and in five minutes it will be in a pond somewhere."

I started to ask him to knock it off with the spooks and shadows bit, and tell me what was going on, but I was talking to a dead signal. He had hung up.

I sat there in bed and reviewed what I knew about Augustus Harvey. I knew his employer. I knew what he looked like, an older man with a faint military bearing and a burr haircut. He chain-smoked. That was about it. Somewhere he had learned the art of picking a lock, but what private eye hadn't?

In sum, he had seemed like a normal guy, maybe a little rougher around the edges than most, but with an experienced set of eyes.

And he also struck me as someone who wouldn't scare easily. And that set my nerves to jangling, because unless I missed my guess, something—or someone—had just scared the living shit out of him.

14

I wasn't going back to sleep anytime soon. It was still dark so I couldn't go for a run. I made some coffee and sat out on my dock to watch the dawn. A great blue heron that I had come to consider my neighbor was perched on a submerged stump about 50 yards from my dock; he was scanning the water intently and ignored me. The sun was beginning to filter through the pine trees and dapple the water.

The big heron came to point suddenly, stretching his neck out, and made a quick, vicious stab into the water. He returned with a fish, which he gulped down quickly. He then flew off to another stump about 50 yards from the first one, and settled back into scout mode.

Once it was light enough, I went for a long run, thinking the whole time about work and Anastasia Primo de Montez. I wondered if George Lamb had a family, a wife and kids who were probably still in shock, and having to struggle through the details of a funeral and burial. I wondered what the hell Randall Clifton was up to, hanging out with clients who were on the bank's shit list, and partying with them on a 757. I wondered whether I was going to get stuck in a year-long bankruptcy proceeding with ECP, or if there still might be some way of selling the company. I wondered if the Little brothers were so low that they would stoop to stealing from the bank, even as their company collapsed and they jetted around the country with hookers in a hot tub. I decided they were.

I wondered if the contagion had stopped Friday, or whether this week it would reach for us, wreck the stock and bond markets, and give me a whole new portfolio of worry.

I finished my run, showered, and went down to work in casual clothes. The parking garage was empty and the bank was deserted on a Saturday morning—except for my suite of offices, which was humming like a bee hive. I had brought bagels and coffee, and I set up breakfast in the small conference room. I went to find Jay and Vinnie.

Vinnie was sleeping in his chair in his office, his shoes off, feet on the credenza. I woke him up and told him there was breakfast in the conference room. Jay was on a couch in the lobby. I did the same with him. They scrubbed their faces in the bathroom, and we had breakfast together, and then we went back to work.

I was on Schedules. A bankruptcy filing is a huge mass of paperwork, a good half of which is schedules that list various holdings and assets of the company. A list of employees. A list of all subsidiaries of the company. A list of all the company's creditors. And on and on. We worked all day Saturday and through the night into Sunday afternoon. At 4:00, I finished all the schedules with Schedule Y, a list of all the employees in the company's benefit plans.

Vinnie and Jay had just overcome one last hold-up. It takes three creditors to sign an involuntary bankruptcy petition; the bank could not just do it on its own. Vinnie and Jay had lined up the asset-backed trustee with no problem; the asset-backed securities were losing money as fast as we were. They had plenty of names for a third creditor; they had gotten a list of all bond purchasers from Melanie. But it was tough finding someone who would even pick up the phone on a weekend. Finally they found a guy in Memphis whom ECP owed $40,000 for office equipment, and he hadn't been paid in seven months. He said he would meet them at the court Monday morning and sign.

After the update, I maneuvered Jay into my office for a private word.

"Auggie called me at 5:35 Saturday morning," I said. "He said he was getting out of town, and not to try to call him, or mention his name to anyone."

"What?!" said Jay. "Where was he calling from?"

"A cellphone. I tried to ask him what was going on, but all he would say is that he was out of here and not to call him. He said he might get back in touch later. Has he called you?"

Jay pulled out his cellphone.

"Yes, it looks like he did, around the same time. I haven't been answering my phone because of this filing. He didn't leave anything on voicemail, though. "

Jay shook his head.

"This is just not acceptable," he said. "I've done a lot of business with those guys over the years, and they've never asked off a job, much less walked away from one without notice. I'm going to talk to Pat Collins right away. He owns the place and he had better have some answers."

I left him alone to make his phone call. A few minutes later he came into my office and sat down.

"I talked to Pat and he is as surprised as I am. He tried to get ahold of Auggie, but the cellphone just rang without even going to voicemail. And get this: his man in Memphis isn't picking up the phone either. He said he was going to get to the bottom of it, and call me back with some answers as soon as he had them."

I sat there silently. After a while Jay said:

"So you're thinking that, whatever scared Auggie also scared the guy in Memphis, right?"

I nodded. "And Auggie didn't strike me as someone who scared easily."

"Me either," said Jay.

I told him about my visit to the plane on Friday night, and the party that assembled on it that evening. I also told him about Ana, and my suspicion that she and Marcos were not who they said they were.

"Well, I verified that they were employees at Santiago Capital. I'm positive that Santiago is a vulture fund with plenty of money, my contact on…"

"No," I interrupted, "what you verified was that someone named Marcos Pereira and Ana Primo de Montez worked for Santiago Capital. But we haven't really verified that these two people up here are those same people."

"True," he said. "I guess we need to dig a little deeper than that. I can get…"

I interrupted him again.

"Look, Jay, I need you focused on this bankruptcy, okay? I will work on our friends from Santiago Capital. You and Vinnie need to get this bankruptcy filing done."

"You're right," he said, nodding. He looked at his watch. "Our plane leaves for Memphis in two hours. We need to start getting this thing organized, copied and packed up."

That evening, after a 36-hour marathon work session, Jay and Vinnie packed up their briefcases with the bankruptcy filing, and took diskettes of the files, too, on the odd chance that the court might take the petition electronically.   It was slapdash, the best we could do in a weekend, but it would hold.

I drove them to the airport. They were going in front of the judge in the federal bankruptcy court in Memphis first thing Monday morning. I was staying in Charlotte. Among other things, the markets would open in turmoil, I had to do some more work on Marcos and Ana, and the Feds would be in Lawson's office first thing Monday over that anonymous letter.

After dropping them off, I went home and sat out on my deck in a chaise lounger with a cold one, listening to water slap against my dock. There seemed to be something chasing the bass out there, and as I thought about going to get a rod, I fell asleep. I woke up around midnight to mosquitoes munching on my ankles and wrists, and the beer, half full, tucked between my legs. I went inside to get a shower and go to bed.

◆

Melanie hailed me from her office when I walked in first thing the next morning. Contagion, she said, had reached our shores. The market wasn't even open yet but futures foretold a 200-point drop on open. Investors in Asia and Europe were fleeing into Treasury bonds and even the best of corporate bonds could not find a bid. The market for exotics like asset-backed securities and preferred stock was simply closed. No buyers meant no transactions.

"You heard about Long-Term Capital Management?" she said to me.

"The hedge fund? Bunch of braniacs from Salomon Brothers left and started their own fund. Quants or something, right?"

"That's them," said Melanie. "They are supposed to be on the ropes. Trades that were supposed to be totally unrelated are all converging. The word up on the Street is they couldn't give away their portfolio. But they are too big too fail, and the Federal Reserve is going to have to bail them out."

"The Fed? Bail out a hedge fund?" I said incredulously. "Don't be ridiculous. What kind of systemic risk can a hedge fund pose? They should just let them fail."

Melanie shrugged.

"That's the word up on the Street," she said. "The Fed might not do it themselves, but they are supposed to be putting a strong arm on the banks that are already involved, to get them to do it."

That might be the word on Wall Street, but there was no way Main Street was going to have anything to do with the Fed bailing out a hedge fund. Nobody was too big to fail, much less a hedge fund that was not FDIC-insured.

Nonetheless, everything was down everywhere, Melanie said. The only guys who weren't totally glum that morning were on the international desk. We had sold their emerging markets portfolio two weeks ago, and barred them from re-investing. They were essentially getting paid to watch TV. I left and went to my office.

After all the hustle and bustle of prepping the bankruptcy, and the rampaging on the trading floor, my offices seemed oddly subdued. Only Sharon and Melanie and I were there. I asked Sharon to get Santiago Capital on the phone. Too early, she told me a few minutes later. There was nothing but an answering machine.

15 minutes later she stuck her head in.

"Still no answer at Santiago Capital, but Lawson just called. The Feds are upstairs."

Oh boy, I thought. Time for a trip to the whipping shed. I put my jacket on and Sharon straightened my tie in a motherly fashion.

"Goodbye Sam. It's been nice knowing you," she said.

"Very funny," I said. "If I come back down here with no ass left in these pants, you'll know it got chewed off up there."

Four government officials were in Lawson's conference room—a guy from the Securities and Exchange Commission, two from the Office of the Comptroller of the Currency, and a lady from the Federal Deposit Insurance Corporation. From the bank's side were Lawson and me, the Monster from the trading floor and two guys from our Memphis office. The govvies were in no mood for coffee and chit-chat, and the senior man from the OCC was in charge.

"This letter," he said, holding up the fax from Anonymous, "is it true?"

"We think so," said Lawson. "We don't know who wrote it, but we have been cross-checking its assertions against ECP's monthly reports, and we have found the discrepancies to which the writer alludes. We have also spoken to the asset-backed trustee, and they have verified the same discrepancies in their reports."

"Have you discussed this with the company?" he asked.

I looked at my watch.

"We are in front of the bankruptcy court in Memphis right about now," I said. "We are pushing the company into involuntary Chapter 11 today. We expect we will have an opportunity to discuss the letter with them after that."

"How long has this been going on?" said the OCC man.

"At least a year," said Lawson, "maybe longer."

"A year? How in the world could this company get away with fraudulent reporting for a year?"

For this, Lawson looked at the Memphis guys. They were responsible for monitoring the line of credit. Both of them turned beet red.

"Uh...well, I guess it kind of slipped through the cracks," said the more senior of the two. "I mean, we were looking at the reports every month, but we just did not notice that 'Wolf River' line. Or, we noticed it, but didn't realize how much the number was growing. Since they were paying promptly until about three months ago...well, I hate to repeat myself, but it just slipped through the cracks."

"Slipped through the cracks," said the OCC man. "You have a $200 million line of credit whose sole collateral is receivables, and you fail to notice that 20% of the so-called collections are in fact nothing but air? Take me through the process that occurs when the receivables report first comes in."

The Memphis guys got a solid thirty minutes of tongue-lashing from the OCC. Then the topic turned to the asset-backed and corporate bond stubs that we owned on the trading desk. The guy from the SEC took over.

"First of all," said the SEC man, "where is George Lamb? He is named in this letter, he must be familiar to the writer. Why is he not here?"

"Um...Mr. Lamb passed away last week," said The Monster. "He was murdered in broad daylight here in Charlotte, actually. My name is Greg Meunster. I am his supervisor."

The regulators all looked shocked, none worse than the SEC guy.

"Well, we uh….we had no idea," said the SEC guy with a rare note of humility in his voice. "And we are very sorry to hear that. Please…um….accept our condolences."

Meunster just nodded at him. I liked him for that. Let that regulator suck on his own clumsiness for a minute or two.

But that didn't mean they were going to take it easy on us. Mr. SEC regrouped.

"Mr. Meunster, how did the bank end up with these ECP bonds?"

"Well, as you know, sir, we were lead underwriter on both the corporate issuance and the asset-backed issuance. We knew the company quite well and decided that these bonds would be good investments for the bank to hold."

"You mean you couldn't sell all of the deal, don't you?"

"No, sir, the deal had a healthy subscription base, and we thought…"

"You couldn't sell the BBBs on the asset-backed, and the last piece of the bonds, so you put it into your trading book and then, when you thought no one was looking, you slid it into the bank's Hold-to-Maturity portfolio. Come on, it's the oldest trick in the book."

"That is not what happened," The Monster retorted. "Like I said, we thought they would be a good investment…"

"A good investment? Neither of those bonds is worth 10 cents on the dollar right now," said the SEC guy.

"They are worth a lot more than that."

"Fine. Sell them today, then."

The Monster shifted in his seat.

"There is a significant market disruption going on right now owing to the Russian default last week and the situation with Long Term Capital Management. It would be tough to get a bid today that accurately reflected…"

"Tough to get a bid? How about impossible? Which means those bonds need to be marked to zero. And before you respond to that, let me tell you that my staff is going over your disclosures in the prospectuses with a microscope right now. I don't need to remind you of what will happen if we find out you knew materially damaging information about this company that you didn't disclose to investors. And you personally, Mr. Meunster, are licensed by this organization, and we will be reviewing the appropriateness of that as well."

The SEC guy rhetorically slapped The Monster about the head and shoulders for another 15 minutes. He was wobbling in his chair when he finished.

But we weren't done, because the lady from the FDIC hadn't had her turn.

"My colleagues are focused on these individual transactions, which of course is their bailiwick. The FDIC is much more concerned about a system-wide breakdown. I'd like to discuss the underwriting and monitoring processes across the entire bank platform."

Lawson took his turn. When the lady from the FDIC found out that I was working on a thorough analysis on the investment bank's portfolio, she insisted on being copied on everything. And I would be her point person for whatever other information the regulators might need.

Three hours after it started, the regulators finally walked out of the room. The three groups had requisitioned office space and would be monitoring not only ECP, but the entire investment bank portfolio, on-site, until such time as they were comfortable that the bank's risk management process was not seriously flawed, as it now appeared to be.

The two guys from Memphis stumbled out behind them. Their careers were finished and they would probably get fired.

The Monster looked small and uncertain as he left; it was not a good look for him. If the SEC jerked his licenses, he was finished in the banking business, too.

"Well, that was certainly enjoyable," I said to Lawson. He had fished his pipe out of his jacket but was just chewing on it.

"Nothing like having the government come in to tell you that the horses have gotten loose and you should have locked the barn door," he said.

"How do those folks expect me to handle this job and also do a bunch of additional reporting to them?" I said. "If I am jumping every time they whistle, I'll never get a thing done."

"Sam, I will handle them. You just keep your eye on the ball. First things first. Get ECP into bankruptcy, get a handle on those deposit accounts, and preserve our collateral base."

I walked back down to my office. Keep your eye on the ball, Sam.

I picked up the phone and called Santiago Capital. This time an operator picked up. I asked for Ana Primo de Montez.

"One moment, please," she said, and then the phone was ringing.

"This is Ana," said an unaccented American voice on the other end.

"Oh...hi," I said. "This is Sam Wilson, I work for Citizen's Union up in Charlotte. I was looking for the Ana who works in your investment group."

There was a puzzled silence on the other end.

"I am the only Ana who works at Santiago Capital," she said. "I work in the operations area."

With a sinking feeling in my stomach, I apologized and hung up. I called the main operator at Santiago Capital again.

"Marcos Pereira please," I said when she answered.

There was a moment of silence on the line.

"You want to speak to our janitor?" she finally said.

◆

The two people who had come to my office and identified themselves as Marcos Pereira and Anastasia Primo de Montez were frauds. They didn't work for Santiago Capital, they had just used the company and a couple of employee names for a background screen. It wasn't likely they worked for any vulture fund. They were in Charlotte and interested in ECP for a different reason. But what?

They were not fools, that was for sure. They talked the talk. They knew how to look like financiers. They were perfectly attired for their roles, had professional business cards, and in their 30 minutes with me they had provided a very professional pitch book on Santiago Capital. Their few stumbles with banking jargon had been easily covered up as translation problems. They were con artists, clearly, but good ones, and the question remained: what were they fishing for?

I looked around all the junk piled in my office and started turning over folders and files until I found their original pitch book. I looked at it closely. Standard vinyl cover, high quality paper, color laser printing with all the requisite charts and bullet points. I riffled the pages through my fingers. Something felt odd. I looked at the first page, which said "Presentation to Sam W. Wilson, Citizens Union Bank, Charlotte, NC." I flipped to the second page, which said "Provided by:" and then listed their names and titles and phone numbers. The third page, though, where the actual information on Santiago Capital began, was printed on a higher-quality, glossier paper. I looked closely at the binding. It looked loose, as if someone had torn it apart and put it back together.

I tossed the presentation back onto a pile. They had stolen it from somewhere, loosened the binding, took out the previous introductory pages, and put the new ones in with my name and theirs on the first two pages—but on slightly different paper. Nobody looked closely at pitch books. Hell, even if I had noticed the paper differences earlier, I would have chalked it up to them being in a hurry. Plenty of real investment bankers do the exact same thing, make the same presentation to multiple parties, changing only the names and companies and titles. Happens all the time.

But why? What were they really after? Inside information on a publically traded company would obviously be valuable to a trader, but by the time Marcos and Ana came to see me, ECP was essentially broke, and everyone in the market knew it. The letter from the disgruntled employee was just icing on the cake. There just wasn't any kind of inside financial play that made sense.

What had they said in that original meeting? I looked through my Rolodex until I found Marcos' card. I had written on the back:

- ABS, CDO, CLO, CBO
- Op. co. w/ intnl. exposure
- Small/med. domestic mfg. co.
- NO R/E

That was supposedly what they were interested in. ECP fit the mold as a "small/medium manufacturing company."

Ana had said something about management then, too. Their "portfolio" of leasing companies had a strong management team, she said, and they had success with replacing weak management teams with their own.

And after the actual meeting with ECP—where she had said absolutely nothing, I remembered—she had said they were still interested in the company, and still thought that management was the problem.

Were they interested in management, for some reason? Did that mean the CFO and his crew? Or the Little brothers? Or was that just more bullshit, part of the smokescreen they had thrown up?

I had given Ana access to the management team at ECP. If they discovered that someone not truly affiliated with the bank was in the room without their permission, their lawyers would throw themselves a party. Sharing confidential information from a public company with an unrelated outside entity—the image of ECP's lawyers banging away at me in some distant courtroom was so vivid I started to sweat.

The phone rang.

"Sam? It's Vinnie. We are done here in Memphis. The judge accepted the filing and as of 10:34 this morning ECP is in Chapter 11."

"Great work," I said. "That's got to be a record on a bankruptcy filing. You guys basically put the whole thing together this weekend."

"Yeah, I'm beat," he said. "Did the Feds come in today?"

"Brother, did they," I said, and told him what had happened in our meeting.

"Wow. That's a shame about those guys from Memphis. I worked with them both on this deal for a while, they were nice guys."

"Yeah," I said. "They just didn't do their jobs. When are you guys coming home?"

"Our flight should get into Charlotte early this evening. I hope so. I could stand to get in bed early.

"Don't feel like you need to come in tomorrow," I said.

"Oh, I'll be there," he said. "Wouldn't miss it."

"Is Jay there with you?" I asked.

"Sure," he said, and Jay came on the line. I told him what I had found out about Marcos and Ana.

"I feel so stupid," he said. "I want to apologize to you for..."

"Come on, Jay, forget about it. You ran a reasonable check on them and it came back fine. They set out to deceive us, and it worked for a little while. I just can't figure out why. Have you got any ideas on that?"

"Not right now," he said. "I'm pretty tired. Let me sleep on it, okay?"

"Sure," I said. "You haven't heard from Collins Investigative Service, have you?"

"No," he said, "but I've had my phone off. Believe me you don't want your cellphone ringing in the courtroom of a federal judge. Hang on."

There was a delay, and then he said:

"No messages from Collins. You want me to call them again?"

"No, give the guy some time," I said. "Have a safe trip home."

"Thanks. We'll see you tomorrow, and talk about our next step, okay?"

15

This North/South thing, with the Civil War references? George's snide remark about HOSOBs, The Monster's not-so-subtle jab about expertise? The chairman's anger at being lied to about the investment banking portfolio, and his firing of two of the most senior people in the bank? My own disgust at investment banking high-rollers looking for government bailouts?

These were symptoms of the problem, not the problem itself. The real problem was that a traditional commercial bank had acquired an investment bank.

Investment banking is essentially a transaction-oriented business. Guys like George Lamb fought tooth-and-nail with other investment banks to win "engagements" from big companies to sell their debt in the bond markets. Once "engaged," they then brokered the selling of the debt to the investment community, arguing constantly over price and term and other conditions of the deal.

When the debt was finally sold, and they collected their multi-million dollar commissions, everyone who had been working 12-hour days for the last three weeks had a big blowout closing party with the client. Steaks, red wine, then a trip to the topless club, all on the bank, and everybody is best friends for the night.

And then the bankers get up the next day and go right back to chasing the next deal. The salary for someone like George was probably in the mid-six figures—but he could make millions in bonuses based on how many deals he did.

Traditional banking is relationship-oriented and very different. Commercial bankers have known some of their clients for 30 years. When they close a loan, they might take the client out for lunch or a beer, but there were no closing parties. There weren't any topless joints. Branch bankers see the same customers every Friday, check-cashing day. I knew a mortgage lender in Greensboro who worked 40 years in the same job and made mortgage loans to three different generations of the same family.

A senior commercial banker might have a low six-figure compensation package, bonuses, stock options and all. Mortgage lenders would be lucky to make six figures. Branch managers made less than that.

So on the one hand you had a fast-moving, hyper-competitive, transaction-oriented business where senior bankers could make millions of dollars a year. And on the other you had a slower-moving, relationship-oriented business where $150,000 a year was considered big money. Putting those two businesses under one roof was causing serious cultural clashes.

I needed to talk to Greg Meunster. I had to know more about what Randall Clifton was up to, with his wining and dining of the Little brothers. It would have been nice to just talk to

Clifton directly, but a) he didn't know me from his maid's housecat and b) with the whole ECP thing, I didn't trust him anyway. So my only alternative was The Monster, who had never expressed any affection for me either. And I had to circumvent this whole commercial/investment banking conflict somehow. We had to have something in common.

Late that afternoon I tapped on his door and he gestured me in without looking up. When he saw it was me, his face grew stony. I sat down quickly, before he could tell me to get out.

"Can we have a truce for a minute?" I said.

He looked at me for a minute, then shrugged.

"I wasn't aware we needed one," he said.

"Fine," I said. "I need to talk to you about Randall Clifton. There are some things he's done recently that don't make a lot of sense, at least from where I'm sitting."

"Like what?" he said. "Because I don't know if you've been reading the papers, but he doesn't work here anymore. And anyway, he's my boss. Or he used to be. So what would be the point of talking about an ex-employee?"

"First of all he does technically still work here—his 'retirement' doesn't take place until the end of the month. Secondly, and this is my issue with him, he signed a modification agreement for the Little brothers and Entourage Capital Partners the other day, extending their bank loan for 30 days. Believe me when I say that that extension was not in the best interest of this bank."

Greg looked puzzled.

"Modification of a bank loan? He's not authorized to do that. Hell, no one in this department including me can do that. That's been made perfectly clear to us. We are a subsidiary of the bank holding company. The bank is a totally separate subsidiary of the same holding company. We can't even sign a letter on the bank's letterhead. And you can't sign one on the Capital Markets letterhead. The two subsidiaries and their officers are totally separate."

"Well, he signed it, and it was not what I wanted to happen. And let me tell you something else. He has been hanging around the Little brothers, going to dinner with them, partying with them. What's the point in that? ECP is bankrupt and the bank's relationship with them is definitely adversarial. Why is the former head of this investment bank still involved with them?"

At this his face darkened.

"ECP? Randall's hanging out with the Little brothers? There is no business for us there, those guys are broke. I can't imagine why Randall would be messing with them. Are you sure?"

"I am absolutely positive he had dinner with them here in Charlotte last week. And he was seen at the airport getting on their private plane this past weekend."

Greg scrubbed his face with his hands, leaving his eyes closed for a few seconds.

"Well, I suppose I can talk to him when he gets back. I'm in charge of the budget for the whole operation now, and don't want to see a bunch of money being spent on private planes and such from him. He can't possibly be doing any business development for us; I mean, would you, knowing that in two weeks you're leaving for good?"

"No, I wouldn't and I don't have any idea what he is up to. Is he personal friends with the Littles or something?"

"I don't know," he said. "I mean, he's my boss. I don't exactly get involved in his personal business. The best I knew, the Littles were George's clients. Clifton knew them, of course, but he also knew the trouble they were in, so I figured he would stay away. The only thing I can promise you is, I'll ask him about it and let him know you guys don't really need his involvement right now. But since I'm technically still his subordinate, that's about all I can do."

"Fair enough," I said. I reached across his desk with my hand out.

"I appreciate your time. I'm sorry if I've caused you any trouble."

He eyed me for a minute, and then, saying nothing, he took my hand and shook it firmly. I left hoping I had repaired a bridge that I might need again.

And with the knowledge that Randall Clifton was running bandit.

◆

I had to go back through the trading floor to get to my office.

Chaos was still the order of the day. Curses were flying, and there was yelling, screaming and the rending of garments.

I guess it wasn't really funny, real money was being lost, but at some point there ought to be a growing awareness that the market had turned down. I saw the trader I called Elvis and asked him what today's hysteria was about.

"Same stuff as last week, but this is verging on historic. I mean *everything* is down. There isn't a single profitable play in the market except betting it will go down further. Stocks are crashing, the bond market is essentially dead, and everyone is running for safety. This Long-Term Capital thing is making it all worse."

"Melanie told me the Fed was going to bail those guys out," I said. "Surely they wouldn't step into a hedge fund problem? I mean, the Feds don't guarantee that money like they do bank deposits. There is no FDIC insurance for hedge funds, so why would they bail out a bunch of super-rich investors?"

"This is not your average hedge fund. It is enormous. They have huge trading positions and lines of credit with every big firm on Wall Street. If LTCM goes down, it takes half of Wall Street with it. Those rich investors aren't going to get a dime back, but the Fed can't let Wall Street collapse because of one hedge fund. So I'd say Melanie's right, the Feds will step in."

I left, shaking my head. How we had gotten to this point, where the Federal Reserve was seriously considering bailing out a hedge fund, was beyond me. Using taxpayer money to save a bunch of Wall Street high-rollers? Not in your wildest dreams, I would have told you before today.

So much for that illusion. It was now crumpled and discarded. I would soon stack several others next to it. I went home at a reasonable hour, and went to bed before dark.

◆

I came into work that morning, Tuesday, to once again find two big men with guns standing in my conference room. Sherman and Lawson were in there too. I recognized Detective Jeffries, who was the black local cop from Charlotte who questioned me about Melanie. The other guy I had never met.

But after a quick look, I thought, he's not local. Nor is he one of those glorified accountants or lawyers from the bank regulators. No, although I didn't recognize him, he looked to be in his late 30s, and with his dark suit pants, his white shirt and sober tie, his athletic build and close-cropped hair, he had a recognizable look.

It said FBI.

"Mornin' Sam," said Sherman. I greeted him and Lawson as well. They both looked serious.

"Sam, you remember Detective Jeffries from the Charlotte-Mecklenburg police department. This gentleman here is Agent McAlister of the FBI. He's the head of the FBI office in Charlotte."

McAlister was clearly Irish-American, with a ginger complexion and reddish-blonde hair. I shook hands with him; he had an iron grip. Everybody sat down.

"What's going on?" I asked. "Is this about George again?"

"Well, Mr. Wilson, we honestly don't know the answer to that," said Jeffries of the Charlotte police. "We were hoping you could help us figure that out."

"You see, Mr. Wilson, what we now have is two more dead bodies to add to that of your co-worker Mr. George Lamb. They were discovered last night at the Charlotte airport," said FBI Agent McAlister.

He took out two photos from a manila envelope and laid them on the table. I looked at them then looked away quickly. There were two bodies. Each of them had been shot twice in the head. Their eyes were both wide open in the photos. I swallowed hard and tried to keep my breakfast down.

"Andrew and Jonathan Little," I finally said.

McAlister nodded.

"We understand that they own...owned a firm called Entourage Capital Partners, and that your bank forced that firm into bankruptcy yesterday."

I stared at the FBI agent, bug-eyed.

"Is this related to the bankruptcy?" I asked. "I mean, two gun shot wounds each—that's not suicide, is it?"

"No, sir," said Agent McAlister. "No, you can shoot yourself once in the head, but twice is tough to do. We are investigating their deaths as homicides. Their bodies were found in a private plane in a hangar in the private section of the airport. They were discovered late last night by one of the airport's employees. We think the bodies were there for at least 48 hours, maybe as much as 72, before they were discovered So we estimate that they were killed sometime this past weekend."

There was a silence in the room as I absorbed that information. I couldn't seem to stop swallowing. Like George Lamb, I had not liked the Little brothers much, but I had certainly not wished them dead. I reached into the conference room fridge for a bottle of water and drank half of it.

"We're going to ask you to account for your whereabouts this weekend," said Agent McAlister. "Before you get upset, that's just a formality. We don't think you did this. We are aware that bankers don't generally shoot their customers, even ones that are going bankrupt. But we do think you can help us figure out who did do it."

I was having a kind of out-of-body experience. I saw myself sitting there, nodding reasonably to the FBI agent and telling him where I had been on Saturday and Sunday. Separately, my head was spinning over another murder...or two, actually. And I was cataloging the enormous problems that the murder of the Little Brothers had created for the bank and me personally.

After I finished the details of my weekend, I asked if I could talk briefly with Sherman and Lawson before we continued.

"I want to give you officers a full accounting of everything I know," I said, "but there are certain bank confidences that I want to be careful not to breach."

"Bank confidences?" scoffed Detective Jeffries. "There is nothing that happens at this bank that supersedes a murder investigation. If you think that..."

Agent-in-Charge McAlister held up his hand.

"That's fine," he said. "Go talk with your attorney and your boss. We understand. We'll wait right here."

Jeffries looked like someone had just jerked on his leash, which someone had. It was the typical tension between the local police and the Feds.

But they allowed Sherman and Lawson and me to adjourn to my office, where I closed the door. I perched a haunch on my desk and Lawson and Sherman sat down in the chairs in front of the desk.

"What is it, Sam?" said Lawson.

"I just want to do a stream-of-consciousness thing about all the trouble we're in. Let me just get through it and we can talk about each point, okay?

"First, I hired a private investigator to track the Little brothers. I was tired of having no contact with them—none of our phone calls or e-mails were returned, we couldn't get to them through the management of the company, they refused to attend meetings that we called. So I got Jay Podolski to hire a P.I. to track them.

"Second, that P.I. called me Friday night, and at his request I went down to the airport. The Little brothers were in Charlotte for a bank meeting that morning, and they flew in on a private plane. You remember, Lawson, I showed you a picture of them and George having dinner here the night before. The P.I. had tracked the plane to a hangar in a private part of the airport, and after he jimmied the lock, he showed me the plane—which is probably the one they were killed in. It was empty of course, the Littles were somewhere else. It was a pimped-out 757 with a movie studio, a wet bar and a hot tub, plus private bedrooms and a shower. I am not entirely certain, but I think it is part of the bank's collateral for the line of credit.

My fingerprints are all over that plane. I mean, literally. I touched several door knobs, opened cabinets, that kind of thing.

"Third, the P.I. and I saw the Little brothers shortly thereafter. They had stocked up the plane with booze and food, and the P.I. thought they were going on a booze cruise in the plane somewhere. Randall Clifton was with them. So..."

"Randall Clifton?!" said Sherman incredulously. "The ex-head of the investment bank?"

"The same," I said. "There were also three young ladies who we thought were hookers. Lawson, you already know that Clifton signed an extension of the ECP loan on behalf of the bank that he wasn't authorized to sign.

"Fourth, the P.I. thought someone else besides him was snooping around the Littles. He didn't know who, but had seen a black BMW too many times for it to be a coincidence.

"Fifth, the P.I. called me early Sunday morning and essentially resigned. He sounded spooked and he did not strike me as a man who scares easily. He got out of town in a hurry. I still don't know where he is or why he left.

"And finally, I discovered this week that two individuals who represented themselves as working for a vulture fund, and who claimed to be interested in buying ECP, were con artists. They don't work for the company they said they did, and I introduced one of them to the Littles and management of ECP at a meeting here at the bank Friday. I don't know what they want with ECP but one of them owns a black BMW like the one the P.I. described."

There was a silence that seemed to last the entire afternoon as they both stared at me. Then Sherman and Lawson started talking between themselves.

"It's legal for us to hire a private investigator, isn't it?" said Lawson to Sherman.

Sherman nodded.

"Sure. Just about anybody can hire a P.I. for just about anything. It's probably not something you want to put in your customer service brochures, or the newspaper, but it's perfectly legal.

"But the FBI is going to want to know about the P.I.," said Lawson.

"Certainly we need to tell them that," said Sherman. "Sam, do you know the firm and the name of the investigator?"

"Yes, both," I said.

"Fine. Let's give them that information, and tell them about the last phone call," said Lawson. "Now, Sam, how did you come to be on that plane again?"

I explained how Auggie had called me because he wanted me to see the plane, and I went down to the hangar with him, and he jimmied the door and we walked through the plane. He took a few pictures, the last one of the tail number, then we left."

Lawson looked at Sherman.

"What say you, Counselor?"

Sherman fidgeted in his chair. He scratched his head several times. Finally he said:

"The FBI will not like that lock-picking, or, in fact, the whole story about how they gained access to the plane. And it doesn't seem to be material right now. It's a risk, but I say leave it out. If they dust the plane...." He paused to think for a moment.

"Sam, have you ever been arrested?"

"No," I said.

"Fingerprinted for any reason?" he said. "Does the bank have your prints on file? You've never been in the military, have you?"

"No to all that," I said.

"I say we leave it out, then," said Sherman. "Even if the Feds fingerprinted the whole plane, and found a clean print of Sammy's, which is highly unlikely, they still don't have it in a database anywhere to tell them who it belongs to."

"All right, but what about his sighting of the Little brothers on Friday night, and the fact that Randall Clifton was with them?" said Lawson. "We can't dismiss that as immaterial."

Sherman fidgeted some more. He scratched his head again and made a face.

"Sam, what was that you said about showing Lawson a photo?" Sherman finally asked.

"The P.I. got onto the Littles' trail Thursday night, and got a surreptitious picture of them having dinner with a third party. He didn't know at the time that it was Randall Clifton, but when he showed it to me, I did. I showed it to Lawson the next day."

"Where is it now? The photo?"

I went around behind my desk and dug into a stack of papers until I found the manila envelope with the photo in it. I handed it to Sherman. He slid the photo out and looked at it carefully.

"So these chubby fellows are the Little brothers?" he said.

"Yep."

He stared at the photo for a while, then his eyes went into middle space for another long spell.

"So this P.I. calls you Friday night and says, come on down to the airport," Sherman says. "You go down there, and after you check out the flying whorehouse, as you are leaving, you see the Littles and Clifton and the hookers come in. Is that how it went?"

"Pretty much," I said. "When I say we were leaving, I mean we were in the P.I.'s car, on the way back to the gate, when we saw a van coming to the hangar. We slid around behind a different hangar and watched the van unload. I remember asking Auggie, what the heck was going on, and he said..."

"Wait. Stop," said Sherman. "You asked the P.I. what was going on? And what did he say?"

"He told me that he thought Clifton and the Littles and the hookers were all going to get in the plane and fly around and party, and that eventually..."

But Sherman was holding up his hand and smiling.

"Sam, you're a smart fellah, you know that?"

"What? Why?"

Instead of answering me, Sherman turned to Lawson.

"We don't want Sammy anywhere near that airplane, if we can help it. We both know he had nothing to do with those two guys getting killed, and the FBI would just be snuffling down the wrong trail if we bring it up. So I just think we don't bring it up."

"Wait a minute, there, Sherman," said Lawson. "That's shaving a little close to the jugular. We don't need to add 'lying to the FBI' to our current slate of problems."

"It's not lying. I propose to have Sammy go in there and say exactly what happened: the P.I. told Sam the Littles were in town. The P.I. gave him a photo of Randall Clifton with the Little brothers. The P.I. told him about the plane, and when Sam asked, the P.I. told him that he thought that those three and the hookers were going on a party cruise. Later on, the P.I. called Sam early Sunday morning, and sounding spooked, essentially walked off the job. You see where I'm going here?"

Lawson took his unlit pipe out of his pocket and began chewing on it. "Yes, I think so. 'The P.I. said, the P.I. photographed, the P.I. told.' You want to make sure the Feds understand that we were getting all of our information from the P.I."

"Right," said Sherman.

"What if they ask me a direct question? 'Were you on that plane?'"

"Answer it truthfully," said Sherman. "Look, I'm not telling you to lie, okay? I'm just telling you what to emphasize with them."

"What about the con artists—you know, Marcos and Ana, the lady I took to the ECP meeting?" I asked.

"Leave it out," said both Sherman and Lawson in unison.

"That's bank business," said Lawson. "One of those bank confidences to which you referred before we left the conference room. That has no bearing on their case, and anything we say would be pure speculation."

"Ok," I said, "but you do want me to tell them that Randall Clifton was there, right?"

"Absolutely," said Lawson. "I don't know if he played any role in the deaths of the Littles. We don't know what might have happened on that flight, or what Clifton might have done or seen. He's going to have to answer those questions himself."

Sherman looked at his watch.

"We've been in here for 15 minutes. Any longer and they'll start to get suspicious. Let's go."

We arose to walk out.

"Don't rush it, Sammy," said Sherman. "Let them come to you. When they do, all the information you got about the Littles and that plane came from the P.I."

Dancing with the FBI again, I thought as I trudged back into the conference room. It was not my first time, but I could not help thinking that there was not a long term future in it. What was the old saying? Like dogs chasing cars and golf pros chipping for pars. No future.

"All right," I said as I sat down. "The Little Brothers and Entourage Capital."

I first described the bank's history with them: all the acquisitions, the stock and asset-backed issues, our ongoing relationship with them—not just ours in SAG, but through the investment bank and the trading desk. How it started to go sour, how we were having workout meetings trying to find a way to save the company, how we had had an impossible time trying to get the Little brothers' attention.

"Anyway, one day last week, I got tired of trying to track the owners down, and asked my attorney to hire a private detective to see if he could locate them, figure out where they were staying, phone numbers, etc... so we could talk to them directly instead of trying to go through ECP's management team."

"You hired a private detective to find the Littles?" asked Agent McAlister

"Yes," I said, "and with a stroke of luck, he did. We had finally gotten the word that they would attend a meeting on Friday morning at the bank. My attorney told the P.I. we had hired about the meeting, and he found out that the Little brothers flew into Charlotte on a private plane Thursday night."

I slid the manila envelope with the photo of the Littles and Clifton having dinner.

"That's Jonathan and Andrew Little all right," said McAlister after he opened the envelope and looked at the photo. "Who's this guy here with the silver glasses and the fancy suit?"

But the Charlotte cop, Detective Jeffries, was looking over McAlister's shoulder. He tapped the photo.

"That's Randall Clifton, isn't it?" he said to me. "The head of the investment bank who just got fired last week. Or 'took early retirement,' as the story goes around here."

"Yes, sir," I said.

"We talked to this guy briefly over the Lamb case," Jeffries said to the FBI guy. "He was not much help."

FBI guy nodded.

"Those bond issues you talked about earlier, when ECP first went public, would he have been involved with those?" asked Agent McAlister.

"Certainly. Others would have handled the details, but he would certainly have known the clients and the issues. It's his job. He appeared to know the folks at ECP very well."

"All right, so this Clifton guy has dinner with the Littles. Then what?" asked McAlister.

"Well, we had the meeting with ECP the next morning, and it didn't go very well. We agreed to give them 30 more days to try to work things out, but afterwards, amongst just the bankers, we started getting our ducks in a row for a bankruptcy. It just didn't look like there was any way to save ECP."

"And this time the Littles were at the meeting?"

"Yes," I said.

"Was Randall Clifton?"

"No."

"So then what?" said McAlister.

"So then the letter came in, not even three hours after the meeting. It was from an anonymous source who claimed he or she worked at..."

"You mean this letter," said Agent McAlister, and reaching into a file, he handed me a copy of the anonymous letter that had alerted us to the collateral fraud.

"Yes, sir, that one," I said.

"And you guys verified the accuracy of the letter through your own reports."

"I see you have been speaking to your colleagues in the other branches of the government," said Lawson.

McAlister nodded.

"We got our own copy of the letter, but yes, I've talked to some of the other agencies that got the same letter. They happen to think your credit monitoring is pretty sloppy, and in this case it's going to cost you a boatload. Sound about right?"

Lawson's eyes narrowed. I saw Sherman give him a warning look. Lawson took his pipe out of his pocket and bit on it, but said nothing.

"OK, ECP leaves with a 30-day reprieve, but that lasts more like three hours, because you get the letter and declare them in default," said McAlister. "Then what?"

"Then," I said, "we spend the whole weekend working on an involuntary bankruptcy petition that needed to be in front of the Western District of the Tennessee federal court first thing Monday morning. It was a double all-nighter."

"Did you hear from your P.I. anytime during the weekend? What was his name, by the way?"

I told them the name of the P.I. and the firm he worked for. McAlister looked at Jeffries, who nodded.

"Yeah, I recognize the firm, they're registered and reputable as far as I know. Been in business as long as I've been on the job, maybe longer. Regional folks. I don't know that particular individual."

McAlister nodded and turned back to me.

"Go on," he said.

"Auggie called me late Friday. He said he had found the Little Brothers' plane at a hangar in Charlotte and had been sitting on it. He said he had never seen anything like it. It was all pimped out with a movie theater and wet bar and a hot tub. He said that Friday afternoon, the plane got stocked with food and booze, then the pilots showed up, two of them, and they had a van full of people that included the Littles, Clifton, and three girls. I asked him what he thought was going on, and he said the girls looked like hookers and it looked like they were all going on a big party cruise.

"Well, Auggie said he was going to stay put until the plane returned, and there was another P.I. from his firm at the airport in Memphis, and he would call us if they landed in Memphis. I stayed here at the bank and kept working on the bankruptcy. This was Friday. Then around 5:30 Saturday morning, I got a call from Auggie again. He sounded spooked, and said he was off the job and would be out of touch for a while. And that's the last I heard from him."

"Did he tell you the plane was back in Charlotte or Memphis at that point? Or was it still flying around the country somewhere?"

"I figured the plane had to be back in Charlotte, because why else would he call me, but he really didn't say. I didn't really get a chance to ask anything. He basically said, this is over my head, I quit, don't call, and then he hung up."

"Did he use those exact words?" said McAlister, suddenly bearing in. "'Over my head?'"

I closed my eyes and tried to remember the conversation word for word.

"No, not 'over my head.' He said he was leaving Charlotte, that I didn't know him and this never happened, and he was ditching his phone right then, so don't try to call him."

"Did this private eye have any reason to harm the Littles? Did he have anything against them, that you are aware of?" said McAlister.

"No," I said.

"Do you have any idea where he is now?" asked Jeffries.

"No," I said.

"Have you got his phone number?" asked McAlister.

I pulled out my cellphone, but before I could open it Sherman interrupted.

"Now wait a minute, Agent McAlister," said Sherman. "This is not a license to go browsing through Mr. Wilson's phone records. Most of the information in that phone has nothing to do with ECP or the Little brothers."

"You realize that the police department has power of subpoena, don't you?" said Jeffries, the Charlotte cop. "For the second time, this is a murder investigation. We can..."

FBI Agent McAlister jerked Jeffries' leash again.

"Let's all take it easy here," he said. "We appreciate your cooperation, Mr. Wilson. All we'd like to see is Augustus Harvey's phone number, and the time, date and duration of his calls to you. You all have my word I am not going browsing through his phone for anything else."

"Fine," said Sherman tersely, and I handed McAlister the phone.

"Here are the two incoming calls," I pointed to them on the cellphone screen for McAlister. "Friday night here, Saturday morning here."

He wrote down the numbers, including when they came in and how long they lasted, and then he gave me the phone back and I put it back in my pocket.

"What else, Mr. Wilson?" said McAlister. "Anything else we should know about ECP and the Little brothers? Or anybody else you might not have mentioned? Is there anyone you know who had something specific against the Little brothers?"

It struck me then that I was being subjected to the old good cop/bad cop routine. Jeffries, the local, was asking the tough questions. McAlister, the FBI agent, was playing good cop, acting like he was restraining Jeffries. I was embarrassed that I hadn't noticed it earlier.

In that situation, contrary to what a lot of people think, you want to watch out for the *good* cop. It's when he's bailing you out, calming the bad cop down and keeping him off your throat, that you become grateful for an ally.

And anxious to answer any question he asks.

So I thought for a minute before answering, and started to shake my head, then stopped.

"One other thing I forgot to mention. Auggie told me he thought someone else was tailing the Littles. A third party. He said he had never actually seen the guy, he must be good at surveillance, but there was a black BMW showing up too often to be a coincidence, and he thought they were following the Littles too."

"Did he describe this person to you?"

"No, he specifically said he had not seen the person, only the car."

The local cop and the federal cop looked at each other for a few minutes. Some exchange took place in that look, and McAlister took over the questioning.

"So you don't have anything to say about the vulture fund that visited you? The big Latino—what was his name?" he said.

Uh-oh, I thought. I reflexively looked at Sherman.

"Mr. Wilson? I'm the guy asking the questions, not your lawyer. What about the Latino from Santiago Capital?"

"Uh...well...what about him?" I said. "I don't think he's got anything to do with this."

"Oh you don't, huh? Is that your expert opinion as a criminologist?"

"I don't think..." I started.

Agent McAlister sat down at the table directly across from me.

"Marcos Pereira. Right now, Mr. Wilson. Tell us everything you know about him and don't leave anything out," said McAlister.

"Agent..." Sherman started, but McAlister cut him off.

"Not now, Counselor. You boys neglected to tell us about your relationship with Pereira and Santiago Capital.

"Why didn't you tell us about this when we first met?" demanded Jeffries angrily. "Do you know how much time Detective Young and I spent looking for George Lamb's killer? And this guy is a prime suspect, only we didn't know a thing about him because you didn't tell us."

"So that's strike two," said McAlister. "So here's the deal. You, Mr. Wilson, are going to tell us everything you know about Marcos Pereira, right now, or I'm going to have you arrested for impeding a federal murder investigation."

I was rocked back on my heels by the idea that Marcos was involved in the death of George. Only then did it occur to me that Max's description (big fellah, pretty black hair, nice suit) fit Marcos quite well. I thought he had been describing George Lamb.

I looked at Sherman and Lawson for some help. Both looked a little worried but Lawson put his hands out palms down, hovering them just over the table. Calm down, he was saying.

"Marcos Pereira came to see me a few weeks ago," I finally stammered. "He represented himself as being with an investment firm named Santiago Capital. He had an associate with him, a young woman named Ana Primo de Montez. At the time they gave me a pitchbook and told me..."

"What's a pitchbook?" Detective Jeffries interrupted.

"It's a sales pitch. It outlines the firm's capabilities, its interests, the amount it has to invest, that kind of thing."

"Go ahead," said McAlister.

"One of the things Marcos said they were interested in was small manufacturers like ECP. I had my attorney check them out, and they came back legitimate. So I introduced them to the management and owners of ECP. Only later, we found out that they were not legitimate. I mean, there is a company called Santiago Capital out of Miami, and they are a legitimate investment company, and there are two people who work for them named Marcos Pereira and Ana Primo de Montez. But that is not who was in my office, or whom I met with subsequently.

"If Marcos has anything to do with George's murder, it's news to me. As far as I can figure, he was working on some con on the bank."

"Describe Marcos Pereira," said Jeffries.

"What?" I said.

"Describe him. What does he look like, how does he dress, speak, act?"

So I gave them the description of Marcos.

"Now describe this Ana...what was her last name supposed to be? Prima de something?"

"Primo de Montez," I said, and then gave them a description of Ana.

McAlister then got up from the table, lost in thought, and wandered over to the windows. Jeffries studied him for a minute and then turned back to me.

"So this con they were running on the bank," continued Jeffries. "What was it?"

"I'm not sure," I said. "At first I thought they might be short sellers..."

"What's a short seller?" said Jeffries.

"Someone looking to profit on a decrease in the price of stocks or bonds. ECP is a publically traded company, with both stocks and bonds outstanding, and a short-seller could get confidential information from the bank and then use that to trade on in the markets. But by the time these two got involved, ECP was already in the shitter. The stock price was in the pennies and the bonds had gotten hammered. The market knew full well that the company was headed for bankruptcy. So there was no profitable short trade."

"So what did they want?" said McAlister.

"I'm not sure. The only thing I can think of is, access to ECP and its management team. Like I said, I took Ana to a meeting with me on Friday, where she met them."

"What do they want with ECP?" asked Jeffries.

"Hang on," McAlister interrupted. "You introduced this Ana Prima-de-whatever to management of ECP?"

"Yes," I said. "The owners were there too."

"The Little brothers were there too," said McAlister ruminatively, and resumed his perch at the window.

Jeffries looked at me leeringly

"That Ana sounds pretty tasty," he said. "Did she give you a little something extra for letting her meet with ECP?"

I felt my face get hot.

"Detective, you are out of line," said Sherman.

"I'm just wondering what was in it for Mr. Wilson here. He seems awfully educated to have been taken in by these two clowns. Maybe there was a little something on the side for him, in exchange for giving these people access to...."

"Do you always make unfounded accusations like that, Detective Jeffries?" asked Sherman. "Because if you do, I can see why..."

"You know, the bank didn't place the responsibility for this portfolio mark on just anyone," said Lawson.

"Don't bother, Lawson," I said. "Detective Jeffries here is just going to ask you what a portfolio mark is."

Jeffries got angry and stood up, and I did too, because I was tired of taking shit from him. But McAlister intervened before it went any farther.

"You gentlemen can go now," he said to us. "I want to know if you find any more information about the link between these two con artists and ECP."

He gave a nod to Detective Jeffries, who looked puzzled and upset. They both proceeded to the conference room door, but Jeffries stopped at the exit.

"I'm sure you've got some big finance explanation for what a mark is, but you know what it is in my world? In law enforcement?" said Jeffries. "A mark is the object of a con, a sucker, someone who gets played. Ring any bells, Mr. Wilson?" he said.

Then he walked out.

My face got even redder and my ears even hotter, but there was nobody to yell at and on second thought I wasn't sure

I wanted another piece of Detective Jeffries anyway. Sherman looked at me and nodded, and the three of us didn't tarry. We left right behind them.

◆

Lawson went back to his office, but Sherman and I reconvened in Sherman's office. I mentioned that Sherman and I went back a ways. In fact, his history as outside counsel and fireman for the bank went back almost 25 years, to when the bank was just a small statewide bank trying to expand out of North Carolina. I was barely out of diapers then. He had been a young lawyer when Lawson was making his bones as a loan officer. He probably could have had a 40-lawyer firm by now, based on the business the bank would have given him, but that was not his style. He was a litigator, and more than that a master negotiator. The bank called him whenever they wanted a problem fixed quietly, which was more and more often as the bank got bigger.

He took off his shoes and his tie, and undid his collar, then sat down in the chair behind his desk and proceeded to wrinkle up paper and shoot paperwad basketballs at his trashcan. He had a little basketball net and backboard that said CAROLINA over the top of the trashcan. There were paperwads littered all around; this was not his first shooting practice.

"You shoot about like your Tarheels do," I said as I sat down. I was still unwinding from the FBI interview. I tried to take deep breaths and slow my heart beat. I could feel my blood pressure in my eyeballs.

"I'm better than that," he said, lobbing up another paperwad that missed everything.

He squared his chair up to the desk. He picked up a newspaper, which he showed to me.

"Did you read the paper today?" he asked.

"The paper?" I said. "Sherman, I have barely had time to read the bankruptcy documents we filed on Entourage Capital last week, and the bank is going to lose $100 million on that deal. No, I did not read the paper today."

He put that paper down and picked up one next to it.

"How about yesterday?" he said. "Did you read the paper yesterday?"

"I'm averaging about three hours of sleep a night," I said, exasperated. "What is in the papers that I need to be worried about?"

He picked up two other newspapers.

"It's what's *not* in the papers that you need to be worried about. Today is Tuesday. These are the Charlotte papers from Saturday, Sunday, Monday and Tuesday. You want to know what's not in them?"

"What?" I said.

He rattled the papers at me.

"A single word about two dead bodies at the Charlotte private air terminal. There is no headline, nor a sub-headline, nor a paragraph buried on Page 27, that says 'MURDER' in it. George's death is in here, on Friday, buried in the local section as a mugging gone wrong. But the Little brothers were killed sometime this past weekend. And there is not a single word about it in the paper."

I smoked on that for a while.

"Let me ask you something else. Did you happen to notice, during our meeting with the FBI and the Charlotte-Mecklenburg police, a point at which Agent McAlister appeared to be disinterested in our discussion?"

"He got up from the table and wandered away," I said. "Went and looked out the window for a while. I was watching Jeffries and he seemed puzzled by that, too."

"Exactly," said Sherman. "Do you remember the point in the conversation where he did that?"

"Not off the top of my head," I said.

"It was after you described Marcos and Ana," said Sherman. "It was almost like he recognized them. Or that he suddenly formed a different idea of the crime, some alternate explanation other than the one he had been pursuing. And right after that, he concluded the interview and kicked us out."

"An alternate explanation? Like what?" I said. "For that matter, what is their current explanation of the crime?"

"Well, they were initially treating George's murder just like the paper said, a mugging gone bad. That's reasonable as far as it goes. His wallet and watch were missing. What he was doing in that particular parking garage isn't clear. It's not the bank's garage, where you and I park, it is over next to the Dunhill Hotel. He could have been meeting someone there, or heading to a restaurant or something.

"As to the Littles, no one has ever said specifically, but I would imagine that, like us, the Feds were thinking Randall Clifton had something to do with it. He was on the plane, he knew the Littles, and while they might not think Clifton pulled the trigger, I bet they thought he knew who did, and why. I'm sure they had some issues with Auggie, the private detective. They weren't solid on motive with him, but every P.I. I ever heard of carries a gun, and knows how to use it. So opportunity, he clearly had.

"But your description of the two Latinos changed McAlister's attitude, I'm sure of it. Sent him down a different path. And I am convinced of three things now that I had no idea about when that interview started.

"Number one, George's murder might not be a mugging gone wrong. They all of a sudden seem to like Marcos Pereira for it.

"Number two, they are covering up the murder of the Little brothers, and when I say 'they' I mean the FBI, because only the Feds have the juice to do that in this town. The locals wouldn't be able to pull it off. But I bet you anything that someone at the newspaper, or a TV or radio station, knows something about these murders, and has been told to stay quiet for now.

"And number three, Agent McAlister recognizes Marcos and Ana from somewhere. He's run into them in some other investigation, or knows them by reputation, or something. And he isn't planning to tell us about it. At least not now, and maybe not ever."

16

"Whenever they are telling you it's not about the money...it's about the money!"

A friend in Special Assets at another bank had sent that to me in an email. She said it sounded like something I would say. I thought it was funny, and liked it enough to print it out and tape it to the cabinet over my credenza.

I stared at that phrase as I sat brooding in my office the next morning. I could not figure out the FBI. "Why" seemed to be on McAlister's mind as much as "who" or "how." The "how" seemed awfully tricky to me—I guess it was simple with George, someone just walked up to him on the street and shot him. Or that was the official line, for now.

But with the Littles, someone had gotten through the gate access, into the locked hangar, and aboard the plane, shot them both, and then escaped back out unnoticed. I mean, the private aviation area at the airport was by no means a SuperMax prison, but it was more secure than that.

Then again, Auggie had gotten in pretty easily.

The "who" was also undecided, but Sherman thought that the FBI was now pointed in the direction of the Latinos. Randall Clifton, Auggie, the hookers and the pilots seemed to have been placed on the back burner.

Whenever they are telling you it's not about the money, it's about the money. Ana had said that recently, I suddenly recalled. When was it? I thought back. It was the meeting that we had had with ECP. The Littles were there, they had pulled that stunt with the extension signed by Clifton. I had told Ana that taking control of ECP's debt would be expensive, and she had lightly scoffed at the idea. It wasn't about the money, she had said. We have plenty of money.

I sat at my desk, tapping my fingers on the armrest of my chair, and staring at that saying. Whenever they are telling you it's not about the money...

I got up and went to Vinnie's office. He and Jay were hunched over some bankruptcy documents. I had told them earlier about the death of the Littles, and they were trying to figure out what that meant for our bankruptcy case. Nothing good, I was sure.

"Hey guys?" I said to them. "You remember when we were getting the bankruptcy filing ready for ECP, and you had to find a third party to join you in the involuntary petition? We had the bank, and the ABS trustee, and we needed one more?"

Vinnie nodded.

"Yeah, we got that office supply guy in Memphis. Nice guy. He met us at the courthouse, signed the papers, and we took them right in to the judge after that."

"I remember," I said. "It was the weekend, you were having a hard time finding someone who would pick up the phone. Here's my question: where did you get the list of people to call? I mean, how did you know who ECP's other creditors were?"

"Well, we had a partial list of their accounts payable from an old financial statement," said Vinnie. "We started digging around for a shareholder list, for the initial public offering. And for bondholder lists, from the corporate and asset-backed sales. We didn't know how useful those would be, there might not be any current creditors in there, but we figured if we really got desperate we could start calling them."

"But those lists were current only as of the day the bank closed the book on the stock and bond issuances," said Jay. "After that the positions obviously could have been resold, so there would be no guarantee that..."

"Was there a name or two from those lists that stood out?" I interrupted. "Someone who had a big stock position, or someone who had bought several different bonds that added up to a big position? Or maybe someone who was in both the stocks and the bonds?"

Jay and Vinnie looked at each other.

"What was that funny name?" said Vinnie. "The one you said meant balls."

Jay laughed at the memory.

"Huevos Investments. Registered in New York. *Huevos* means eggs in Spanish, but is also slang for balls, like a guy with big balls has big *huevos*. So we couldn't decide whether someone named the company to say something like 'nest eggs,' or to say that he had big enough balls to take risky investments."

"Right," said Vinnie "They had positions in everything, didn't they? I've got those lists somewhere."

He turned around and started digging on his desk. Then he stopped suddenly and looked at Jay with a weird expression on his face.

"Melanie," he said.

"We got those lists from Melanie," Jay finished for him. "The guys on the trading floor hold that information pretty closely. George was very wary of their customer lists getting into the hands of the competition. But it was nothing for Melanie to get it. She just punched in a few codes from her trading station. She gave us a copy, and when we were finished, she asked us to return it."

I picked up the phone, dialed Melanie's extension, and when she picked up I asked her to join us in Vinnie's office. When she got there I asked her:

"Do you know these guys, Huevos Capital? Do you know what they invest in?

She shook her head.

"I never met them. Mr. Clifton brought them into the bank before I started working here, then apparently he turned them over to George. They are pretty active investors, but they were definitely a house account. George and Mr. Clifton wrote their orders, nobody else. As to what they invest in, I gave a list of assets they had bought from us to Vinnie."

Vinnie had been digging around in the stacks of documents on his desk, and finally found the paper he was looking for.

"The stock issuance of ECP was initially $300 million. Huevos Investments bought $25 million of that."

He flipped the page.

"The corporate bond issue was $100 million, they bought $10 million of that."

"And the ABS issue, that was $200 million total, they bought double As and single As both there, $30 million total. What's that, $65 million?"

"That's a lot for a boutique capital firm," I said. "Is there anyone else bigger investing in this company?"

"Us," said Vinnie sardonically.

"Yeah," I said. "Melanie, did they ever invest in anything else? Surely it wasn't all ECP?"

Again she shrugged her shoulders.

"I don't know. They never bought anything else I worked on, that I was aware of, but that doesn't mean much. There were plenty of other deals they could have been involved in and I wouldn't have known. I can look around, I guess."

"Did anybody ever figure out who they were? Who owned Huevos Investments?"

"Not us," said Jay. "We were just looking for one creditor, and when we found that guy in Memphis, we dropped the search for anyone else."

"Not me," said Melanie. "Like I said, that was a house account, George or Mr. Clifton only. They never came into the office while I was there, or toured the trading floor or anything like that."

"OK. Here's the deal. I need to know who owns that company. Right away," I said.

"What's up, Sam?" said Vinnie.

"A hunch," I said. "And please keep it quiet while you're looking for the owners."

"We'll get on it right away," said Jay.

"Are we any farther on figuring out what the death of the Littles does to our bankruptcy case?" I asked.

Vinnie nodded.

"We think the court will have to appoint a trustee, almost like a guardian, to represent the Little's interests. Both brothers had wives and children, so we are assuming their estates will get the ECP interests that each of the brothers owned. Eventually the estates will represent themselves, but until the estates are both settled, this guardian/trustee will do it."

"Does the court even know about the deaths of the Littles?" I asked.

Vinnie and Jay looked at each other, then Vinnie shrugged.

"I don't know," he said.

"Well, I guess we better tell them," I said. "I'll talk to Sherman and handle that."

Two simple items, you would think. Figure out who owns the big investor in ECP, and tell the bankruptcy court that the Littles were dead. Like that butterfly in chaos theory who supposedly starts a deadly hurricane with the flapping of his wings, I had no idea what I had just unleashed.

It didn't take long to figure it out.

I was sitting in the small conference room with Jay and Vinnie, talking through the ECP bankruptcy, when there was at tap at the door. I looked up and Sherman was standing there, wearing one of his expensive, go-to-court suits.

Oh shit, I thought.

"Sam? Can I see you for a minute?" he said.

I got up out of the chair.

"Better get your jacket," he said.

"Why?" I asked as got my jacket and walked out with him. "Where are we going?"

"Down to the FBI offices. Agent McAlister wants to talk to us again," he said.

"What is it now?" I asked.

Sherman shrugged.

"He said something about a photo lineup. I thought you could handle that on your own. But he said I ought to come because there were some other things 'of a general nature' that needed discussing. So I'm going, too. Lawson is tied up with the other Feds right now, the regulators."

We walked a few blocks over to the FBI offices. We were shown into a ratty conference room; I swear I had been in there before, a few years ago, when I was talking to a different agent about a different fraud. The place hadn't changed at all, still run-down government issue furniture and coffee stains on the carpet.

After a short wait Agent McAlister and two others came into the room. One was a Latina lady, tall and slender, with short, jet black hair. She was losing a fight to a mustache that was blooming under her nose. She was casually dressed in jeans and a golf shirt and held a large briefcase. She did not have FBI stamped all over her like McAlister did. The other was a lumpy, medium-sized white man in a suit and tie. McAlister introduced them as Agent Martinez from "the Miami office" and Mr. Stein "from D.C."

"No local police anymore?" asked Sherman.

"What we're talking to you about today is all a part of the federal case," said McAlister. "The locals were involved only because of the murder of George Lamb. But we now believe that his death may not have been a random act. It may be related to the deaths of the Little brothers, and, of course, all three are related to the bank. So right now we are proceeding under the jurisdiction of the FBI."

"All right, Agent McAlister," Sherman said. "You are in charge today. We understand."

"What do you mean, George's murder was not a random act?" I said.

"We'll get to that," said McAlister. Then he nodded at Agent Martinez. She put her briefcase on the table and withdrew from it two large photo albums. She laid one of them in front of me and said:

"I am going to show you some photos now," she said. "We think we know who 'Marcos Pereira' and 'Ana Primo de Montez' really are, based on your descriptions, but we want to make sure. So please go through this first book, and see if you can identify the man who claimed to be Marcos Pereira."

The photos were an odd mixture. Some of them were obviously mug shots taken in a jail. Others seemed to be taken surreptitiously, where the subject did not know that his photo was being taken. And a third category I could only classify as "official:" a photo that was taken for a college yearbook, or the military, or for inclusion in a professional directory. When I was promoted at the bank a few years ago, they instructed me to go get an official photo, for publication in the local paper, and it looked just like those: stiff, formal, the subject usually in a suit and tie, standing before a draped curtain background or a flag.

I quickly browsed through the first few pages, and in the middle of the album I stopped and pointed at Marcos. His was an official photo; he was standing against a light blue background, in a jacket and tie, wearing a stern look. His hair was much shorter then.

"Are you sure? This is the man who identified himself as Marcos Pereira to you?" she said.

"Positive," I said. "He wears his hair a lot longer now, down past his shoulders, but this is him."

She nodded, then slid a second photo album in front of me. "And now for the woman," she said.

Same drill, same odd mix of mug shots, long photo angles and official shots. I went through it slowly. There were all kinds of women in there, dark-skinned and fair, fat and skinny, lovely and less so. Like the men's book, even the shots that appeared surreptitious had a professional quality to them. They were not accidents from a tourist's camera.

But there was no Ana.

"She's not in here," I said, closing the album and sliding it back to Agent Martinez.

This occasioned a good amount of eye contact, grunting, and other non-verbal communication from the FBI folks.

"Look again," said Agent Martinez. "Take your time. Look at facial structure, okay? Keep in mind that people can change certain things about themselves with plastic surgery or clever makeup. Hair length, eye color, birthmarks, even noses can all be changed easily these days."

I looked again, slowly, thoroughly, and came to the same conclusion.

"She's not in here," I said again.

Agent McAlister let out an exhale of frustration. They had clearly expected me to identify Ana in that book.

"Let's go through the description again," he said. "Height?"

"I am 5'10". Even with just flats on, she could look me right in the eye. So she was tall for a woman, 5'8" at least."

"Weight?"

"No idea, but proportionate to her height."

"Race?"

"Hispanic. She spoke English with a Latino accent."

"Eyes?"

"Brown."

"Hair?"

"Long black hair, halfway down her back, very shiny."

"Build?"

"She had a very nice, fit body."

"Was she...well endowed? Did she have...you know, a big butt, or large breasts, or was she more the skinny type?"

"Curvaceous, is how I would describe her."

"Curvaceous?" said Agent Martinez, a bit loudly. "She was definitely not flat-chested, and didn't have a skinny little ass? Is that what you mean?"

"Yes, I guess so," I said.

"Don't guess, Mr. Wilson," barked Stein from DC suddenly. I had almost forgotten he was there. "This is a murder investigation."

"Then I'll stick with curvaceous," I barked back. "You're the ones trying to put words in my mouth."

There was an awkward silence, with Stein seething in my general direction, and Agent Martinez in particular looking frustrated.

"Her breasts," said Martinez. "Were they real?"

"Real?" I said incredulously.

"Yes, real," she said. Her face had reddened but she persisted. "As opposed to implants or plastic surgery of some kind."

"Agent McAlister, exactly what the hell is going on here?" said Sherman, standing up. "My client saw this woman on a financial matter, he did not custom-fit her for a bikini."

My thoughts drifted to that night with Ana in the hotel room, and her naked body framed against the window. Stein looked away and rubbed his eyebrows. Agent Martinez looked at Sherman angrily, but said nothing, and after a time Sherman sat back down. Finally McAlister exhaled and said:

"Look. We think we know who this Marcos is. Sam identified the guy we thought he was from the photo book. And we thought we knew who this Ana Prima-de-whatever is, too. Because she and Marcos work on...these cons frequently. As a team. Only 'Ana' is right in the middle of that book, and Sam passed on her twice."

He looked at Martinez.

"And as Agent Martinez is alluding, the woman who is a con partner to Marcos fits part of your description—she is tall and attractive with long black hair. But she could not in any stretch be called curvaceous. She has the body of a marathon runner.

"So cut us a break here, Mr. Wilson. We're now trying to figure out whether we were barking up the wrong Latina, so to speak, or whether she may have altered her appearance. So...were her breasts real, to the best of your knowledge, or could they have been recent implants?"

"They were real," I said.

"And her butt?" said Agent Martinez. "Her butt was real too? Not padding in her skirt or something like that?"

"Yes," I said. "And she didn't have those emaciated arms or hollow faces that you see on marathon runners. She was not fat by any means, but she wasn't razor thin either."

Martinez looked disgusted. She glanced at McAlister, shrugged, then picked up her photo albums and left the room.

There was a long silence, as McAlister puzzled over how to proceed.

"Who are those two, really?" I asked McAlister.

"Con artists. Criminals," he said.

"OK, but what kind of criminals?" I asked. "What else have they done?"

He ignored the question and sat down.

"There is another issue we would like to discuss with you," he said, addressing himself to Sherman more than me. "We want you to agree not to mention these two...con artists, the assault on George Lamb, or the death of the Little brothers, to anyone outside the circle that already knows."

Sherman considered this for a minute.

"Agent, the bank is certainly in no hurry to publicize its involvement with the two con artists, as you call them. But George's assault is already a matter of public record. The local police would have filed a report on it, which is a public document, and the newspaper has already reported on it. And as for the murder of the Little brothers...well, two of our customers are dead, their company is in federal bankruptcy court, and the bank isn't really able to cover that up."

"We can deal with the local police report on George's death," said McAlister. "The FBI is not without resources. As for the murders, any mention of them could jeopardize our investigation. We have to insist that you honor our request, and if you like we can make it official by getting a court order for...."

"It's impossible," I said flatly, interrupting him.

"Son, do you really want to get on the wrong side of the Federal Bureau of Investigation?" said Stein from DC, this time breaking his silence to take a few steps in my direction.

He and I just weren't getting along at all.

"First of all, my name is Sam Wilson," I said, "and so you can call me Sam or Mr. Wilson. Not 'son.' Second of all, I know you think the FBI is tantamount to God on Earth, but in fact you are the fifth federal agency I've dealt with in the last week. And you all have the same attitude—you are here to be obeyed. Well, I don't work for you, I work for the bank, and my obligation is to them. If you think you can put me in jail for that, go right ahead."

Sherman kicked me under the table...which was a good thing, since I was getting ready to go into how my taxes paid his salary, which was guaranteed to get any civil servant riled up so bad you would never get anything accomplished with them ever again.

Mr. Stein did not like the little bit I had said, much less what I was planning on, and his teeth were clenched and a vein on his bald head popped out. He sat down at the table and put his forearms in front of him.

"Suppose you tell me why it's impossible, Mister Wilson," he said, placing a heaping amount of disdain on the 'Mister.'

"Because Entourage Capital Partners, the company that the Littles founded and still partially own, is in bankruptcy. And their deaths are material events. So material, in fact, that the federal bankruptcy court judge in Memphis will be quite interested in knowing about them, and he will have my ass in a sling if I don't tell him in a prompt fashion. So you can save your threats. We *have* to tell His Honor."

"You have to avoid impeding a federal murder investigation," began Mr. Stein.

"Let me tell you what you have to...." Agent McAlister was trampling all over Stein to get to me.

"Gentlemen. Gentlemen!" Sherman said. Everybody piped down.

"Mr. Stein. Agent McAlister. How long do you need us to keep quiet on this?" said Sherman. "If, for instance, we could get you two or three days, even through this weekend into next week, would that be long enough?"

Stein and McAlister looked at each other. There was quiet in the room for a moment. Finally Stein spoke up.

"Into the middle of next week would be a minimum."

"Sam, you need to notify the court officially, we all understand that," said Sherman. "But a phone call won't do. You need to get a letter together. You need to write to His Honor at the bankruptcy court in Memphis that you have heard from the FBI that the Little brothers are dead. As your attorney, I will need to review the letter. I will probably need to make some changes. There might be several drafts. It probably wouldn't go out, registered mail of course, until Thursday afternoon. Maybe even Friday morning. The court wouldn't receive it until Tuesday at the earliest, maybe Wednesday or even Thursday of next week. But as long as we get that letter in the mail this week, nobody will be able to accuse us of being less than prompt. And we won't be in any trouble from the federal court judge in Memphis."

Stein and McAlister both nodded.

"Everyone happy?" said Sherman.

'Not just yet," I said. Sherman looked at me stonily but I pressed on.

"I'd still like an answer to the question I asked earlier. Has the explanation for George Lamb's murder been changed from 'mugging gone bad' to 'related to the Little brothers?"

McAlister looked at Stein from DC, who, after a pause, nodded.

"It is possible—only possible, not probable, not likely—that the three murders are related. Both George Lamb and the Littles were connected to your bank. There are some other...similarities in the murders, which may simply be coincidence. We are looking into those now. "

As I was absorbing this, Sherman touched my elbow and stood up.

"Thank you, gentlemen. It was nice to meet you, Mr. Stein. We're going to head back to the bank now. Y'all have a nice day."

◆

We went back to Sherman's office and he kicked off his shoes, loosened his tie, and proceeded to shoot some more paperwads at his TarHeel trashcan.

"You know what your problem is with cops?" Sherman said, his attention focused on the basket more than me.

"I wasn't aware I had one," I responded.

He looked at me sarcastically.

"Don't give me that. You know damn well that every time you talk to the police or the Feds, both sides end up with hard feelings. You know why?"

"Why?"

"Because you think you need to score points on them."

"Look, if you're talking about that crack I made about the FBI being God on Earth, Stein started that whole…"

"I'm talking about that," Sherman cut me off, "I'm talking about the mark-to-market comment you made to Detective Jeffries, and I'm talking about every other interview I ever sat in with you and the cops. You have got to start understanding, Sammy, that *they have to win.* All you need to do is tell them what they need to know, and get out of there."

"I'm not playing a game with them Sherman, but neither am I going to sit there while they treat me like some sleazy pimp they picked up on Wilkinson Boulevard."

Sherman shook his head in exasperation.

"One of these days, I'm not going to be there to smooth things over for you. Then they will put you in jail, just to teach you some manners. Now please, from now on, I want you to do your dead-level best to avoid arguing with them, all right?"

I realized with a shock that what he said was true. I did treat Sherman as my crutch. I was cockier than I normally would have been when he was there, because I knew he would look out for me. I wondered if that was what it felt like to have a big brother, or a guardian angel. It made you more mouthy than you should be.

"All right," I finally said.

"Good. Now, I told you it was odd that there was no mention of the murders in the paper," he said. "I guess you stay in this business long enough, you see it all. The FBI wanting to hush up a hit job. Beats anything I ever saw."

"You would expect them to be asking the community for help, if they don't know what's going on," I said.

Sherman paused and looked at me, then wrinkled up another sheet of paper and shot it. This one finally went in.

"That's right," he said. "So what does that tell you?"

"I don't know," I said.

"It tells me that they do know what's going on. What did you make of Agent Martinez?"

"She didn't look FBI to me," I said.

"Martinez. Dressed casually. Out of Miami. With a book full of mug shots, some of which looked to be undercover photos. You know what that sounds like to me? It sounds like the Drug Enforcement Agency."

"The DEA? You think there's a drug connection here somewhere?"

He shrugged.

"Maybe. Or maybe not, since you failed on Ana's identification. Martinez didn't like that one bit—she was sure those two were in her books. What was your take on Stein?"

"I figured that was McAlister's boss, from Washington."

"Nope. I've met McAlister's boss. So have you, for that matter. Remember Agent Grummel? From the last time you talked to the FBI? He was Agent-in-Charge in Charlotte at the time."

"Big guy, late 50s, balding?" I asked.

"That's him. He got kicked upstairs to DC, and McAlister reports to him now."

"So who was Stein?" I said. "Financial Crimes?"

"Good guess, but wrong again. I've met the Financial Crimes people several times, too. As you can imagine, with all these banks headquartered here in North Carolina, they are down here quite a bit. Stein is not with them."

"So who is he?"

Sherman quit fiddling with the paperwads and turned in his chair to face me. He grabbed his left index finger with his right hand.

"One, I don't know who Stein is, but he is somebody pretty senior in the FBI structure, which means this is a bigger deal than your garden-variety financial fraud."

He grabbed another finger.

"Two, the FBI wants us to keep our mouths shut about what appears to be a professional hit job on two respectable businessmen. And before you argue with 'respectable,' I know your feelings about the Little brothers, but there is nothing at all to suggest they were criminals. Or at least not the kind that would interest senior people at the FBI. Not to mention being silent on the death of one of our employees, which now might not be a random mugging, but might be a professional hit as well."

"Three, these two con artists, as the FBI described our Latino friends, are well known to the FBI. Or at least, Marcos is. They are now chasing their tails on Ana, but if she is in the system anywhere, you can bet they will find her."

He was on his pinky now.

"And four, the DEA out of Miami seems to be the repository of their photos, and perhaps their cases."

"So what does all that mean?" I said.

"I don't have the slightest," said Sherman, smiling at me. "Except you sure know how to stir things up."

17

I tossed and turned that night, in one of those stages where you're not really awake but not really asleep either. I had bad dreams but when I would wake from them, they would slide off and disappear, and I couldn't remember what I was scared about. Finally, about 2:00 in the morning, I fell into a deeper sleep, only to be startled awake a few hours later by a chilling thought.

I looked at the clock. Just after 6:00. I got up and using my laptop logged into the bank's computer and accessed my email account. I browsed through it until I found what I was looking for. I then found Agent McAlister's number on my cellphone and called it.

He answered, sounding tired but like he was already awake.

"McAlister," he said.

"Agent, this is Sam Wilson of Citizen's Union. Do you have a secure email address?"

"Yes. Why?" he said.

"Because I just remembered that I have a photo of Ana Primo de Montez. She sent it to my work email address a few days ago. I can forward it to you if you like."

The photo, of course, was the one Ana had taken of herself, in her smoke-gray lingerie, with her tits spilling out of the front of her bra and a come-get-some look on her face. I was not dying to be sharing it with the FBI, but I had no choice. And if she had anything to do with two or maybe even three murders, then she deserved to be riding a gurney on death row, damn any embarrassment to me.

"Why did Ana send you a photo of herself?" asked McAlister.

"Well...I think she was flirting with me. You can kind of tell that by the nature of the photo."

There was a long silence on the phone.

"When was it taken?" he said.

"She sent it to me sometime last week, before George was killed."

"I'm almost afraid to ask this, but when was the last time you saw her?"

"Friday night," I said, wincing.

I could almost hear him gripping his phone tighter.

"Friday night? Where? What time?"

"We were at a bar on Lake Norman, having a drink. She took a phone call, and said it was Marcos, and she had to go back to work. She said they were working on an analysis for potentially buying ECP, and there were some problems with it that she had to go fix."

"What time was that?" said McAlister.

"About 9:30," I said.

"Where was she going 'back to work' at?"

"She said they had gotten a conference room at a downtown hotel, she didn't say which one, but she and Marcos and some other people on her staff were staying there."

"And you believed her?" he said.

I got a little hot at that, but then heard Sherman in my ear saying "...the FBI has to win."

"I'm sorry, I did. At that time we still believed that she and Marcos were legitimate employees of Santiago Capital."

There was another pause.

"OK, send the photo," he finally said, spelling out an email address that I wrote down.

"Do you have a phone number for her?" he asked.

"Yes, both work and cellphone."

"Let me have the cellphone," he said. I read him the number.

"Ok, now let me give you some very sincere advice. Stay away from this woman from now on, understand? Do not go near her."

"Well, what's the big deal?" I said. "If she's a con artist, then who cares if..."

"Sam? Stay away from her unless you'd like to get yourself thrown in jail. Or worse. Is that clear enough?"

"Thrown in jail?" I said. "For what?"

"Believe me, I will think of something. And we are not done talking about your relationship with this woman either."

He hung up, and from my laptop I forwarded to his email the photo of Ana with all her assets showing.

I thought smugly that at least we would not be having any more discussion of whether her tits and ass were real.

Then I thought of my discussion with Sherman earlier, when he said that if I didn't start watching my attitude, I was going to get thrown in jail. I didn't feel so smart after that.

◆

Jay Podolski was waiting on me when I got into the office that morning. Over the last few weeks I had become impressed with his even keel and calm demeanor, but that morning he looked grim and stressed. And his senior partner, His Gravitas Counselor Wickham, was with him and looked every bit as serious. I walked into my office, and Jay got up and closed the door behind me. They both sat down across from me at my desk.

"Well, you want the bad news, or the worse news?" Jay asked.

I sighed.

"Ease me into it," I said. "I haven't even had coffee yet."

"I talked to Pat Collins, the owner at Collins Investigative Service. He has talked to both Auggie and the other P.I. who was stationed at Memphis. Both of them have resigned. Pat said they wouldn't give him any real reasons, but the guy in Memphis said something like, 'this job is a lot more dangerous than what I thought I was signing up for.' Anyway, Pat is really sorry, and has offered to send us two more guys, and of course he isn't charging us anything, but the bottom line is, they are gone and they are not coming back."

"Does Pat know where Auggie is?"

Jay shook his head.

"Not according to him. He said Auggie only called him yesterday, and the conversation lasted less than a minute."

"Well, then he can tell that to the FBI," I said. "I sure ain't taking a bullet for him. And he has no idea why these two guys are running scared?"

There was a pause.

"No," said Jay. "But we might."

"What?" I said.

Jay looked at his senior partner, who took over.

"Huevos Investments," said Wickham.

"Right," I said. "The guys who invested all that money in ECP. What's that got to do with the P.I.s?"

"You asked us to find out who actually owned Huevos Investments. And we have."

I waited.

Jay handed me a sheet of paper on it that had several corporate names on it, as well as three personal names. I looked at them; they meant nothing to me.

"Okay," I said. "Who are all these folks?"

Wickham adjusted himself in his chair.

"Long story short, Sam, skipping all the corporate screens and the legal cut-outs, Huevos Investments is nominally owned by one Ignacio Aragones. He is an American citizen who currently resides in Miami and lists his profession on his income tax return as 'investor.'"

"Miami?" I said. "I thought Huevos was headquartered in New York."

"It is," said Wickham. "Most investment companies are, there and the Cayman Islands. But Mr. Aragones is a resident of Florida and currently lives in Miami."

Wickham paused again. He seemed to be drawing this out for some reason. I waited again.

"In Miami," he said again. "In a very large, ocean-front estate on Key Biscayne. It's real close to where Nixon used to vacation."

"Nixon?" I said.

"Richard Nixon. President Nixon," said Wickham.

I was running out of patience.

"Look, are we playing a board game or something here, where I'm supposed to guess letters until I come up with the right answer? Just what is it you are trying to tell me?"

"Well, formally, I guess we've told you what you asked us to find out. Huevos Investments is owned by Ignacio Aragones. That's that."

"But there's more, isn't there?" I said.

Wickham squirmed in his chair some more.

"Let's say that we have come by some information—informally, you understand, nothing that we would put in writing—about how Mr. Aragones makes his money. And let's say that, off the record, while it doesn't appear the he himself is doing anything illegal, it might be the case where his associates would be."

I looked at Jay.

"Would you mind translating here?" I said.

"Ignacio Aragones appears to be a front man for an organized crime syndicate," he said.

"Organized crime?" I said. "You mean the Mafia?"

"No," said Jay. "Miami is an open city. Neither the Mafia nor anyone else is fully in charge down there."

"So who does Aragones 'front' for?" I asked.

"According to our information, Aragones is a lawyer, and he works for narcotics smugglers. Drug lords out of Columbia, mostly."

My mouth opened involuntarily. I clapped it shut. I looked at Wickham, then at Jay.

"So now you know why we think Auggie and his associate quit and left town," said Wickham "We think they may have recognized someone that works for the *narcos* while they were watching the Little brothers. Auggie may have even seen the Littles killed."

"Look, Sam," said Jay, "I know this is tough to fathom, because we had a difficult time with it too. But Huevos Investments is owned by this Aragones guy, who is in fact a lawyer for the *narcos* in Miami. As a lawyer, he's had a grand total of 12 cases in the last 10 years. Every one of them has been defending a drug smuggler caught with serious weight. Which means that the money invested by Huevos Investments, whether it belongs to Aragones or his 'investors,' is drug money."

"What in the hell are drug smugglers doing investing in asset-backed securities and corporate bonds?" I said. "I thought these guys used Cayman Island and Panamanian bank accounts to launder their money."

"We understand that this has been going on for the last several years now," said Wickham. "American and Caribbean banks have really tightened up their reporting procedures for loose cash, and the big drug runners are having a hard time laundering their money through the banking system. They've figured out that there is less regulation in the stock and bond markets, so they've opened up brokerage accounts and started investing all over the markets: stocks, bonds, futures, options, everything. Presumably they have financial advisers just like corporations or wealthy individuals might have."

"Huevos Investments, owned by drug smugglers, invests in the stock and bond markets? And took a huge position in ECP? As if it was an investment, like a mutual fund or something?" I asked.

Jay and Wickham both nodded.

I mulled this over for a minute. Then I said:

"And George Lamb sold them all the stuff they bought, didn't he? Corporate bonds, stocks, the asset-backeds. All of that came out of the investment bank we now own, didn't it?"

They both nodded.

"Is there any evidence that George Lamb, or anyone else here, knew that Huevos was backed by drug money?"

"We haven't really looked into that, Sam," said Wickham, averting his eyes. "That would be well outside our area of expertise anyway."

"Jay, what's the loss going to be on Huevos Investment's positions in ECP? Has Vinnie looked at that?"

Jay nodded.

"Worse than ours," he said. "The same percentages on the asset-backed deal would apply, and the unsecured corporate bonds, but we don't have any stock in the company. Huevos has $10 million. Vinnie figures that for a dead loss. He says absolute best case on that position would be 10 cents on the dollar. That means that, total, Huevos is going to lose $35-40 million on an investment of $65 million."

I stared at Jay and Wickham.

"These *narcos* are going to lose $40 million on a position of $65 million. I can't imagine that is going to make them very happy," I said.

"No," said Wickham. "It's not making the bank very happy either."

"We do this for a living," I pointed out. "Nobody likes taking losses, but everyone understands it's part of the business. I doubt drug dealers are as understanding as we are. I imagine they would treat this as if somebody just stole $40 million from them."

"Yes,' said Jay, "it would probably make them really angry. So angry that they might shoot the owners of the company."

"Yeah," I said. "For that matter, they might also be so angry that they would shoot the guy who recommended ECP to them. Which I gather is what George Lamb did."

Both of my attorneys stared at me blandly, as we all contemplated the thought that the second biggest investors in bankrupt ECP were drug lords out of Miami.

◆

So it was back to tell the FBI. I called Sherman but he wasn't in, and neither was Lawson. I walked down to the FBI offices myself, and asked to see Agent McAlister. I was shown to a conference room, and twenty minutes later he came in.

"So, Mr. Wilson, what happy surprise do you have for me this afternoon?"

I gave him a copy of the document that Vinnie and Jay had gotten from Melanie.

"This is a list of all the initial investors in the corporate bonds, the asset-backed bonds, and the stock of Entourage Capital Partners. You will see one name that is common to all three issuances in there, a company called Huevos Investments out of New York. They invested a total of $65 million in ECP over the last few years."

"Okay. So?" said McAlister.

"Huevos is actually owned by a lawyer out of Miami, a man named Ignacio Aragones."

"Ho!" said McAlister. "Ignacio Aragones? Hold on a minute."

He left and re-appeared a few minutes later with Agent Martinez in tow, the lady from Miami whom Sherman speculated worked for the DEA.

"Tell her what you just told me," he said.

So I did, and she had the same reaction when I named Ignacio Aragones.

"Oh, Señor Aragones is well known to us in Miami.   And since you are here, I suppose you know who he is?"

"I am told that he is a drug lawyer and a front man for this Huevos Investment company," I said.

"He is that, and a lot more," said Agent Martinez.   "He controls the money for a large family of drug dealers. I had heard of this Huevos Investments, but $65 million is a lot of money even for the *narcos*. Señor Aragones will be very upset to hear that some of the money is at risk. What did you say the loss would be on his investments?"

"I didn't, but since you ask, we are guessing somewhere between $35-40 million."

On Agent Martinez's face bloomed a grim smile.   She looked at Agent McAlister.

"$40 million, huh?" she said.   "Señor Aragones is in some big trouble. The Garridos brothers don't like him anyway. I would bet you that Sr. Aragones will be in need of a friend very soon. If you understand my meaning."

McAlister smiled back at her.

"I understand you exactly," he said.

Martinez motioned to McAlister and they went into the corner for a whispered conference. McAlister gave a small nod of his head, and Martinez left. She came back in a few minutes with a laptop, a set of headphones, and a file.

"What's this all about?" I said.

"Let's talk about Ana Primo de Montez for a moment, yes?" she said.

Oh great, I thought.

She pulled out the lingerie photo that Ana had sent me, and that yesterday I had forwarded to McAlister.

"This is her? I can see why you were so adamant that her breasts were real. She seems to like you quite a bit, to send you a photo like this."

I looked for the question in there, realized she hadn't really asked one, and said nothing.

"Tell me, what is she like?" said Martinez.

"Well, I don't know her all that well. I only met her two weeks ago."

"Yes, but you have a relationship that is…closer than normal for two weeks. What is she like?"

"Well, she's very pretty, and she knows it. She takes her work seriously, I guess, but seems to have time for fun. She is from Columbia. She likes rum. "

"And handsome American bankers, yes?" said Martinez, feigning innocence. McAlister chuckled and I got the feeling they were mocking me.

"You said she is from Columbia?" said Martinez.

"That is what she told me. She said she and Marcos were both from Columbia, in my first meeting with them."

"Yes," said Martinez. Then she rattled something off in Spanish very rapidly.

"*Puede hablar o entender español? O otros lencuas?*"

Do you know or understand Spanish, or other languages?

"*Conozco un poco de español,*" I replied. I know a little Spanish.

"*Bueno,*" she said. "But I doubt you understand the different accents of Spanish?"

"Accents?" I said.

"Yes, just like English, Spanish speakers have different accents, depending on where they are from. Mexican Spanish sounds a lot different than Bolivian Spanish. So I want you to help us identify Ana's accent. You see, we don't think she is from Columbia. Marcos is, but your Ana…well, we think she is from somewhere else. So put these headphones on, please, and I am going to play you some different accents. We do this as a training program for our new agents. You will hear a different woman saying the same few sentences. Stop me when you hear an accent that sounds like Ana's."

She plugged the headphones into her computer, hit a few keys, and I heard a woman speaking in Spanish. She was telling her husband that she was gathering the children, getting in the car and going to the store in the city, even though it was raining.

Woman #1 sounded like the Spanish I had heard my whole life. It had to be Mexican Spanish.

Woman #2 spoke a clearer, more distinct Spanish in which soft c's (like in the word "city") and z's were lisped and sounded like "th:" "ciudad" sounded like "thiudad." It sounded a lot like my college Spanish professor. She was Castilian. That was Spanish Spanish.

After that I had no idea. Some of the speakers turned *yo,* the word for "I" that sounds just like it looks, into "Joe." Others turned words with double lls, like *lluvia* (rain), which I had been taught to pronounce as "you-vee-ah"," into "juvia" or even "chuvia." I had no idea where these speakers were from and in one case the words were pronounced so strangely I barely understood them.

And then, on the sixth or seventh voice, I heard Ana's accent. There was something similar to the rhythms of Ana's speech. I raised my hand.

Martinez punched a few keys.

"This one?" she asked.

She replayed the same speech again.

I nodded and took off the headphones.

"That sounds a lot like the way she talks. Something about the rhythm of her speech and where her accents fall on certain words. What is she? I mean, what country is she from?"

"That," she said, "was not a Columbian. In fact, she's not even Hispanic. That was an Italian speaking Spanish."

She looked at McAlister.

"Which means that maybe you are correct. Maybe the *narcos* are working with the *mafiosos* in Miami now, and the...."

McAlister shook his head quickly at Martinez, and she clammed up. He gestured to me.

"Thanks, Sam, we appreciate you coming in. You can go now. Only listen. If you get the slightest peep from Ana or Marcos, a phone call, an email, anything, you call me immediately. And stay away from them, okay? Consider them armed and dangerous. We do."

I left with my skin crawling.

18

I stopped at the China King in Latta Arcade and had a bowl of soup noodles for lunch, standing at the counter.

Call me stupid, or maybe just slow, and I wouldn't have much of a defense. My only excuse was, my work load was so heavy that I was forgetting the obvious things. But what the FBI had made an effort not to tell me, I had finally figured out on my own.

People who run con games on white-collared bankers are generally not "armed and dangerous." It kind of defeats the purpose—they're trying to steal money *without* using a gun. So if the FBI was saying that Marcos and Ana were armed and dangerous, then it was because they were complicit in the murders of the Little brothers.

And maybe George Lamb's death, too. But regardless, the FBI wasn't sweating Marcos and Ana because of some supposed con they were running on me and the bank.

Friday night, Ana had left The Green Room unexpectedly and in a hurry, after receiving a phone call. She said it was because of work, and indeed maybe it was—her real work of killing the Little brothers. They had died sometime that weekend. Perhaps Marcos had called her and told her, I found them, it's time to go to work.

There were still a lot of questions rattling around in my head, chief among them being "where are Marcos and Ana now?"

I finished lunch and walked back to the office. Sharon saw me as I came in.

"Lawson is looking for you," she said.

I turned on my heel and went up to his office. He had just finished lunch himself, and was throwing the remains in the trash.

"I'm sorry I have been unavailable the last few days," he said as I sat down. "These regulators have been…a little voracious in their need for information. I understand you and Sherman have had another chat with the FBI."

"Yes," I said, "and I just got through with a second one."

"Do tell," he said. "In fact, if you wouldn't mind, I would appreciate a full summary of this situation. You know, we only have a few days until we report to the chairman on this. It seems like a good time to start working on an executive summary."

"Okay," I said. "As near as I can figure, the ECP situation goes like this:

"A few years ago, Randall Clifton brought a new client to the investment bank in the form of Huevos Investments. Huevos was eager to get involved in stocks, bonds and everything else, and had plenty of money. Whether Clifton knew that the money behind Huevos was Miami drug money, I don't know. I would guess he did, and didn't care. Anyway, he turned Huevos over to George Lamb to…."

241

"Drug money? How do you figure that?" Lawson interrupted.

I told him about the search that our lawyers had done on the true ownership of the company, and who the owner was connected to.

"So why do you speculate Clifton knew?" Lawson asked.

"Because the account was a house account. That's code for 'senior attention only,' and Melanie confirmed to me that only Clifton and George worked with Huevos, no one else.

"Clifton, and possibly George, put these Miami *narcos* into Entourage Capital Partners heavily: stocks, corporate bonds and asset-backeds. Things went along fine for a while. George and Clifton hung out with the ECP folks and took trips on the corporate plane, snorted coke and banged hookers and generally did all the things...

"Whoa!' said Lawson, "wait a minute. You're telling me that the president of our investment bank and our head bond salesman were snorting coke and banging hookers? Where'd you get an idea like that?"

"Well, I told you and Sherman that I saw Clifton get on that plane with a bunch of hookers and the Little brothers. I can't say I actually saw him snorting coke and banging whores, but when I was in that plane Auggie found some hand mirrors and razor blades that are usually used for cutting up and snorting cocaine.

"So I don't think they were up there playing Monopoly. As for George, just about everyone knew he had a coke problem, and Melanie told me that George had been bugging her to go along on these plane rides, too."

"It's still a stretch to me," said Lawson. "At least regarding Clifton."

"Ok, then let's say Clifton reluctantly went along with all that in the name of client relations. How's that? Anyway, Clifton and George were the only two links between ECP and Huevos Investments. It all worked fine while ECP was making money. Huevos was happy to be feted by such senior bankers, and was also happy to receive nice interest and dividend payments on their investments. ECP was also happy to have senior contacts at the bank, and a smooth ride for their capital needs. So I imagine this period of time was like a honeymoon for both them and for us, too."

"Fast forward two years, to right now. In the interim we bought Clifton's investment bank. Right around the time that the financial situation in Russia started to collapse, so did the one at ECP. The two aren't related, the timing was just a coincidence. Clifton was doing what he could for ECP to keep things afloat, including that sneaky little extension he pulled on me, but it was pretty clear to anyone who could read a balance sheet that ECP was going under.

"I suppose that Huevos got word of the problems around then, because I think that is when they sent Ana and Marcos in to see me, under the guise of being vulture capitalists who might be interested in buying ECP from us. I'm pretty sure Ana and Marcos worked for the *narcos* down in Miami. Perhaps they suspected they weren't getting the real skinny from George and Clifton, and the *narcos* can read stock prices in the paper as well as anyone.

"Anyway, Marcos and Ana were not, we now know, vulture capitalists. I think they came in here with two goals: figure out what the true financial situation is, and if it was as bad as they were hearing, kill the Little brothers. This ain't professional investing, Lawson. It's organized crime. When someone loses that much of your money, you pretty much have to kill them. Otherwise you're laughingstock on the streets.

"As you know, while they were figuring all this out in Miami, we were having a problem finding the Littles, which is why we hired the private detective. Something Auggie saw spooked him so badly that he quit his job and ran. My guess is, he saw the Littles get killed, and he told his P.I. buddy, and they both folded their tents and left."

"Hold on," said Lawson. "Under normal circumstances, if you are a private eye, aren't you going to let the police know about the killings?"

"I'm getting there. The FBI hasn't said so directly, but like I said earlier, they too seem to believe that both Ana and Marcos are working for the Miami *narcos*. It's possible that Auggie figured this out, and that's why both of those P.I.s took off. Neither one of them wanted to tangle with the drug lords. Who would?

"In addition, the FBI is hedging its bets on George's death. They think it could be related to the killing of the Little brothers, and maybe it was done by the same people."

"Why," asked Lawson, "would anyone want to kill George Lamb? I did not particularly like the man, but I just cannot explain how sick it makes me that he died over this nonsense."

"I think it was because he was the one who put Huevos Investments into ECP. I think Clifton brought Huevos into the bank, and turned them over to George, and then George sold them a bunch of bonds that turned into shit. So they killed George because they figured he was equally responsible for losing their money. That's all speculation, of course.

"The Feds are now calling both Ana and Marcos 'armed and dangerous,' and have told me to stay away from them. Meantime, our bankruptcy case is going to come to a screeching halt in a few days, as soon as the judge finds out the Little brothers are dead. Jay and Vinnie think he will have to find someone to represent the interests of the Little estates, some type of guardian or trustee, and that is going to take weeks."

Lawson sighed and got up from his chair. He was chewing on his unlit pipe again.

"I can't pretend to think like a Miami drug criminal, but if you were out to avenge these financial losses, and you held both the company owners and the bank's bond salesman responsible, would you also not hold Mr. Randall Clifton responsible as well? According to your theory, he was the one who introduced the drug dealers to the bank."

I nodded.

"Seems consistent to me," I said.

"Then I would not want to be in Mr. Clifton's shoes these days. I don't suppose you have any good news for me, do you?"

"Well, I think the bond portfolio has stopped hemorrhaging, if that is any help. The worst thing in the loan book is obviously ECP, and we knew about the loan portion of that before this all started, so we have already set aside reserves for some of it. After that, there are a handful of riskier clients, but nothing that seems to have bankruptcy written on it quite yet. The asset-backed portfolio is actually pretty solid. There are four bonds, a position of about $10 million total, that we should probably sell, and we will take a small loss on those. But the rest are from high-quality issuers in pretty liquid categories, and they should pay out fine. And we're out of Russian debt and emerging markets entirely until you put us back in."

"When will you have a set of loss estimates for me to look at?

"I can have them by the end of the day," I said. "They are mostly done, I just need to put them in some kind of recognizable form. If you want good news, that's it. The losses other than ECP are not going to be that bad."

He was filling up his coffee from his side credenza, and he paused and took his pipe out of his mouth to say:

"Sam, you folks have done a damn good job here. I am sure the chairman will tell you the same thing. I know ECP is a mess but that is not our fault. You made the right call on the emerging market debt. You've done a great job getting a handle on this in a short period of time."

"Yeah," I said as I got up. "And we only took one casualty doing it."

He looked at me, eyes brimming with sympathy.

"Sam, you know you can't blame yourself…."

But I had walked out. I was sick of Miami drug lords, crooked bankers and sleazy company owners who snorted coke and flew hookers around in 757s with hot tubs. I felt like I needed a shower.

◆

I went into the bathroom and got myself together. I washed my face and hands, and went down the elevator to my office. I went in and shut the door, and went to work on the final loss estimate.

Five hours later, I had a two-page memo outlining the losses in the bond, loan, and exotics portfolios. I treated ECP as a separate line item. The whole loss, counting ECP, came in at about $190 million. I sent the memo to Lawson, turned off my computer, and looked at the clock. It was after 10:00. I got my jacket and toured my suite of offices. Nobody was around. I got in my Jeep and went home.

As I got to my neighborhood, I could see that the lights in Curtis's house were still on. I decided I wanted some company. I pulled into his driveway and lightly tapped on his screen door in the back. He was sitting in his living room watching TV and was surprised by the knock. I went in before he got up.

"Hey man," I said. "What are you doing up?"

"Man, I took a nap this afternoon, and now I can't go to sleep. Are you just getting in from work?"

"Yeah," I said, loosening my tie. "Long day. Got any beer in the fridge?"

He pointed to an empty bottle on a side table next to him.

"Last one," he said, "but we can run out and get some more."

"You want to go up to The Green Room and shoot a little pool?" I said.

"That sounds good," he said, looking at the clock on the wall. It was not quite 11:00. "They open?"

"They should be," I said. "Even if they're not, Bill is still there cleaning up. He'll let us in."

"My boat or your car?" he said.

"Let's take the boat," I said. "The moon's out tonight, navigating will be easy."

So we got into Curtis's fishing boat and cruised down to The Green Room. We docked in a berth of the otherwise empty dock. The docks have a view of the parking lot of The Green Room, and I noticed the headlights of a car pulling in. The headlights illuminated the only other two cars in the lot, which I recognized as belonging to Bill Ritchie and Big Max Buford. Good, I thought. If Big Max was still there, and a couple of new customers were coming in, then Bill would be in no hurry to close up. He was open as long as he was making money, and

Curtis and I would be able to shoot pool all night if we wanted to.

The guy in the car got out and went into the front entrance of the pool hall. Curtis and I tied off the boat and walked up the stairs to the back entrance.

"Shit," I said, tapping my pockets. "I left my wallet in the glove compartment of the boat. I'll be right back."

Curtis went on in through the back doors. I headed back down to the docks, got back in the boat, got into the glove compartment and fished around until I felt my wallet. Then I walked back up the stairs to the pool hall.

I walked across the back porch and in through the back doors, only to find that no one was there. The hairs on the back of my neck stood up.

The place was lit up. It looked like it was still open for business. A few overhead fans were whirling. The tables had all been cleaned and the balls racked. There was a broom out by the bathroom area, as if someone had decided to start sweeping up. But there was no one there. No Bill Ritchie. No Big Max.

And no Curtis.

I took a step into the poolroom and felt a jab on the side of my neck. It suddenly felt like I had plugged myself into an electric socket. I collapsed onto the floor and flopped around. I'm not sure if I lost consciousness but I was cognizant of being in a lot of pain: neck burning, severe spasms in my legs, arms, and abs. I was unable to control my mouth—my lips burned and I was slobbering as I rolled around on the floor. I banged my head against a pool table leg, and am pretty sure it hurt, but I couldn't control the spasms racking my body.

They subsided after a minute—or was it an hour? I was seriously weakened, unable to even think about getting up. I looked around and realized where I was, and then a voice behind me spoke.

"Well, if it isn't Mr. Big-Time Banker. You sure flop around on the floor pretty good. Do they have a name for that dance here in Charlotte?"

I felt some strength returning and was able to pull myself up into a sitting position, leaning my back against the wall. My eyes slowly focused on the long, strong silhouette of Marcos Pereira, who had apparently been waiting behind the door for me. He was dressed more casually than I had seen him before, in jeans and a tight black t-shirt with some kind of logo on the front. He had on a long black trench coat of some lightweight fabric, and low-ankle hiking shoes. In his hand he held a Taser.

"Pretty amazing device, huh?" he said, gesturing at the Taser. "Two small batteries and you get 10,000 volts a pop. The only problem, you have to be close to the target, within the reach of your arm. But other than that, it is perfect."

"Fuck you," I tried to say, but it came out as blurry nonsense.

"Still can't talk, huh? Don't worry, it will come back in a few minutes. That's another great thing about this Taser—no permanent damage. I mean, you can shoot someone, or hit them with a sap, like I did that guy there..."

He gestured toward one of the pool tables across the room, and my heart skipped a beat as I looked over and saw Curtis, unconscious, his legs splayed wide apart, one of his arms twisted behind him, lying under one of the pool tables.

"Fuck did you do to Curtis?" I said loudly. This time it seemed semi-intelligible.

"He didn't want to go all the way down after the Taser, so I had to hit him with this sap I have here and...hey, did you say

Curtis? Is that his name? So you know this guy, huh? Maybe he's a friend of yours?"

I realized I had bumbled and said nothing more.

"Not talking now? Okay. That will change when I give you another taste of the Taser, yes? Because I have some questions to ask you.

"You see, I need to know what you have told the FBI. You are surprised, eh? That I know you have been talking to them and that *puta* from Miami, Martinez? The DEA lady? Yes, I know she is here in Charlotte, looking for me. You put her on to me, *sí*?

I mumbled into my shirt and purposefully drooled a little.

"You are still feeling the Taser, I see. It's okay, we have plenty of time. I will check on the bossman, yes?"

He walked up front, and reached down behind the front counter. He dragged Bill Ritchie's body out several feet. I panicked at the thought that Bill was dead, but then I heard him snort. Marcos was kneeling over him as he said to me:

"I had to give him a little taste of the Taser too. You have to be careful with the older gentlemen. Sometimes they have a heart condition that you don't know about, and...well, this one will be fine."

I had faked the dumbness and the drooling a little. My body had returned to normal and I was thinking clearly. I looked over at Curtis. His eyelids were fluttering. He would be up and conscious very soon. Marcos and his Taser were in for a nasty surprise.

Marcos left Bill and started walking back toward me. There were pool tables in between us, and I carefully timed his approach. I slowly stood up as he cleared the second to last pool table.

"Well, there he is, feeling a little better now, yes? Good. Then perhaps we will..."

And I reached under the pool table in front of me and pulled out the bridge. It is nothing more than a long pool cue with a metal bracket at the end. It is for those extra-long shots that you can't quite reach—you lay the bridge on the table and slot your cue through the bracket at the end of the bridge, and you can reach an extra couple of feet with it. Every pool table at The Green Room has a bridge on hooks underneath the table. It is invisible to people playing on the tables above. But I used to work at The Green Room, and played pool there all the time.

Marcos had walked to the last table separating us, and was looking at me with a puzzled expression, as if something had just come to his mind. It didn't deter me. I whipped the bridge out across the table and hit him right in the face with the metal bracket. It caught him in the left cheek and knocked him back two feet. He almost went down, and I would have closed, but he had the Taser out and the bridge had snapped in two. I now had about four feet of cue left in my hand. It was a good club, with a splinter of broken wood on the end that could leave a cut or even a puncture wound, but I was keeping a close eye on that Taser.

"Curtis!" I shouted. "Can you hear me? Get up, Curtis!"

His eyes were fully open but I could tell he wasn't processing yet. He reached around and felt the back of his head. He rolled out from under the pool table.

Marcos reached up and wiped blood from his face.

"You have scarred me," he said. "I will kill you for that."

"Did you kill George Lamb?" I said.

"Who? Oh, that cocaine-head who cheated my bosses? Yes, of course."

He said it with the wave of his hand, like he was talking to a waiter. Yes, of course I'll have another drink.

"You bankers are amazing to me. It used to be an honorable profession in this country. Not glamorous, it is true, but an honest way to make a living. And then you put these people like George in charge of things, and now it is like doing business in Mexico. Everywhere there is a hand out for some personal money. This George of yours cheated my bosses out of millions. What a fool! Did he think my bosses would do nothing? And when I confronted him with this, he sneered at me. At me, Marcos! Told me that I was 'an errand boy' and to go back to Cuba before he whipped my spic ass! He is lucky that all I had time to do was shoot him."

Marcos wiped the blood from his hands on his pants. Out of the corner of my eye I could see that Curtis was up and back in the game. He had a bridge in his hand, too, I could see it under the table. I started to slide around the table toward Marcos. I had only one thing in mind—hit Marcos with the stick again.

Curtis was slowly angling to get a shot at him too. We were both wary of the Taser, but if that is all he had, he was in deep shit, queued up for a serious beating.

So of course he reached into his jacket pocket and pulled out a gun. He smiled at us.

"Those sticks are not such a good option now, no?" he said.

The gun looked like a long-barrel .22 caliber. A killer's gun. He laid the Taser on the pool table in front of him, then from his other pocket he pulled out a suppressor and quickly screwed it onto the gun. He put the Taser back in his pocket.

"So...we were saying?" he said.

The gun changed things. Now it seemed like a good idea to play for time. I had sensed his vanity earlier, and thought that if I could keep him talking about himself, he might not shoot me.

"How did you know I would be here?" I said.

"I followed you from your office," he shrugged. "I saw you go to your house, and get in the boat and leave. I took a guess about where you were going—Ana had told me about this place—and I got lucky to find you here."

He didn't seem to know that that wasn't my house, it was Curtis's, and he also didn't seem to know that Curtis had been in the boat with me.

"Well, who else has the master assassin killed?" I said, trying to keep him going.

"Master assassin? You try to irritate Marcos? I tell you, it will not work. Others have tried this, too. They are all dead.

"But you surely know by now that I came here for the Little brothers? They stole large amounts of money from my employers, that they would never be able to repay. They had to be punished. They were fools."

"Why?" I said. "Plenty of businessmen start companies that don't make it. Do you think they should all be killed? I mean, your employers, as you call a bunch of *narcos* , down in Miami, invested in a start-up company. There is a certain amount of risk there."

Marcos shook his finger at me.

"No, no," he said. "Your bankers came to my employers, the *narcos* as you say, not the other way around. My employers were introduced to them by George Lamb and this other man who works for you, Clifton. They told my bosses what a wonderful company the Littles had and asked my bosses to invest with them. They promised them significant returns. Everything was supposed to be very safe. They pitched them a business plan. They made my bosses look like...what do you say, suckers? They made my bosses look like suckers. You do not do that to my bosses, believe me."

"So a little while ago, my bosses asked this Clifton, so how is our company doing? We have heard some things on the street, that they are having problems. And Clifton, he was not telling them the truth. He was being *evasivo*. He told us that the bank had taken our account out of his hands, and given it to this George, and we should talk to him. So my bosses talked to him, and he was being a liar too."

"So, they sent Ana and me up here to see what we could find out, and to find the Littles and ask them directly. After the meeting you had with the Littles and Ana, we knew where they were staying, and we also saw them take off in the plane. I knew all about that plane. My bosses had flown in it, too. They found it for me, told me exactly where it was and when it was going to be there."

"My bosses made the decision that the Littles had to be taught a lesson. Otherwise, who would respect them? So I waited for the plane to come back, and when it was sitting in the hangar, and the pilots were being switched out, I snuck onto the plane and took care of them. They were so pathetic when they found out who I was! So scared of Marcos! I told them, you should never have cheated my employer like this. Did you think they would do nothing? They begged and cried for their lives, but it was no use. They are lucky, even. Marcos was told to make it painful for them, but there was no time for that. My bosses will be disappointed."

And that, I thought, is how a psychotic killer thinks. In the third person, mocking the emotions of others as signs of weakness.

I noticed that during Marcos's talk, Curtis had succeeded in inching even closer to him, and now was almost close enough to get his bridge into play. Unfortunately, Marcos noticed it too. He took a half-step back.

"You move very well, Curtis. Perhaps you have done this type of work before? No matter. Stay where you are and take your hand off that stick. Put your hands on the pool table. You too, Sam." He waved the gun at us to make sure we understood.

We did as he said.

"Now, Sam, I need to know everything you have told to the FBI and that *puta* Martinez."

I said nothing, just continued looking at him. He sighed.

"Listen, I respect you, okay?" said Marcos. "I know you didn't have anything to do with my employers losing their money. You are just cleaning up the mess, I understand this.

"But here we are. You have answers and I need to know them. So if you don't start talking, Marcos is going to shoot this man here in the knee." He gestured the gun at Curtis.

Curtis made an involuntary move forward, as if to rush him, and Marcos reflexively took another half-step backward.

"You know, I got distracted when we were talking earlier, but you two are friends. You both came in the back door, from the docks. There is your boat there, eh Sam? So maybe you two came together in the boat? I think so, yes? So the question is, there are two cars in the parking lot. One of them belongs to the owner up there. But who does the other one belong to? Sam? Who owns the other car?"

"Don't say shit to him, Sammy," said Curtis.

I maintained my silence.

"Sam?" he said. He aimed his silenced .22 at Curtis's knee. "You better start talking to me."

255

19

Marcos's two half-steps backward, caused by Curtis's earlier threatening moves forward, had taken him right to the doorframe of the bathroom entrances. It was from there he pointed the gun at my best friend's knee.

There was a broom propped up against one side of the frame, the one that had led me to speculate, when I first came in, that someone was sweeping up in preparation to close. Otherwise it was just a normal bathroom entrance—turn right and you open the door to go to into the men's room; left was the ladies,' and in the middle was the janitor's closet.

And as Curtis and I watched in silent fascination, the huge hand and long arm of Big Max Buford snaked out from behind the doorframe and grabbed Marcos's gun hand.

Marcos grunted in surprise and tried to turn, but Max had nudged him out into the pool hall slightly and reached his other arm around and got Marcos's throat in the crook of his elbow. Marcos was struggling to loosen himself from Max's grip but it was like watching a little boy play with his dad.

"Wyatt, this here's the feller that was looking for you the other day, in his fancy car," said Max. "What say we drop the gun, big boy?"

And he slammed the back of Marcos's hand repeatedly down on the slate of the pool table surface until we could hear the bones break. Marcos finally yelled out in agony and dropped the gun.

The pain seemed to energize him, though, and he first tried to flip Max over his back. He bent at the waist and slid a leg backward, between Max's legs, but he might as well have been trying to flip a dump truck. Max was simply too big for flipping. Marcos abandoned the idea and decided to start kicking backwards, trying to catch Max in the knee. He missed several times, then caught him a glancing blow on the shin.

Then Max got mad.

"I don't know where you learnt your manners from, boy, but you don't come into my favorite bar, which I have been coming to for going on 15 years now, and which belongs to my good friend up there at the front, and start shocking people with a Taser."

Max let his hand go and grabbed him by the hair. Then he slid his other arm off Marcos's throat and grabbed him by the back of his pants.

And he picked him up off the ground like that and slammed Marcos's head straight through the wall.

The wall was in fact nothing but painted wallboard on a wooden 2x4 frame, and Marcos's head went all the way through it, up to the shoulders. Max pulled him out and he was dazed but still conscious, with dried plaster and pieces of wallboard all over his face and hair. Marcos seemed to be trying to get his hand into his other pocket, where the Taser was, but there was no time for that. Max walked him down the wall another three feet, picked him up sideways like a man throwing a bale of hay onto a hay truck, and slammed his head straight through the plaster again. When he pulled Marcos out the second time, his eyes had rolled up inside the lids and you could only see the whites.

The third time Max backed him up about four feet, got a running start, and had Marcos a foot off the ground when he slammed his head into the wall. This time, though, his head hit one of the 2x4 studs coming down from the ceiling. The stud cracked and so did Marcos's neck. When Max pulled him out the third time, Marcos was dead.

Max didn't seem to notice, and was fixing him up with a fourth heave into the wall, but Bill Ritchie, who had recovered enough to walk the length of the pool hall to watch what was going on, put his hand on Max's shoulder.

"Max?" he said. "He's dead. You can stop now."

"What?" Max looked at Marcos closely. "Oh. Well, so he is."

Then he dropped him on the floor like he was dropping off a bag of trash off at the dumpster.

"You okay, Bill?" said Max, scrubbing the plaster off his hands.

"Yeah," he said, rubbing his neck. "I took a Taser shot back when I was still on the job at CMPD. Volunteered for it. It hurt then, but I swear it hurt more this time. I must be getting old."

"Wyatt, how about you?"

I rubbed my neck like Bill had.

"I'll be fine," I said.

"Curtis, he hit you pretty good with that sap," said Max.

"I could use some ice," he said. "I've got a knot the size of a large egg back behind my ear."

"I'll get you some," said Bill, and we all walked over to the bar.

"I want to apologize to all three of you for taking so long to get to him," said Max. "I should have moved a little faster, but when he pulled out that gun...well, I had to wait for the right time. I'm sorry if that scared you."

"Max, you saved my life," said Curtis. "Or at least my knee. There's nothing to apologize for, big man."

I noticed that under the bar there was still a half a bottle of the Havana Club that Ana had given me. I walked around and got it out, and got out four glasses. I poured the rum into the glasses and slid them around to everyone. Curtis took the plastic bag of ice Bill had given him, and gingerly put it behind his ear. And we all sat there and had a drink, like we had probably done a dozen times in the past, and looked at each other in silence. The only thing different was, there was a dead body with a broken neck near the back door.

◆

I called Agent McAlister at the FBI. He was up there in 30 minutes with two dark-windowed SUVs and a dark panel van.

And the glowering presence of "Mr. Stein from D.C.," who arrived separately in a white government-owned sedan.

Several other people followed them into the pool hall, including two who looked like medical personnel. McAlister saw Marcos's body and gestured to the two of them; they went to the back of the pool hall and bent down to examine the corpse.

McAlister and Stein then peeled me off from the others and took me over to a corner.

"What happened?" said Stein.

I explained to him how Marcos had come in zapping and sapping, how he confessed to the killings of George and the Little brothers, his affiliation with the drug gangs in Miami, and how Big Max had gotten behind him and broken his neck.

They looked at each other, and then walked down to look at the three big holes in the wall, including the last one with the 2x4 cracked almost in half, the bottom part still hanging by a shard to the top. They examined but did not touch the silenced .22 lying on the pool table. I noted with detachment that the body of Marcos whatever-his-real-name-was being loaded gently into a body bag.

McAlister and Stein finished their conference and came back to me.

"Let's go up front and talk to your friends," said McAlister.

As we walked forward, he put his hand on my shoulder.

"You know, Sam, you probably don't realize it now, but you guys have done a hell of a service for your country."

He gave my shoulder a little squeeze.

Oh boy, I thought. Best buddies with the FBI. I couldn't wait to see where this was going.

At the bar up front, Stein took over.

"You guys okay?" he asked. "How's that knot on your head coming, sir? Do you need to go to the hospital?"

Curtis put the ice bag down in the sink.

"The swelling's coming down. I'll be fine," he said.

"How about you, sir?" he addressed himself to Bill Ritchie. "You're the owner of this establishment, aren't you? How are you feeling?"

"I'm 60 years old," said Bill. "I just got Tasered. I feel like shit."

"Do you need to go to the hospital?" said Stein.

"No," he said. "I need another drink."

Mr. Stein from D.C. picked up the Havana Club bottle, which still had a few fingers left in it, and poured some more into Bill's glass.

"Then another drink you shall have, sir," said Stein.

He set the bottle down and then addressed himself to Max.

"Sir, I would like to shake your hand," he said.

Max thought it was a joke for a second. So did I. I mean, Max had just turned a grown man's brain into mashed potatoes. But Stein stuck his hand out, and after a second Max put his big paw out and they shook.

"I want you to know that you...all of you...have done your country a fine service. That...gentleman...back their on the floor is a very dangerous man. The FBI has been looking for him for quite some time. He is a known killer and the world is a better place now that he is dead. I'm sorry that it happened this way to all of you, but believe me when I tell you that you have saved us, and the taxpayers, and even his future victims, from a lot of trouble."

He turned back to Bill Ritchie.

"Your bar has sustained some damages from this fight. I noticed that your glass liquor case is broken, and that the felt on one of your tables has been scratched through to the slate. And obviously there are those holes in the wall. Please send any and all bills related to the restoration of The Green Room to Agent McAlister. He will see that they are paid promptly."

It seemed like a fair thing to do to me, and Max didn't look like it was any big deal to him. But Curtis has spent eight years in the U.S. Army, and Bill had been a cop on the Charlotte police force for 20 years. Both of them had their mouths open in shock.

"You're telling me that the federal government is offering to pay for the damage to my bar?" said Bill incredulously.

"No," said Stein, "the FBI is *insisting* that it pay for the damage. As well as any medical bills any of you might have related to this. If you wake up tomorrow with a headache, or a sore neck, and want to go see the doctor, go ahead and send the medical bills to Agent McAlister. He will take care of them, no questions asked."

"Does that mean I don't have to go downtown and answer any questions about all this?" asked Max.

"Downtown? Questions?" said Stein. "Agent McAlister, do you see any evidence that a crime has been committed here?"

"Me? No, sir," said McAlister on cue. "I mean, obviously this Marcos fellow is guilty of busting up this bar, but he has...well, let's just say he's already paid the price for that. And after that, it's as clear a case of self-defense that you'll ever see. From all these folks. No, sir, there is nothing that happened here that would require any of these gentlemen to come downtown or answer questions."

It was a whitewash, but I wasn't about to object to it. Neither, I thought, were any of my friends.

One of the med-techs from the back of the room came up and said something quietly to Stein. He nodded, then turned back to us.

"Agent McAlister is going to take care of hauling that trash out of here. I thank all of you again for your service. Mr. Wilson, if I might have a minute with you outside?"

McAlister walked toward the back and the body of Marcos, which was now in a black body bag. The gun was bagged up and McAlister put it in his outside suit pocket. I walked outside with Stein. We walked to his car, and he opened the passenger door for me. I got in, and he walked around to the driver's seat. I hadn't seen him as a smoker, but he lowered his window slightly and lit a cigarette, which he kept close to the window as he spoke.

I had only interacted twice with Stein. The first time was in that meeting where he seemed to be playing the tough guy, insisting that we keep our mouths shut about the deaths of George and the Littles. The second time had been just now, where he played the glad-hander with the fat checkbook. I looked at him closely now, and thought for a second that I saw a glimpse of cop-sense in him. Bill Ritchie had been a cop for 20 years and from time to time I would see it in him. It is not just street smarts, although there is a component of that in every good cop. It is also the belief that every single person in the world is guilty of something, and if he can just figure out what you did, he will have a lever he can use to pry you open. Anyway, he seemed a different man now: older, more tired, mean even. While he talked, he looked straight ahead through the front windshield, but if I took my eyes off him I would catch him stealing glimpses of me through his peripheral vision.

"I figured for all you've been through, we owe you a more complete explanation," he said. "I won't even bother with the normal denials or don't-tell-anyones. You're smart enough to figure that shit out for yourself.

"The first thing I want to say is, I'm sorry. I'm sorry we got off on the wrong foot when me met, but most of all I'm sorry that you had to get involved in this. I know you are a good guy just trying to do his job. And you and your friends just wanted to have a few drinks and a few laughs tonight.

"And you ran into Marcos. Which actually is his first name, only his last name is not Pereira, and I'm not going to tell you what it really is. Wouldn't matter anyway.

"You want to know who he is, I'm sure. Well, it's just like he told you. He's a killer. He's done wet work—excuse me, he's killed people—on three different continents. We can confirm that he has killed 5 different people, not counting the Little brothers and George, and we suspect him in at least a half a dozen others. He has kind of an exclusive killing contract with the drug lords in Miami. He only works for them, and they pay him very well.

"His *modus operandi* has always been to use an advance girl. Like a sniper uses a spotter. In this case, Ana. And I don't know her real name yet, but I will soon enough.

"Anyway, when Marcos has a target identified, he usually sends the girl in to get close to him. 99% of the killings he does are of men, so he uses a pretty girl to get next to them and lower their guard. You'd think a guy with a price on his head would not be fooled by that kind of approach, but you'd be wrong.

"His main spotter was a Mexican woman we'll call Julia. They worked together for years. She would get close to the target, tell Marcos about his habits, where he lived, what his routine was, all that, and then one bad night Marcos would swoop in and kill him. Julia got caught in some nickel-and-dime con in the south of Spain last year, and got sent to jail for a couple of years. So Marcos needed a new partner; he doesn't like to work alone.

"Anyway the *narcos*—and you know those are all Latinos involved in the drug trade—asked the *mafiosos*—and those are mostly Italian-Americans involved in drugs and everything else—if they could help. Turns out the *mafiosos* had just the girl. Your Ana. An Italian who looked Hispanic and spoke perfect Spanish and very good English. So they paired her with Marcos on this deal, and they sent them both to Charlotte.

"Why did they come to me?" I said. "Here? If their object was to kill the Littles, why did they come to the bank?"

"The *narcos* were having the same problem that we all were having. They couldn't find the Littles. They thought that you or someone else at the bank, like George Lamb or Randall Clifton, might know where they were. Plus, they were unsure about what the financial situation really was. They had heard it was bad, they could read the ticker tape just like anyone else, but they wanted to know exactly what kind of losses they were looking at on ECP before they made any decisions.

"We think that is probably why George was killed...," he was continuing, but I interrupted.

"You guys are going back and forth on this. First George's death was a random mugging, now Marcos killed him. Which is it?"

Stein looked at me silently for a moment, then stared out the window some more. He lit a new cigarette with the old one and tossed the butt.

"Look," he said, "the fact is, there is kind of a split in the law enforcement community on this one. It's basically two factions. The locals are in the 'Of Course Marcos Did It," camp, for several reasons. The gun used in George's murder was a .22. George got it exactly like the Little brothers got it—two in the head. The shooter took his brass with him. Those things all point to a professional, like Marcos, and the locals want it to go on the books like that.

"The second camp, which has some of my federal law enforcement brethren in it, you could call the "No Hard Evidence" camp. With no empty brass casings, we couldn't match up the gun from George's killing with the gun from the Little brothers killings, even though we might have just found it in there on Marcos. But nobody saw Marcos with George, nobody heard any shots or saw any cars driving away. And the wallet and the watch were missing, which is more consistent with a mugging. And Marcos didn't swipe any watches or wallets from the Littles. So according to my fellow officers, Marcos didn't do it. Or at least you can't build a winnable case that he did."

"What do you think?"

"What do I think?" said Stein. "What I think is, we've got the locals wanting to close a case, to make their crime stats look better. And the feds don't want the case to get closed on their books, because that would mean George's death goes into body count on drug-related deaths in this country. So my guess is, it will stay on the books just like it is, a local mugging gone bad, and the Charlotte cops will toss it into their cold case file and forget about it."

"Because they know Marcos did it," I said. "And he told me he did it in there, before Max killied him.

Stein didn't look at me, but he nodded to the windshield.

"And so George's family never knows the truth," I said. "That he got killed by a professional assassin working for Miami drug dealers.

Stein turned on me angrily.

"Firstly, George Lamb doesn't have much of a family—no kids, no wife, parents deceased. Secondly, don't you think that maybe George had something to do with his own death? Packing that white powder up your nose every chance you get is expensive...and guess who gets the money from it? That's right, the Miami drug dealers. If it weren't for people like George, the druggies wouldn't have enough money to make investments in the stock markets, and to buy beachfront real estate, and to hire professional killers.

"And that wasn't enough. Apparently George thought it was a good idea to sell these same drug smugglers a piece of a bullshit company that was run by two inbred cretins from

Tennessee. Like these drug smugglers got rich and are still free because they are stupid. And they would not eventually figure out that your bank was selling them crap bonds, and come looking for payment.

"I tell you, I cry no tears for George Lamb. Nor the Little brothers either. They all knew who they were dealing with. You get into a game with the *narcos*, you better realize it is the biggest of the big leagues. They throw hard and inside, they slide with their spikes up, and they do not ever, *ever* hand out intentional walks. If you can't hit in that league, you end up with two holes in your head, cooling off in a Charlotte parking garage like a piece of meat in a freezer. Or crumpled up on the floor of your private jet, with a look of surprise on your face, and the last thing that went through your head before that bullet was 'how did this come to pass?'"

He made an obvious effort to calm down. I felt like I was getting lectured by my father. After a few minutes he continued.

"Where was I? Oh yeah—the *narcos* finally figured out that their financial loss was a big one. In fact, after you told us about that Friday night you were up here with Ana, we wondered if they might have been targeting you next. But Marcos found out where the Littles were around the same time, we're not sure how exactly, and called Ana to come help him kill the Littles."

"His employer told him," I said distractedly.

"What? How do you know that?"

"He told me in there. He said his employers had been on the plane before, and I guess they were tracking it, because they told him when it was going to land in Charlotte."

"Well, that fills in a blank. Thank you," said Stein.

"But why was Marcos still here, then? Why didn't he take off this past weekend, after he killed the Littles?"

"We think he was cleaning up loose ends.   Several jobs ago, he let a few things slip, and we almost caught him because he left too clear a trail back to himself. So we think he is being a little more meticulous now. Or was being, I guess I should say. That's why he came up here looking for you."

There was movement in the corner of my eye. The FBI team was leaving The Green Room. The med-techs had Marcos's corpse in the body bag and were loading it into the panel van. Agent McAlister looked over at Steins' car, and Stein rolled down his window. He tossed his cigarette butt out and said:

"I'll meet you downtown, okay?"

McAlister nodded, got into one of the SUVs, and the FBI SUV caravanned out of the parking lot. Stein left his window down and lit another cigarette.

"So what's the need to keep all this a big secret?" I asked. "Why is there nothing in the paper about two psychos running around killing people in Charlotte?"

Stein eyeballed me sternly for a long minute. Then he sighed.

"I guess I could tell you that we didn't want people frightened over something we had under control. That would be true. Or I could tell you that we didn't want to spook Marcos and Ana with what we knew, because they might run. And that would be true, too. We figured they would stay around after the killings, to clean up those loose ends I was talking about, and we still had a chance to catch them."

"Under control?! I was one of the loose ends!" I said angrily. "I almost got cleaned up in there tonight!"

"I know. I'm sorry for that, but would an article in the paper have changed anything? We told you to stay away from him, that he and Ana were armed and dangerous."

"You didn't tell that to my friends in there," I said. "They almost got cleaned up, too."

Stein sat silently for a minute, then he turned to face me in the car.

"Look, I'm going to tell you something that I probably shouldn't. Then you're going to keep your mouth shut about all this, okay?

"Marcos used to be one of us. He was trained and employed by...well, by a U.S. government agency, let's put it that way. We used him for undercover work, to get inside the South American drug gangs. He was a damn good undercover man. A few years ago, he almost got caught in Honduras, and he had to run, and we got him out of there and into the States. We got him set up with a new job and identity in Miami. Things seemed to be going fine for him.

"Then, about 18 months ago, he went rogue. He went to work for the *narcos* down there. Why? Who knows? Maybe it was the money, or maybe he missed the excitement. That happens. But that's why we had to take care of this ourselves, and quietly. Because otherwise we would all be sitting in front of a Congressional subcommittee answering questions under oath about a rogue government agent killing Americans."

"And Ana?" I said.

He shrugged.

"This is the first time we've run into her. She's gone now. We had her hotel and her phone, but she left without checking out last night and the cell phone is probably in a ditch somewhere. But she's in the system now. If she stays in this country—hell, even if she doesn't—we'll find her.

"One nice side benefit of all this is now those *narcos* and the *mafiosos* down in Miami are at each others' throats. Of course the *narcos* are pissed off about the money, and they are going to be even hotter when they find out their main hitter is dead. And we've got their main mouthpiece, this lawyer Aragones, ready to chirp in return for immunity from prosecution. With just a little luck, we might get a full-on intramural shooting match down there. So I guess we have to thank you guys for that, too.

"But like I said, we don't need this on the street, via the newspapers or the TV or just idle talk. So we need you to keep this to yourself, okay?"

I mulled over this for a few minutes. Stein smoked his cigarette and alternately looked at me and stared out the window of his car into The Green Room parking lot and at the lake beyond it.

"I'm just having a hard time with the way you put me and my friends at risk," I finally said. "That just doesn't sound like responsible law enforcement to me. I felt like I was put out there like bait. And what about Randall Clifton? Don't you think he deserves to know that a drug cartel is killing bankers who were involved with ECP and Huevos Investments.?"

Stein gave me another hard eyeball and this time his anger seemed to reach across the seat and grab me by the throat.

""I don't seem to be getting through here, Mr. Wilson, so let me drop the 411 on you on a couple of items. First, Mr. Randall Clifton is desperately in need of a friend. He knows it, and so do we. You ever heard of the Witness Protection Program? Yes? Then enough said. He's got lots of information on money laundering at investment banks. In return for telling us all of it, we're going to hide him in East Gibipp somewhere.

And try to keep those boys in Miami from killing him. Because believe me, they consider him unfinished business.

"Now, another guy who really needs a friend is Ignacio Aragones, the aforementioned mouthpiece for the *narcos*, the guy who ran Huevos Investments. He figures he is on the hit list too, and he is not wrong. So guess who he wants to be friends with?"

"You," I said. "Obviously."

"Amazing how popular the federal government becomes once the bodies start stacking up, isn't it? So we've got those two bases covered, okay? Now, there's a third party who needs a friend, only he hasn't quite realized it yet."

He reached into his jacket pocket and took out a piece of paper. He handed it to me.

I unfolded it. It was a copy of two thumbprints. One was unmarked, the other had some kind of serial number or identifier above it. Both were obviously computerized; I was looking at a paper version of a digital file of two thumbprints.

"Care to take a guess what those are?" said Stein.

"Two thumbprints," I said.

"Very good," he said. "Any idea who they belong to?"

"I'm afraid to ask," I said.

"The first one is a thumbprint we took from the interior of the Little brothers' 757—you know, the one with the movie theater and the hot tub? Came from a countertop by the bar, as a matter of fact.

"The second thumbprint we got from the SEC. Anyone who gets a license from the SEC has to go through a background check, and to do that they have to give the SEC a thumbprint. You remember that process, don't you? You used to have a Series 7 license from the SEC when you worked on Wall Street."

I looked down at the paper again and felt like I was going to throw up. I had forgotten about that fingerprinting in New York. It was a long time ago, right after business school, a part of one big hurried process to get licensed and get all the badges and security clearances and access cards necessary to start working in the investment banking world. It had taken all of two minutes eight years ago, and I had forgotten all about it.

"As you can see, the two thumbprints are an exact match. The one on the right, with the number above it, is your print from the SEC. The one on the left is from the plane. So we're looking at some pretty solid evidence that you were on that plane, and you didn't tell us about it."

He took the paper back from me.

"So we're done with the lectures on responsible law enforcement, okay? My question for you is this: would you like a friend?"

"I guess I need one," I said.

"You do," said Stein. "So here's the deal. Marcos used to be our boy. That's why we don't want this out in the public domain. It would make us look bad, and even worse, inept. We can't have that. Plus, he's dead now, so he's no threat to anyone.

"We're not asking you to do much. In fact, we're asking you to do absolutely nothing. You're not going to tell the newspaper, or the TV stations, or anyone else, anything at all about what happened up here tonight. You're going to ask your three friends to do the same. Publically, none of you are ever going to mention any of this, okay? If some reporter comes looking for you, or some curious co-worker wants the inside scoop, you have one response: 'I don't know what you're talking about. Marcos who?'

"What I'm going to do for you, in return, is make sure this thumbprint match disappears. I can't erase your thumbprint from the SEC files, but there's not going to be any link between it and this case. Now is that a deal?"

What else could I say?

"Deal," I said.

Stein tore the fingerprint ID in half and handed it to me.

"It's been a pleasure doing business with you, friend," he said.

I got out of the car, and he fired up the engine and started to back out. I thought of something and tapped on the window. He rolled it down.

"Why is the FBI involved in all this foreign drug stuff? Isn't that someone else's territory, like the CIA's or something?"

"I never said I was FBI," Stein responded. He drove away.

I stood there for a few minutes, then went back inside The Green Room, throwing my thumbprints away in a nearby trash can.

The guys had finished the Havana Club and were drinking beer now. Bill got me a longneck from the cooler.

"So what did the FBI guy say?" said Bill, handing it to me.

"He said we should all keep our mouths shut. He said the situation was cleaned up and there wasn't going to be any publicity about it, and if there was it better not come from us. He said we don't know shit about what happened up here tonight, or Marcos, or anything else related to it."

"What did you say?" asked Max.

"I told him we would not tell a soul about it."

The three of them looked at me, and then Curtis raised his beer bottle.

"Here's to keeping our mouths shut," he said. And we all clinked bottles.

20

A few mornings later, I was careful in my dress. I shaved closely and calmed my unruly hair as best I could. I shined my shoes and made sure I had on my best suit, and a clean shirt and tie.

I drove down to the bank and met Lawson in a special basement parking area. We checked in with a guard, and then took an elevator that had only one button on the panel. It went straight to the top floor of the bank. We stepped out into a reception area, where another guard was expecting us. He escorted us into a waiting room with a stunning view of Charlotte and the surrounding area. You could see for 50 miles easily. Was that Grandfather Mountain in the far distance?

There were only three rooms on the top floor of the bank. We were sitting in one of them, the reception area. The Executive Dining Room was off to the right, a 30-top private restaurant reserved for bank executives and their most valued clients. It had a private chef and a world-class wine cellar. Almost nobody in the bank knew about it. I had been up there once, when I was being recruited to return to the bank after I left Wall Street. I had dined on fish soup, filet mignon and a fine California Cabernet Sauvignon. But I had never been back—my clients did not tend toward the type that were eligible for the Executive Dining Room, and I was not invited on my own.

The other area was the chairman's office. While we were waiting to see the man, Lawson said:

"Sam, I've been thinking about something. It troubles me that these two people, Marcos and Ana, got so close to the bank so easily. I don't like the idea that a couple of con artists got this kind of access to the bank's confidential opinions of ECP. And I don't like the fact that Ana got into a meeting with ECP's management."

"She signed a confidentiality agreement," I said. As soon as it came out, I realized it sounded defensive.

"Yes, I got a copy of that, " said Lawson. "That's fine, as far as it goes, but she ought not have been in there at all. If ECP were ever to make an issue out of it, we would be in a legal pickle, make no error. As I'm sure you know."

I nodded.

"So why did you put her in there?"

I didn't have a very good answer to that, and while I was trying to think of something, Lawson said:

"Sherman said the FBI implied that there might have been some kind of personal relationship between you and Ana. Is there any truth to that? Did you know her before all this started?"

"No," I said. "I met her and Marcos the same day that those firings were announced, right after you and I had the conference call with the chairman about taking over the portfolio. In terms of after that, she and I..."

Lawson held up his hand.

"I don't care to know any details, Sam. Your personal life is your business. I just need to know that it's not interfering with your work responsibilities, or impairing your judgment. Is it?"

"Lawson, the main reason I put Ana in that meeting with ECP was because she had expressed an interest in the company, and at the time I thought she and Marcos were legitimate. I was starting to realize how bad ECP was going to be, and I was desperate to get some alternatives to bankruptcy. I had initially hoped to just sell them some of the asset-backed bonds, but Vinnie suggested giving them a look at the whole company. A vulture fund that was willing to buy the whole company, even at a big discount, would have helped tremendously. In retrospect, maybe that looks like wishful thinking. But it has nothing to do with my relationship with Ana. It has to do with us being under a lot of pressure to get these portfolio problems solved quickly."

Lawson watched me closely and after a while, nodded.

"Yes, I thought as much. Just keep in mind, from now on, that we have procedures in place to govern how we introduce outside parties to our customers. They are designed to protect us. In this case, I doubt that anything will come of it because..."

"...because the Little brothers are dead," I finished for him. "There's no one to complain."

"Indeed," Lawson said.

A receptionist came out and gestured us into the chairman's office. As we stood up Lawson said:

"Sam? Let's keep this incident to ourselves, all right? No need to burden the chairman with it."

"Thank you, Lawson," I said

Mr. Christopher Avery was slender, not quite six feet tall, with a mane of black and silver hair and a bushy mustache to match. He was elegantly attired, but it was a very conservative look: starched white shirt with collar points, dark gray suit with barely-visible chalk pinstripes, dark blue tie and black wing-tips. He came forward and shook Lawson's hand first.

"Good morning, sir," said Lawson.

"Good morning, Lawson."

"Good morning, sir," I said, sticking my hand out. "Sam Wilson."

"Of course, Sam," he said, shaking my hand and smiling warmly. "Your reputation precedes you. Come on in, both of you, let's have a seat over here."

He led us to a small round conference table, where we were all seated. He and Lawson made some small talk, and then finally he turned to me and said:

"Well, Sam, how bad is it?"

I wish I had a dollar for every time someone asked me that over the last eight years.

"Not as bad as you might think," I said. "ECP is a nightmare, and we are going to lose a lot on that. As you know it is already in bankruptcy and...well, you know about the deaths of the Littles and George Lamb."

He nodded sympathetically. I knew he was going to speak, because he had a habit of pregnant pauses after someone else finished speaking, and you could tell he wanted to say something. It was not a stutter. It was a pause to consider his words. I think somewhere along his career, someone had told him to always think before he spoke, and he had taken it literally.

"I am very sorry about those murders," he said finally. "I have been in this business for 30 years and have only seen a banker killed once before, over banking business. The Littles...well, I don't know about them, but it certainly is a distressing thing. What is the latest from law enforcement on this, Lawson?"

"The FBI has wrapped up its investigation. Their official line is that George was killed in a random mugging, and the Littles were killed by drug lords who had invested in ECP. These *narcos* were upset about their losses and felt like they had been duped. They hired a person or persons unknown to kill the Little brothers. Full stop. They have not said as much to us, but we believe Randall Clifton was somehow involved in this, and he is now under FBI protection."

"Would that mean the Witness Protection Program?" said Mr. Avery.

Lawson shrugged.

"They were not specific, but I would guess that is the case."

The chairman sighed, and paused again, and I waited for him to speak.

"Well, if Clifton was implicated in the 'theft' from the drug lords, so much that he is in a witness protection program, then how can the FBI believe that George Lamb's murder is unrelated?"

Lawson squirmed in his seat a little.

"I don't know, sir. I tend to agree with you. But perhaps they don't want people in Charlotte upset about the death of a local banker. George was not married, had no children, and both of his parents are deceased. There is not really anyone to object."

The chairman considered this, then let out a small sigh.

"Very well. So, to the loan portfolio. It is not that bad, except for ECP, which you say here..." he looked down at the presentation I had sent him earlier..." is likely to lose over $100 milion. It is in bankruptcy now in Memphis, and the judge is standing still until this issue of a guardian for the estate of the Littles can be settled, is that correct?

"Yes, sir," I said.

"Okay," he said, making some notes on the presentation. "Now..." another pause...."the corporate bond portfolio."

"The corporates have all been marked-to-market and we can get that price if you told us to sell them today," I said. "The loss would be as we have outlined in the presentation. As you can see, there are two reasons we think a hold strategy here would lower our losses. The first is, we have already sold all Russian debt and all emerging market debt. We took small losses on those positions—I think maybe $6 million on $120 million bonds on the emerging market stuff, a bit more for Russia—and we would be looking at a whole lot worse if we were trying to sell them now. The situation in Russia is bad, but we are not exposed to it at all anymore.

"The other corporates, and indeed some of the asset-backeds, are being dragged down by this situation with Long-Term Capital Management in New York. You may have heard, it's this big hedge fund that...

The chairman looked up and wanted to speak again. I shut up and waited. Finally he said:

"Yes, my understanding is that situation will be rectified soon. The Feds are going to force those banks who participated in LTCM, who loaned them money to take all these risky derivative positions, to bail them out. They are going to be required to fund even more money to keep LTCM afloat, until they can place the company into an orderly wind-down. I am happy to report that our bank had no involvement with LTCM."

Lawson gave a low whistle.

"Now how do you reckon the Fed got all those big investment bankers to agree to that?" he said.

Our chairman grinned.

"I imagine that the Fed told them it was that, or a free-fall bankruptcy, which meant that at least half of Wall Street would cease to exist, and the other half would be mortally wounded and barely able to survive as bond trading houses. I imagine they were told that no less than a market meltdown would occur if LTCM went under, and the Federal government would have very little sympathy towards those parties who allowed it to happen."

"In other words, pony up a couple hundred million each, boys, or the Fed window is going to close and you are going to go out into the cold, gray world on your own," said Lawson.

The chairman smiled and nodded. I silently wished I could have been a fly on the wall of the Fed meeting where all the banks were told to pony up some more for their stupidity. Then the chairman said:

"So, Sam, your mark on the corporate and the asset-backeds does not take that into account, is that correct? By 'that' I mean the potential solution to the Long-Term Capital situation."

"Correct, sir," I said. "This is what we could sell those bonds for today, and the market has not priced in any fix to that situation as of today. If there is a fix that the market believes will work for LTCM, then you could see a significant rebound on these values."

"How much?" he asked.

"I don't know, sir. Maybe as much as half. It would depend on the fix, and what else was happening in the world."

"But right now, today, this is the mark? This is what we can sell for if we flipped a switch this morning and said 'sell it all?'"

"Yes, sir," I said.

"And this number here, this $187 million, is your estimate of the total loss in the whole portfolio: loans, bonds, asset-backeds and everything else?"

"Yes, sir," I said. "As you can see it already includes the $6 million we have taken to dispose of the emerging market debt. It also includes the estimated loss in the ECP bankruptcy, and assorted other bond positions where we have small losses and recommend selling."

The chairman studied the report for a while, asked a few more questions, then leaned back from the table and thought for a while.

"You know, this is not as bad as I thought it was going to be. I mean, it's bad, but I thought it was going to be worse. Your folks have done a great job, Lawson. I know it wasn't easy and I appreciate all the time you have put into it."

"Thank you, sir," he said.

"I will need you on the earnings conference call a week from today. These are your numbers, obviously, so you need to be there to defend them. We'll need to have a dress rehearsal before the actual call. My staff will get you the details."

I watched with bemusement as my boss squirmed uncomfortably in his seat again. The man was generally unflappable but it was obvious he didn't want to be on an earning call fielding questions from skeptical stock analysts.

"Uh, well, sir, I've never actually been on TV before. Perhaps we should..."

The chairman smiled.

"It's just a teleconference, Lawson. There won't be anyone in the room but us. The analysts will all be in their offices in New York or wherever. The questions will come to us over the speakerphone. Big Ken from Credit and our CFO will be here, too."

"Oh," said Lawson. "Well, that doesn't sound so bad."

"No, " said the chairman, "nothing you can't handle. Just make sure you know the ins and outs of all those numbers. We are going to be taking a one-time charge, and the analysts are going to want us to break it down as much as we possibly can."

"Of course," he said.

"Now, would you excuse us? I'd like a few minutes alone to talk with Sam."

Uh-oh, I thought.

"Yes, sir. Good morning to you." Lawson got up and left.

The chairman picked up the phone and requested coffee and croissants for two. It arrived instantly. He invited me to help myself, and he picked up a cup of coffee and a chocolate croissant. I stuck with just the coffee, which was delicious.

He chewed on his croissant and drank his coffee, all the while keeping a close eye on me. Eventually he put them down.

"Sam, you have done a hell of a job here for the bank. The first thing I want to say is, thank you. I'm confident that with your analysis, we can put these investment banking issues behind us, and get back to focusing on our customers.

"The second thing I want to say is, I'm sorry. Sherman has kept me up-to-date on what has been going on with the murder investigations, and your role with the FBI. Obviously this is not something we ever anticipated or foresaw, but I do appreciate you handling yourself professionally with them."

He didn't know about the thumbprints, then. I let go of the breath I was holding.

"Have you asked yourself what you'd like to do at this bank? Long term, I mean?"

"Ah...well, no sir, not really. I mean I enjoy my work in SAG, and I like Lawson and the people I work with there a lot. So I was just planning to continue in that group as long as I can."

The chairman paused to brush some crumbs off his pants and dab at his mouth with a napkin.

"SAG does very important work here, Sam. Loss mitigation is not an easy profession. It definitely takes a certain skill set to make a good SAG person.

"Only I'm wondering if you don't have talents that exceed that. I'm thinking we might be wasting you in the minor leagues, so to speak, when you could be pitching in the majors."

He watched me closely and suddenly burst out laughing.

"You look like Lawson looked when I told him I needed him on that earnings call. Listen, just think about it, okay? There's nothing immediate I have in mind, and I know we might be getting a little outside your comfort zone. But this bank is growing, and God knows we need talent right now. You have a diverse skill set: investment banking, commercial banking, SAG work and now a good look at the trading operation here. I wish I had 50 more just like you. Just give some thought to what you'd like your next opportunity to be. I don't think we can afford to have you in SAG much longer."

He then reached into his pocket and handed me an envelope.

"Inside the envelope is a deposit slip, showing that this morning a one-time bonus of $50,000 was paid into your personal checking account. That's the bank's tangible expression of its thanks for your work on this project. I have also authorized another $50,000 to be paid to your subordinates in the project, as you see fit."

He stood up and I did too, a little dazed.

"You did a fine job for us, Sam. I'm sure we'll have some bigger fish for you to fry before too long."

We shook hands, and I walked back across the carpets to the reception room elevator and left. I got all the way into the basement, where my car was parked, before I realized that I would have to leave that area in my car, go back to my parking garage, and get in a different elevator to get to my office. $50,000 in cash muddles the mind like that, or at least it did mine.

21

In the days after that meeting, the bank held its conference call. I was busy with the ECP bankruptcy, but listened to a taped version of it later. The analysts had mostly been positive about the investment bank's portfolio, but had a lot of questions about the direction of the investment bank going forward. Lawson handled his part well. Mr. Avery made it clear that we were going to continue to be aggressive and grow the business; we were just going to do it with different people.

Ana Primo de Montez, or whatever her real name was, disappeared into 'the howling storm,' as William Blake had called the world outside these protected walls. I guess she had done the job on me she had been paid to do. I had no doubt that she had marked me for Marcos, because he had known to find me at The Green Room. "The mark" was how I thought about myself for a while, and that does not do a lot for a man's self-esteem.

I heard later, through Sherman, that the FBI had found that BMW M5 in a covered parking garage close to the Miami airport. Of course Miami has more flights to South and Central America than any other airport in the country, and so Ana was gone for good.

◆

I cannot say I missed Ana much. The rowdy sex aside, I could not have long been with a woman who was constantly looking at herself in the mirror, much less one who was in her line of 'work.'

But I did have to make an effort not to become fascinated by black leather belts and short plaid skirts. I'm shaking my head right now, trying to get those thoughts out of there.

And I found myself unable to delete that photo she had sent me, in her smoke-gray lingerie, leering into the mirror. Finally I printed it out and showed it to Curtis, who drooled over it. Then I stuck it on my refrigerator at home with a magnet, but after a few weeks it got old and I took it down and tossed it in a drawer.

But I couldn't bring myself to throw it in the trash can. So maybe I did miss her after all.

◆

The FBI confirmed, weeks after the fact, that the anonymous letter we received, that had put ECP in default, was legitimate and did come from an employee who used to work there. They wouldn't tell us the person's name, but they did say the person knew about the bank meeting we were having with ECP, and intended the letter to arrive while the Littles were still in the building, so we could brace them with it. Apparently he or she didn't like the Littles much either.

◆

A few days after Mr. Avery's earnings conference call, I had Vinnie and Melanie and my secretary Sharon out to a bar after work, and gave them each an envelope containing their bonus, courtesy of the chairman. I made a little speech about hard work and results and I can't remember what other fatuous nonsense; money temporarily renders some of us sanctimonious. But I was pleased at the shocked look on their faces as they opened the envelopes, and the party lasted so long I had to call a cab for a ride home. It was nice, and rare in my experience, to be able to instantly reward someone who has done a good job for you at the bank.

◆

Mr. Stein's histrionics aside, I knew damn well that my thumbprint match was somewhere down at the FBI. It might only be in his desk drawer, and not in one of their massive computers, but I knew if I ever stepped out of line with them again, it would get brought up. And it was at the SEC too, which I kicked myself for forgetting. Once the government has your prints, they were in the system for good.

I was owned. I wasn't happy about it, but perhaps it would make me a little more humble. I had a feeling, Sherman's presence or no, that I would have to deal with the Feds again in my career.

◆

Counting Marcos, four people died over the Little brothers' fraud. I hope that the drug lords in Miami and everywhere else got the idea that stocks and bonds were not a good place to put your money. I sure didn't want to deal with any of them ever again.

◆

The trading floor, indeed the whole investment bank, was re-organized. Someone else from the outside came in to take the place of the Witness-Protected Randall Clifton, and The Monster stayed where he was as head of the trading operation. A bond trader was moved up to take George Lamb's old job, and Melanie Bissell slid into the trading spot that he left unoccupied. She left my department the day after the earnings call and happily took up her spot in trader's row, working the phones and punching up bonds on the computer and otherwise making a market for that bond, right now, today. She was the trader she had always wanted to be.

It is nice to have a friend on the trading desk now, and sometimes I will stop down there and visit with her for five or ten minutes (before the market opens, of course). The trader's world is a man's world, as she had said, and it bespeaks a toughness in that tiny Carolina girl that she survives and even enjoys it. Whether she will make a good trader or not, time will tell. The market renders a brutal but fair judgment on one and all; it makes a clear distinction between the worthy and the stray.

◆

Damn if The Woodrow didn't give out. I was running errands in Troutman one weekend when I went to pull out of the dry cleaner's parking lot, put it in gear, and it went nowhere. It sat there humming as nice as you please, but it wouldn't move an inch no matter how much I mashed on the gas pedal. I tried changing into lower gears, but the only gear that would work was reverse. So I stuck it in reverse, put the blinkers on, and drove about a half mile down the road to Max's Used Car Emporium. Maxwell D. Buford, Proprietor.

Big Max himself was there, as he always was. He fooled with The Woodrow himself for a while, then put it on the lift and had one of his mechanics look at it. He and I had a cup of coffee and swapped stories until the mechanic came back in.

"Transmission," he said. "It's shot. It'll take a brand new one, if you can find one for a Jeep that old."

"Damn," I said. "Well, Max, how long will it take you to find one?"

Max shooed his mechanic off and put his arm around me.

"Come on let's take a walk around the lot, Wyatt."

We went outside to his car lot, in the bright sunshine of a summer morning on Lake Norman, North Carolina.

"Wyatt, I remember when your Daddy got that Jeep. He bought it from me, you know. He was proud as anything of it, used to drive your mama to church on Sunday like he was driving a Cadillac. And he was proud to give it to you, too, after you got to college. Kept it in the family, was the way he looked at it. And you got a good long ride out of it, didn't you?"

I nodded. It was a good old truck.

"But here's the deal," said Max, squeezing my shoulder "It's dead, Wyatt. The transmission is shot. Even if I could find one, it would cost you more than that whole heap is worth. I've replaced the belts and tires on that thing so many times you could have paid for a rubber plantation by now. And it doesn't have air conditioning. You're not replacing that transmission. It's time for you to buy another vehicle."

"Now look here what I've got for you."

And he patted his hand on what looked like a brand new Jeep.

"This here is called the Grand Cherokee. It's four-wheel drive. You can see it's got the big tires on it. It's only two years old and has 32,000 miles on it. It's got a great cooler, you won't believe how much you're going to like air conditioning in the summer. And looky here—it's Duke blue! Now what else could you ask for? I've been saving this just for you, turned down an offer yesterday 'cause I knew you would want it."

So we went for a test ride, and when we got back to the office I said I'd take it.

"You ain't even asked what I want for it," Max complained.

"What do you want for it?" I asked.

He told me and I said, fine, I'd take it.

Max was upset by this.

"Aw, hell, now, Wyatt. Everyone has done told me that you are some big negotiator down at the bank, now come on! Work some of that negotiating stuff on me. Beat me down a little."

"Max," I said. "You saved my life not a month ago. I think it would be a little ungrateful to argue with your price on a car. I'll just pay you cash for it, okay?"

I took my checkbook out and Max looked at me suspiciously.

"You don't want to finance it with me? I can give you good terms, five years, six, whatever you want. Interest rate cheaper than what you can get at the bank."

"No, Max, I prefer to pay cash if you don't mind."

He stared at me, then a knowing look came over his face.

"You got me anyway. I woulda given you a higher price if I'da known I wasn't going to make any money on financing. Hell, nobody pays cash for a car these days. They told me you was tricky!"

And he laughed uproariously, and had to tell all his staff about how clever I was, and what a tough negotiator I was, and how I had baited him into giving him a lower price without him even knowing it. It took me thirty minutes of this to get him to take my check so I could get out of there.

But I have to admit, I did enjoy the ride home. The new Jeep was quiet. But I turned the air-conditioning off and rolled down the windows; who wants A/C when you can feel the summer breeze on your face?

◆

Not long after that, the markets recovered on the news that, as Mr. Avery predicted, the Fed forced Long-Term Capital's banks to bail it out. Russia was still in default, of course, as were a few other emerging market countries, but the widespread fear of a financial collapse disappeared and markets slowly regained confidence. We handed control of the investment banking portfolio back to the investment bank, with the exception of a few credits from the loan book that we kept because they were probably headed toward bankruptcy.

The biggest of those, of course, was Entourage Capital. Even though the owners were dead, and the *narcos* in Miami had extracted their revenge, there was still a lot of value left in the company, and it all belonged to the bank. Vinnie and I worked on it every day, and then slowly I dropped off and turned my attention to other things, and lawyer Jay and his staff returned to their offices. It was the dirt nap for ECP, as some of my more cynical colleagues in SAG liked to say, except it would take a long time and a lot of money lost to get them in the ground.

◆

Curtis and I were fishing over in Terrapin Creek that Saturday evening, casting up close to the bank with worms and night crawlers and trying to coax out those big bass that hang out under the ledge. It was close to dusk and the sun was just beginning to set behind the tall Carolina pines on the bank.

"So all three of those people, the guy who worked at your bank and the two brothers that owned that Memphis company, they got killed by that guy who was holding a gun on us up at The Green Room?" said Curtis.

"Yep," I said.

"And that chick you were banging, who liked that ass spanking, she was working with that guy? And setting you up?"

"Yep."

"And she's gone? They can't find her?"

"Lost her at the Miami airport," I said.

"And it was all because of those drug guys in Miami investing in the company, and losing their money?"

"Yep."

"And you think the investment bank president is in Witness Protection now?"

"Well, you didn't hear it from me, but yes, that's what the FBI told me."

"But he wasn't really an FBI guy, you said. Who did he really work for?"

"I don't know," I said. "DEA maybe? Somebody else? I don't know."

"And you don't believe him about the fingerprints, do you? You think they're in the system somewhere."

"Well, what would you think? You were in the Army. Does a federal agency ever turn loose of a piece of information like that? I'm not saying they think I did anything. I'm just saying, that's insurance for them against anything I might do later. It might not be in the FBI's computers, but I I'm pretty damn sure they didn't just throw it in the trash."

"Well that was a slick operation up there at The Green Room, I have to say," said Curtis. "Not a police car or light or siren or anything. Reminded me more of an Army Special Forces op. They had that body out of there, and the blood mopped up, and the gun out, in 20 minutes flat. That's not something you'd ever see from the local police. They would have had it all taped off with yellow tape and a helicopter in the air and..."

Just then a big pontoon boat, filled with about 20 people went chugging by. We could see a keg of beer on board and a grill pluming smoke. There was a lot of hooting and hollering and a woman in a bikini pulled her top up and flashed her tits at us.

Curtis and I watched as the boat faded into the distance.

"You know, this used to be a nice, quiet place," he said. "Now it's turning to shit."

"Yep," I said.

Something hit my line hard, and I felt a little surge of adrenaline that told me he was hooked good, and he was big. I jerked up a little to make sure the hook was well set, and then started to reel. He fought hard, trying to get back under the ledge and maybe snag my line on something, and in the middle of the fight he breached for a second and tail-walked across the water. I saw a brief flash of liquid gold, silver and green, and then he went back under with a splash and I thought:

Well, it's not all that bad up here.

THE AUTHOR

Stan Meihaus lives with his wife Ellen in the Lake Norman area of North Carolina. His first book, SKIP, won the 2011/2012 Independent Book Award for Best New Suspense/Thriller. He spent 15 years in both commercial and investment banking in North Carolina.

Made in the USA
Lexington, KY
13 October 2013